Nine Brides for Cowboy Creek

Volume 2
Carrie & Bridget

by

Teresa Slack

Other Titles

Nine Brides for Cowboy Creek

Rennie
Eliza
Carrie
Bridget
Katie
Marianne
Scarlett
Rachael
Amelia

Four Sisters Ranch

Priscilla's Promise

Willow Wood Brides Series

A Promise for Josie—
Available free to newsletter subscribers
A Lawman for Lisette
A Love Letter for Jessa
A Dream for Harper
A Wedding for Felicity
A Hero for Ellie
A Cowboy for Meggan

Jenna's Creek Series:

Streams of Mercy

Redemption's Song
Evidence of Grace
A Jenna's Creek Wedding: *A Christmas Novella*
Legacy of Faith

Tender Blessings Series:

Love Begins
A Little Goodbye

Stand Alone Novels

The Ultimate Guide to Darcy Carter
Runaway Heart
Joy Redefined
Cheater, Cheater: Lindsay's Turn

What Readers are Saying

"Teresa Slack is a one-click author for me!!"

"Compelling story with fun new slant on the mail-order bride genre."

"Great romance & suspense read. ...will keep you turning the pages and won't let you put the book down. Highly recommended. I recommend the entire series as well."

"Outstanding series will have you binge reading!"

"From stagecoaches and sheriffs to outlaws and saloons, your cowboy loving heart will be satisfied."

"...Loved this book. Teresa's characters are interesting and real. This book hooked me in the first pages. I can hardly wait until the next book comes out."

"...Suspense, intense action, and tender moments to warm your heart. Well written...and the ending wrapped everything up nicely. I highly recommend reading it." –

"A good balance of action, life in the West, danger and romance. The characters were well developed, and the settings described so well that the reader feels right there."

"Another wonderful read... These kinds of stories keep you intrigued, wondering how the love story will pan out."

To Ralph. With Love. Always.

Nine Brides for Cowboy Creek, Book 3

Carrie

TERESA SLACK

Chapter One

"You keep that thieving little brat outta my store, or next time the police'll get here long before you do. You hear me!"

The red-faced shopkeeper thrust the girl at her mother and stormed back inside.

Humiliation, anger, and indignation fought for dominance as Carrie Rhoades grabbed her daughter's coat collar and dragged her down the street. She wanted to tell the shopkeeper and all her nosy neighbors craning their necks to see what was happening that her daughter wasn't a thief. Candace was a good girl. A little confused for sure, running with the wrong crowd, but a good girl nonetheless who had been raised better than to take something that wasn't hers. There must be a mistake.

Immediately, Carrie realized she wasn't so sure. This wasn't the first time Candace had gotten into trouble of late. The girl's teachers no longer found her charming and precocious. Carrie had witnessed mothers shuttling their little ones out of the way when Candace and her pack of new friends sauntered down the street. How had this happened? Candace turned twelve last week. Surely, she wasn't old enough to be a...a juvenile delinquent! Carrie picked up her pace while avoiding the gazes of her neighbors. She wanted to believe the new friends were the problem. She wasn't sure of that either. Maybe her daughter was the one influencing *them*.

Without a word to the girl hurrying stiffly beside her—head down and a hank of cornsilk blond hair covering her face—Carrie marched to the faded brick apartment building. She didn't speak until the door swung shut behind them. She had been too mad and mortified at being the center of attention with the shopkeeper's accusations hanging in the air to think about what she would say to her daughter. Too mad to think of anything except getting off the street.

She whirled Candace around and released her iron grip on the girl's coat. Her fingers ached from the pressure. "All right, young lady. What was that all about? And you better tell me the truth."

Six months ago, Carrie's tone and the embarrassing encounter on the street in front of the entire neighborhood would've reduced Candace to remorse. Not this time. She pulled herself up to all her just-turned-twelve-years of height and squared her narrow shoulders.

So pretty, Carrie thought. The stubborn set of her jaw reminded Carrie of the girl's father. Too bad she also possessed his insolence and poor judgment.

"Nothing happened. Joanna, Millie, and I were in the store looking around. Millie was holding a pair of earbobs to her ears to see what they looked like in the mirror. We were joking and laughing, and she forgot about them and slipped them into her pocket. Mr. Steiner saw her and he went crazy."

Carrie gasped. "She stole them!"

Candace's cobalt blue eyes flashed. Her lips pulled into a sneer. Carrie nearly drew back. How many times had she seen that look on Johnny Rhoades's face before he drew back his fist?

"She didn't steal them," Candace said between clenched white teeth. "She forgot. Haven't you ever made a mistake?"

Carrie hid her trembling fists in the folds of her skirt. It wouldn't do for Candace to see how close her mother was to slapping that cheeky look right off her face. Carrie needed to diffuse the situation instead of making it worse if she hoped to get through to her daughter.

"She didn't forget, Candace," she said evenly. "She was stealing them. That girl's a thief, just like her sisters and her mother. That's the last time you're going to spend any time with her. Joanna too."

As soon as she spoke, Carrie knew she shouldn't judge Millie by her family tree. She couldn't help herself. Every word of it was true and the whole neighborhood knew it.

Candace's own fists clenched. She trembled with rage. "You can't do that! They're my friends. The only friends I have left, thanks to you. You're always following us around, accusing us. You don't trust me."

Of course, I don't trust you, Carrie wanted to shout. *No mother in her right mind would trust you.*

She swallowed hard to rein in her anger. Getting into a screaming match with her strong-willed child wouldn't change the situation. She wanted to get through to Candace that she was going down a wrong path she might not be able to get off, not alienate the girl forever.

"Candace, honey, they're not the kind of friends you need. They ditch school. They steal. The other day I heard they were tormenting poor old Mr. Hirsch outside his building. That old man can't even walk. He sure doesn't need to be bullied by a bunch of fresh-mouthed girls."

A flash of empathy skittered across Candace's face. She had always liked Mr. Hirsch. Carrie was hopeful. Her daughter wasn't completely lost, though she would be soon if something didn't change.

Candace's compassion evaporated as quickly as it appeared. She folded her skinny arms over her chest. Her faded gingham dress strained across her shoulders. Carrie fought down the urge to burst into tears. Her baby girl was budding into a young woman. A young woman with nothing ahead of her but poverty, desperation, and crime if Carrie didn't come up with something to stop it.

"They were just messing around," Candace said in defense of her friends. "Mr. Hirsch should've minded his own business. They were throwing rocks at a mama cat hiding under the building so they could get close enough to see her kittens."

"They could've hurt someone throwing rocks. Or they could've killed the mama cat. Then what would've become of her babies?"

Candace shrugged without uncrossing her arms.

"How do you know so much about why they were throwing rocks anyway? Were you there?"

"She's always with those girls."

Carrie looked for the first time to the bedroom door. Eight-year-old John Thomas, as blond and pale and skinny as his sister, stood in the doorway.

"Mind your own business, crybaby!" Candace screamed.

Candace deserved a swat for yelling at her brother, but Carrie didn't want to make the situation bigger than it already was. "John Thomas, go in the bedroom and read your mathematics book."

"I already finished my assignment. Candace was yelling at Mr. Hirsch, too. She was about to throw a rock at him when Mrs. Worstell came out and chased them off."

"Shut up, tattletale!" Candace shouted again and lunged at her brother.

John Thomas wisely ducked into the bedroom and closed the door.

Carrie grabbed her daughter's arm and pulled her to a halt. How long before she could no longer manhandle Candace into obedience? What was happening here? Things would be so much easier if she didn't have to figure this out alone. If her children had a father who could help with the heavy lifting. Carrie wouldn't let her thoughts go down that road. Her children had a father all right: he just lived on the other side of town with another woman who claimed to also be his wife.

"You were throwing rocks—at Mr. Hirsch, no less?"

"I wasn't going to hit him with it. I just wanted him to mind his own business."

Carrie looked down into her daughter's once angelic face, now twisted with anger and indignation, and wondered what in the world she was going to do to save her family from the danger and violence and poverty around them.

"Mr. Hirsch has only been kind to you, Candace. Even if he hasn't been, there's no excuse to treat an adult in such a way. For treating anyone that way."

Candace exhaled and rolled her eyes. Carrie tightened her grip on the girl's shoulders. It took every ounce of resolve she possessed not to shake her like a ragdoll. Maybe that was the only way to get through to her.

"Do not leave this apartment for the rest of the day, young lady. Do you hear me?"

Candace's upper lip pulled back from her pearly white teeth. "Like I have anywhere to go. You insulted all my friends."

Carrie exhaled, exhausted. She pulled the coal bucket out of the corner. "Clean the ashes out of the stove and then go down to the basement for more coal. Tell Mr. Higgins I'll pay for it on Friday."

"I thought you said I couldn't leave the apartment," Candace sneered.

Carrie glared down at her daughter. Candace finally seemed to recognize she had pushed her mother about as far as she dared. She grabbed the bucket from Carrie and stalked over to the heat stove.

Carrie glanced at the timepiece on her bodice. She needed to get back to work. She was already going to be in big trouble, but what was another five minutes?

She went into the bedroom. John Thomas lay on his side on the bed. She sat beside him and brushed his still baby-fine hair out of his eyes. He'd been crying. "Is Candace still in trouble?" he asked.

"Yes, sweetheart, but don't worry. Mrs. Higgins said she'd check on you later. I'll be home from work in time to fix your supper."

John Thomas sat up and wrapped his arms around her. "I'm sorry you're sad, Mama."

She hugged him and kissed the top of his head. "Don't worry about me, John Thomas. I'll be home as soon as I can."

She thought of the letters in her bureau drawer that had come from the man in Cowboy Creek, Colorado. Philip Whitamore. A man she had never met but already felt like she knew as well as any man she ever met. Yesterday she had received a third letter. She'd begun crafting her reply in her head but so far hadn't had time to sit down and start writing. Hopefully tonight when she got home.

Last month Nan Canfield, a kindly older woman whose charity group brought food and hand-me-down clothes to Carrie's church sometimes, had told her about a group of men in Colorado looking for brides. Carrie had blushed furiously and looked around to make sure no one else was within earshot. Why had Miss Canfield singled her out? Did she look that desperate? Hopeless? Destitute?

"I'm no bride," she told Nan with a nervous laugh. At thirty, she felt like an old woman. An old woman with the life sucked out of her.

Nan had smiled kindly and pushed the letter into her hand. "From my understanding, few of the men in Cowboy Creek are youngsters. They're hard-working ranchers and businessmen, trying to carve a life out of the wilderness. They can't do it alone. They're looking for equally hard-working, resolute women ready to leave the city behind and build a better life for themselves and their families."

Carrie had stared at the letter and wondered if it could be the answer to her prayers.

She took the letter home and kept it hidden from the children in the highboy drawer. She had read it so often the folds had begun to come apart. Every time she read it, she prayed for the man who'd written it and the other cowboys in Cowboy Creek. She also prayed for herself and the children. Could she have a life in that faraway place with a stranger? Would it be the salvation of her family?

She turned her back to John Thomas so he wouldn't see and pulled the first letter out of the drawer.

My name is Philip Whitamore, it read, *but everyone calls me Whit. Rase Canfield, Nan Canfield's nephew, said it would be easier for his aunt to make matches between us men and the women interested in coming if she knew a little about each of us. This here's my introduction to whoever ends up reading it.*

I'm older than most grooms. Maybe too old for thinking about taking a wife. But I hope you don't think so. There's only a handful of us living here. All men, except for our preacher's wife. On Christmas Day we men decided we'd like to build Cowboy Creek into a regular town with a school, a proper church, and a few stores. It can't be done with just us cowpokes. We need brides.

Carrie stopped reading and smiled as she always did at that point in the letter. She didn't know anything about this man, but he seemed honest and genuine with a sense of humor. The kind of man she always hoped for but didn't think existed. She continued reading.

I run the local gristmill. It's a small operation, but it keeps me fairly busy. Busy enough to support a family, I believe. My hope is as Cowboy Creek turns into a proper town, the gristmill will become a prosperous operation. Cowboy Creek is a beautiful place to raise a family. Green and big with wide open spaces. The mountains make a man recognize the majesty of our Creator and provide plenty of places for young ones to find adventure. When I close my eyes, I can imagine kids running across the fields whooping and hollering the way I did when I was young. Been so long since I heard little ones playing, I almost forget what it sounds like.

If you're reading this letter and think you might want to come here to build a family and a future with me, please write and tell me a little about yourself. I hope we can get to know each other and you might decide to come and meet me in person.

Carrie folded the letter and slipped it back into the drawer with the other two. Whit's words about longing to hear little ones playing had filled her with hope. As soon as she read the letter for the first time, she understood why Nan had given it to her. This man was very forthcoming about what he wanted. A family. Children. If he and Carrie got together, he would get that is spades.

She knew poor John Thomas was teased around the neighborhood and at school for his small stature and sensitive demeanor. He needed a strong male role model to take him under his wing and teach him what it meant to be a man. Candace needed away from the group of girls she had become part of. Carrie knew the child was looking for acceptance and a place to belong. The only problem was she was looking for it from girls more broken than she was.

But marriage?

Carrie wasn't sure she was ready for that or ever would be. She married Johnny Rhoades when she was seventeen to get away from the poverty of an overcrowded home life. The only thing Johnny seemed to have enough gumption to do was make babies. He began skipping work and leaving the house when Candace was still an infant. He would disappear for days at a time and return smelling like booze and cheap perfume. When Carrie complained or asked where he'd been—or worse, if he had lost another job—she found herself on the receiving end of his wrath.

Johnny's absences grew longer and more frequent. Carrie found she didn't mind so much. She knew how to earn a living, and things were much more peaceful with Johnny out of the house. Then she realized she was pregnant with John Thomas. How could she have been so stupid to let her husband back into her bed when she knew he was unfaithful? She had the biblical basis to file for divorce, but she wouldn't consider that. Divorce was out of the question. Especially for women. Women were meant to stay with their husbands, regardless of the circumstances. She accepted her fate and knew she'd never escape Johnny.

Soon after John Thomas's birth, Johnny lost all interest in her and the children. He came home occasionally, three or four times a year. He always had a pocketful of candy for the children and a small token for her. He would laugh and throw the children into the air, and they wouldn't even think to ask where he'd been. Carrie knew better than to ask. She let him in every time, hoping things would be different. This would be the time he changed and settled down into a respectable life with his family. Then the day came when she learned the reason Johnny couldn't be part of their family. He already had a family. And other children. Johnny hadn't been cheating *on* her. He'd been cheating *with* her.

She did what she swore she'd never do and legally freed herself of Johnny Rhoades. Did she want to latch onto another man who could end up just as terrible? It was impossible for a woman to know what she was getting when she accepted a man's proposal? Regardless, the time had come when Carrie needed to think of what was best for her children. John Thomas needed a father. She smiled as she pictured his skinny legs growing stronger climbing over rocks and jumping across mountain streams. She imagined Candace's pale cheeks warmed by the sun, her gaze turned toward Heaven as she contemplated her place in a world where she was loved and cherished.

Of course, Carrie would have to tell Whit the whole story. He needed to know what happened to her husband—or the man she had considered her husband. No one in this neighborhood knew she was divorced. They assumed she was a widow and her children fatherless. It had been too complicated and humiliating to explain the situation, so Carrie never tried. But Whit would need to know, even if she couldn't begin to think how to tell him.

She grabbed her heavy shawl from the bedpost and wrapped it around her shoulders. She'd worry about all that later. For now, she needed to do some serious thinking and praying over the matter. Maybe she'd already received the answer to her prayers. Maybe the answer and a new life for all of them was waiting in a place called Cowboy Creek with a man called Whit Whitamore.

Chapter Two

The stage rattled to a stop. Carrie's stomach lurched. Her head pounded. The entire trip had been exhausting and trying, but the last twenty miles from Ruby City to Good Hope had easily been the worst. John Thomas suffered from motion sickness nearly the entire trip. His shirt was stained and reeked of vomit. The smell and sounds of him gagging had sickened Candace and done little to improve her surly mood.

Since the moment Candace learned they were leaving Cincinnati—the night before the departure since Carrie wanted to limit the eminent arguments and sulking to as small a window as possible—she had fluctuated between crying, screaming, arguing, sulking, and sneering. Carrie quickly learned she preferred the sulking and sneering. They were quieter.

Between dealing with Candace's temper tantrums and John Thomas's heaving, Carrie barely had time to second-guess her decision to come west to see if she could share her life with a complete stranger. Still, she managed. Now her head throbbed, and she feared she would lose her lunch from this morning.

She climbed down from the coach and reached back to help everyone else. As expected, five-year-old Annie Fairchild leaped into her arms and clung to her neck.

Carrie suppressed a groan. What was she going to do about this child? What would Whit think when he found out Carrie had brought along a foundling? She had written that she had two children. She couldn't very well keep them a secret. But three? If there was any truth to his letters, he liked children. She could only hope he would accept the little girl without complaint.

She hadn't had time to write another letter to explain Annie's situation. She had already accepted the money from the men of Cowboy Creek and bought their tickets. Fortunately, thanks to her frugal nature, she had enough traveling expense money left over to buy a third child's passage. It would take at least a week to get word to Whit about Annie. By then, they'd be here. Surely, once he heard of how the little girl had been left in the streets by her own father, he would understand why Carrie had no choice but to bring her along.

"Here, sweetheart, let me breathe."

She leaned forward until Annie's feet touched the ground and then disengaged the child's arms from around her neck. "I have to help everyone else."

Annie was a darling child who only wanted the security of Carrie's presence, but Carrie was beyond exhausted.

Annie whimpered. She hadn't spoken more than a few words since Carrie literally picked her up off the street and marched back to the apartment with the child in her arms. Carrie still seethed in anger at the sight of little Annie sitting on the stoop of the tenement building where she lived. Carrie had knocked on the child's apartment door until her knuckles were raw. She even tried the door when a neighbor told her Annie's pa sent her outside early every morning and wouldn't let her back in until nighttime, if then. According to the neighbor, Annie's mama died the week before. Her papa claimed he couldn't afford to keep a girl too small to work. He didn't want her, but he couldn't be bothered with taking her to the church or the authorities.

Different neighbors in the building took her in as much as they could, especially at night when her pa forgot or just didn't open the door, but they were all old and couldn't afford to keep her. It didn't help her cause that all she did was cry for her mama.

Carrie had hailed a policeman and told him the child's plight. "You people are like cats; making more babies than you can afford to feed. Pathetic," he added as he walked away.

The second officer Carrie approached had shaken his head in despair. "Here, give her to me. I'll take her to the precinct, and somebody will get around to taking her to the orphanage. It'll go hard for her there with nothing to eat and the older children who abuse the little ones. But she's a pretty thing. Maybe she'll get adopted before she starves."

He reached for Annie. "Come on, kid. I ain't got all day. It's freezing out here."

Carrie had gasped and clutched the child against her. Over her dead body! She knew the city's orphanages were dismal places, but she never dreamed Annie would be better off fending for herself on the street than going to a facility where the staff and older children could do whatever they wanted to her until she starved or died from sickness.

She had practically run with the child back to her apartment. There had been no time to tell Whit. She could only pray he wouldn't begrudge another mouth to feed.

"Excuse me, Mrs. Rhoades?"

Carrie took John Thomas's hand as he jumped to the ground, then turned, leaving Candace to disembark herself. She knew without asking Candace would not appreciate her help or even the touch on her hand.

"Yes," she began.

Her heart sank at the sight of the old man. White hair stuck out in tufts over his ears, which were red from the cold. While he still possessed most of his teeth, they were stained with age and his blue eyes had lost much of their color.

In his first letter Whit had joked that he was older than most grooms, but he hadn't said he was old enough to be a grandfather. He had also written that he looked forward to children. Maybe he meant Carrie's children. How old could a man still father children? In the Bible, Abraham had been a hundred when God promised he would become the father of many nations. But that was a long time ago.

Please, God, she prayed. *Don't let my future husband be a hundred.*

The old man stuck out his hand. "I'm Daniel Dodds, but everyone calls me Preach. My wife and I own the trading post in Cowboy Creek. We also serve the residents' spiritual needs. You'll be under our care while you get to know Mr. Whitamore."

Carrie hoped the relief didn't show on her face.

"Mr. Dodds." She stuck out her hand. "It's a pleasure to meet you. I'm Carrie Rhoades. These are my children Candace and John Thomas. And Annie," she added, remembering the shivering little girl at her knees. The wind had picked up and Annie looked half frozen. Carrie held out her arms. Annie jumped into them in a move that had been perfected over the last week.

The man's forehead puckered for a moment, counting heads. Whit must've told him to expect a woman and two children. Not three.

"My wife sends her apologies," he said. "She stayed home to fix a nice supper for all of you. Since you were bringing children, we hoped you wouldn't mind the ride back without an official chaperone."

"Oh, of course not." Carrie would never think of this kind-eyed, white-haired man as a threat. She glanced around. "Where's Mr. Whitamore?"

A shadow flashed across the preacher's wizened face. "Whit, that's what we all call Mr. Whitamore, he's unfortunately been indisposed and asked me to come in his place. A belt slipped off a piece of equipment and he had orders to fill so he stayed at the mill to fix it. He's a busy man."

Carrie's stomach sank lower than it had when she thought her groom was an old man. Everyone was busy, including Mr. Dodds. What kind of man would leave his intended without a ride to Cowboy Creek so he could work on a piece of machinery? With great effort, she pushed aside her dismay. This wasn't Cincinnati. A broken piece of equipment required a lot more to repair or replace than walking down the street to procure another one. It could bring an entire operation, not to mention the town's economy, to a grinding halt. She wouldn't judge Whit too harshly. He *had* arranged a ride for them. That was something.

She helped Mr. Dodds—or Preach, as he reminded her several times—load their baggage in the back of the wagon atop some farming implements and bags of feed and seed that had apparently been the preacher's other motive for coming to town. The children piled into the back amidst the luggage, and Carrie climbed onto the front seat next to Preach.

"I appreciate you taking the time out of your day to pick us up."

"Wasn't no trouble, Mrs. Rhoades. I come to town at least once a week—weather permitting—to buy things for the trading post and fill orders for everybody in Cowboy Creek. The missus and I sure were happy to hear you have children. A place gets mighty lonesome without them. You young'uns are going to like Cowboy Creek," he said over his shoulder.

He clicked his tongue at the team of horses. "We don't have a school yet, but hopefully you can get along without one for a spell."

"It'll suit me just fine," John Thomas exclaimed. Carrie gaped. He was usually reserved around strangers and seldom spoke to adults unless he couldn't avoid it. She was heartened to see the light of adventure and excitement in his blue eyes.

"How far is it to Cowboy Creek?" he asked.

"Round about an hour. We'll pass a few farms. Might even see some Indians out hunting."

"Indians?" all three children said in unison. Even Candace perked up at the prospect.

Preach laughed at their reaction, then sobered. "We don't see them around much anymore since our settlements pushed the game farther west. More's the pity if you ask me. Folks need to learn to share God's bounty and learn from each other if we hope to carve a strong nation outta these mountains."

As the wagon moved out of Good Hope, the landscape stretched in front of them with no sign of life. The farms he mentioned were so secluded, Carrie and the children could barely see rooflines and barns among the trees and gentle slope of the land. Soon enough, even those signs of civilization were left behind the wagon's turning wheels. Carrie marveled at the isolation. She didn't want to consider what Candace was thinking of it all.

Preach pointed out geographical features along the way. Finally, they reached a line of trees and gradual sloping land. "We're getting close," he announced. "Up around this bend you can look down into a little valley where you can see the house and barn of some of your new neighbors, Jacob and Rennie Campbell. I expect you'll be wanting to meet Mrs. Campbell," he told Carrie. "She was the first bride to come to Cowboy Creek."

He raised his voice so the children could hear over the creaking of the wagon wheels. "We never got around to giving our little town a proper name. Two cowboys were the first to settle this area. They lived here for a couple years, ranching and raising a little of this and a little of that until the day they discovered gold in the river."

"Gold!" John Thomas cried. "Was there really gold here?"

"Yessiree. There sure was. Nuggets as big as your fist." He winked at Carrie. "As soon as word got out, a whole city cropped up along the riverbank. That's why we call it Cowboy Creek. Didn't your mama tell you? The gold made us all rich. Now we live in mansions along the shores of Cowboy Creek and wile away the hours in idle pursuits."

"Really?" John Thomas squealed.

"Really?" Annie echoed, surprising Carrie further. She was still unaccustomed to the sound of the child's voice.

Candace drove an elbow into John Thomas's ribs. "He's just joshing."

Mr. Dodds nodded and grinned. "You're a right smart girl there, little lady. There ain't a flake 'a gold left in that whole stream. The gold lasted about eleven months before it played out. Nobody got rich. Not even the fellas that discovered it. Soon enough, everybody pulled up stakes and hightailed it outta there 'cept Marla and me and the nine fellas who decided to stay and ranch the area. You'll see why once we get there. It's about the most beautiful place on earth. I can't understand the folks who didn't stick around. I don't know what they hoped to find that'd be any better. Me and the missus were doing all right with our trading post, and we didn't have anywhere else to go so we stayed put."

"Don't you have any children?" John Thomas asked, surprising Carrie again by his lack of shyness.

Preach laughed. "Naw. Marla and me's too old. We had us two boys, but they both went on to their reward." His voice softened. "They're with Jesus now."

"That's so sad," Candace said quietly.

Carrie tried not to stare. Candace had barely said two words to Carrie in the last three days, but she still had a compassionate heart to express sympathy to a stranger.

"Yes, it is," Preach said, his eyes on the road ahead of them. "For Marla and me. We try to remember our boys are having a time in Heaven right now, and we'll be reunited someday."

Carrie followed his gaze to the horizon. Parenthood was the toughest job the Lord ever put on a body. Especially when one's children were called home first. All a parent could do was raise them up as best they could, teach them right from wrong, to respect their fellow man, and love God. What happened beyond that was up to them and God's grace. Sad and terrifying. But also rewarding and exciting. Now she'd share that responsibility with Philip 'Whit' Whitamore.

Nagging doubt assailed her for about the hundredth time since accepting Nan's offer to come west. Just how invested was Whit in this proposal? He had seemed enthusiastic in the letters they exchanged, but he hadn't shown up at the stage stop to meet them. She would feel more confident in the likelihood of their success if he had picked her up himself.

She allowed her mind to drift as they rode along, half-listening to the preacher's stories. John Thomas peppered the man with questions, no longer bothered by his earlier motion sickness. Even Candace seemed interested in the stories and asked a few questions of her own. Yes, this might be the best thing for all of them. Annie was still quiet, but her reticence faded as she became more adjusted to her new reality. Weariness finally won out, and she rested her head in Candace's lap and fell asleep among the feed sacks. Carrie looked forward to getting to know the little girl better once her true nature revealed itself. She hoped Whit was as accommodating.

"Yup, we're getting real close now," Preach announced, just as Carrie thought her tired back couldn't take one more bone-jarring bounce in a wheel rut. "Look through those trees there and you'll see Adam and Eliza Waring's place. That means we're less than a mile from home. You'll be staying at the brides' house in Cowboy Creek. It's next door to Marla and me and just down the road from the gristmill."

The gristmill. Their new home if things worked out between her and Whit. She didn't know anything about milling. Like anything else, she figured she'd learn quickly enough.

What if things didn't work out? What if Whit couldn't take Candace's belligerence or John Thomas's skittishness? Where would they go then? How would she explain it to the children? They had uprooted their entire lives. She couldn't very well take them back to Cincinnati. There was nothing to go back to. She glanced over her shoulder, her gaze resting on Candace. The twelve-year-old was craning her neck to see through the trees, a modicum of interest lighting her vivid blue eyes.

Her stomach tightened. *This has to work,* Carrie told herself. *We don't have anything else.*

Chapter Three

"Is this it?"

"Candace," Carrie hissed in warning, though she was wondering the same thing. The knot in her stomach rose to her throat, threatening to cut off her airway. Not another living creature was in sight, including Whit. She counted three lopsided, sun-bleached structures that looked like they hadn't seen human occupation in decades. The wagon rolled past without slowing.

"It sure is." Preach's voice rang with pride and proprietorship, apparently not recognizing the dismay in Candace's voice or the tightening of Carrie's shoulders. "Welcome to Cowboy Creek." Another handful of buildings stood haphazardly arranged, creating a narrow street of sorts. One had a tree growing out of a side window. A large portion of roof had been peeled back on another as if a fierce wind had decided to make its own entrance.

Cowboy Creek looked lonely and forgotten. But the longer Carrie looked, she sensed an air of hopefulness about the place, as if it was just waiting for whoever had erected the flimsy walls to walk back inside, throw open the windows, and start living again.

Two of the buildings and a large barn didn't look as dilapidated or abandoned as the others. Over the door of one was a rough wooden sign that read: *Trading Post* in faded, crooked lettering.

Out of sight on the far end of the street came the ringing of a hammer on metal. The metallic scent of soot hung in the air. The sound and smell encouraged Carrie. There must be some prosperity in the area if the settlement was big enough to support a blacksmith shop.

Annie roused from sleep and joined the other children on their knees looking in every direction. Preach wagged his head toward the sounds of the blacksmith shop. "The smithy's just around the bend up that way. Lonnie Fanshaw, our blacksmith, farms a little patch of land but we keep him mighty busy smithing. On up the road is the Whitamore house and the mill."

Through the trees Carrie saw the roofline of a house and a two-story structure beyond it. After seeing the buildings along Cowboy Creek's only street, she wasn't sure what to expect of Whit's house. The porch of the trading post was swept clean as was the approach of the building directly across from it. Someone had gone to some trouble to neaten the place up, though it still looked terribly deserted and lonely. If not for the ringing of the hammer from the blacksmith shop, she would wonder if

Preach was the only real person left on the planet and he had fabricated everything else.

Real fear pushed aside Carrie's disappointment. Whit's absence shouted volumes about his level of interest in her arrival. She understood an emergency keeping him from meeting the stage, but certainly he could spare a few moments to greet her and the children. Just how committed was he to a possible relationship between them.

"On the other side of the barn is the brides' house," Preach said, pointing. "It ain't much, but it's suitable living for a short time. We men fixed it up for you brides to stay in until you—well, while you get settled to the area. It's tight and warm. We tried to make it as comfortable as we could. Rounded up a few pieces of furniture. If there's anything else you need, just holler and we'll see what we can do."

Carrie murmured her thanks. She didn't know what to say. She felt as overwhelmed as the children looked as they gazed around the deserted street of abandoned buildings. It would help if Whit were here to put her mind to ease. She didn't know what she'd do if he had changed his mind about taking a wife.

She felt nauseous and knew it had nothing to do with the last few days of travel.

The wagon creaked to a stop in front of the trading post. "How about I take the young'uns into the store to warm up and meet Mrs. Dodds?" Preach suggested. "She sure is excited about meeting you all. We'll have supper around six, but for now, I reckon they could stand a bite. Marla baked up a sponge cake yesterday and I think she has some punch cooling on the back step. I'll introduce them and get 'em something to eat if you'd like to take the opportunity to walk up to the mill to meet Whit."

Apprehension struck Carrie's breast at the thought of knocking on Whit's door like a street urchin begging for a handout. Especially if he'd changed his mind and didn't want her. She shook off her worries. He'd simply been detained from meeting the stage. She wouldn't allow her imagination and insecurity to read a whole lot of other reasons into it.

She took a deep breath to still the pounding of her heart. "That sounds fine. Thank you."

Preach nodded encouragingly and climbed down from the wagon. "Me and the young'uns can move your bags and things into the brides' house while you're gone. When you get back, you can unpack." He helped her to the ground before circling the wagon and lowering the tailgate for the children.

Carrie followed him and held out her arms for Annie. The child wrapped her arms and legs around Carrie and snuggled against her. It was a good idea to meet Whit first without the children. She needed a chance to explain why she had brought a third child who wanted to be carried everywhere she went. She needed to warn Whit about Candace's anger over coming. More than anything, she wouldn't subject the children to Whit's rejection should he decide his life was fine the way it was, and he didn't want them after all.

Preach must've recognized her apprehension. He gave her a reassuring smile. "Remind Whit he's expected for supper too. He already knows Marla doesn't cotton to anyone turning down her fine cooking."

Carrie thought about telling him she was too tired to partake in a prearranged supper with anyone. She wanted to wash her hair and climb into a real bed and sleep for twenty-four hours—not that she could with three children hanging off her. She looked at their tired, dirty faces. They needed a good hot meal, which she currently didn't have the means or energy to provide. How would they eat after tonight? Was there a stove in the brides' house? Where would she buy food? Would they take all their meals with the preacher and his wife until she and Whit decided they were suited for marriage?

Oh, so many details she should've investigated before coming across the country.

With no immediate answers in sight, she set Annie on the ground and smoothed her dark hair out of her face. She placed the child's tiny hand in Candace's. "You go with Candace. Mind your manners, all of you."

Annie's lower lip trembled. Candace's lips pressed into a hard line. Only John Thomas looked eager to follow Preach around the side of the building. At least one of their moods had improved since arriving in Cowboy Creek.

Preach gave her another smile for courage before turning the children toward the building. "You ever been fishing? There's a right nice fishing hole down the creek a ways. Can't fish till the water goes down, but you'll like it once the weather warms up a bit."

Would they still be here when the weather warmed up? Carrie wondered. Would she and Whit have fallen in love by then? Or would they realize neither had better options and they may as well make the best of the situation?

Only one way to find out.

She took another look behind her as the children followed Preach around the corner of the trading post. Her heart sank at the defiant set of Candace's jaw. She was a child trying so hard to prove she was grown up enough to make her own choices. Carrie knew the bravado masked the girl's fear and uncertainty. To leave her friends behind was hard for any young girl, but to end up in a place with no other children her own age—no other children at all but her little brother and a foundling—was beyond comprehension. It must seem like she'd been dropped into a completely alien world, and she would hate everything about it.

Carrie nearly felt the same herself.

"Oh Lord, may this not be the biggest mistake of my life," she prayed under her breath.

She prayed Candace would give it a chance and make the best of the situation. She vowed to be extra patient and understanding with the girl. Before she worked herself into a fretful lather over how to help Candace, she needed to meet Whit Whitamore.

She lifted her chin in the same way Candace had done and started toward the gristmill. The creek at the side of the road provided directions. The noise of rushing water grew louder as she walked under the bare branches of tall, thin trees. She passed the blacksmith shop. The door stood open to the small building, but she didn't see anyone moving about.

The slope of the hill leveled off and the trees cleared to reveal a large house. It was an unpainted, unadorned lap-sided two-story structure. It looked like it had at least three rooms downstairs and three more up. The children would be ecstatic to have their own rooms instead of being crammed together like they were in the city, sharing a two-room apartment and two small beds.

A three-step stoop led to the front door. Carrie imagined a wide front porch running along the entire length of the house. She loved the look of a front porch on a house. It made her think the house was smiling in welcome to all visitors.

She'd never had a porch to sit on. She loved the idea of sitting in a rocking chair in the evening with her knitting or mending with Whit in a chair beside her and the children playing in the yard. Candace would someday entertain beaux here—if other families moved to the area from which she could find a beau. John Thomas would learn to whittle on the front porch in the shadow of his adopted father. Annie would cut out paper dolls and listen to Carrie's stories and songs as she grew confident and secure, enveloped in the love of her new family.

A smile played across Carrie's lips. She was tempted to leave the path and go to the window for a peek inside. She resisted. This wasn't her house yet. It may never be. She'd have to wait and see how she and Whit got along. They seemed compatible in their letters, but she wasn't the best judge of that. She thought she was compatible with Johnny Rhoades when he first came courting. After they married, he found all sorts of reasons to pick fights with her and leave home for days on end.

She obviously had no idea what men wanted and how to get on with them.

She heard the whir of machinery coming from the mill just past the house. She allowed the gentle slope toward the creek carry her in that direction since her legs seemed to have lost their strength. The knot was back in her stomach. What if Whit took one look at her and changed his mind? She wasn't a girl. Brides were supposed to be young. Virginal. She wasn't either of those. She was stubborn and independent after spending most of her adult life doing things the way she wanted. She had driven off one husband. What if no man could live with her?

She picked up her pace before she lost her nerve. She hesitated at the large door, wondering if she should knock. Even from outside, it was so noisy, she knew no one would ever hear her. She let herself into the cavernous interior. The building was cold and drafty. Carrie tightened the collar of her coat around her neck. On the far side of a large room, a bay door was open to the rushing sound of the creek. Outside her field of vision, though she could hear it, a wooden paddle slowly moved the water and turned a belt that slid along the length of the bay door.

At the opposite end of the room a man fiddled with the gears inside a large wooden box. He must not have heard her come in over the sound of the water and machinery because he didn't pause in his work. His coat was off, though the interior of the building was nearly as cold as outside. His sleeves were rolled up, revealing thick forearms corded with muscle.

Carrie headed across the floor, making a circuitous route so he would see her coming before she got right on top of him. She didn't want to startle him and make him fall into the creek or swing the huge wrench in his hand at her. She was still half a dozen steps from him when he spotted her and stopped his work. He straightened and turned. The first thing she noticed were the deepest brown eyes she'd ever seen. He had a wide nose, narrow lips, and a strong, square jaw, hidden by the scruff of about a week's-old beard. His toffee brown hair with the slightest hint of red was neatly cut considering he probably had to see to it himself. He ran his hand through his thick hair, calling attention to a hairline just beginning to recede. He looked somewhere in his late thirties, though he had aged well. Carrie nearly laughed in delight, remembering her earlier fear that Preach was the man she had come to wed.

Whit set down the wrench and took up a rag to wipe his hands as he crossed the floor toward her. Suddenly self-conscious, Carrie resisted the urge to reach up and smooth her hair and her hat. She had been so focused on getting the children settled, she hadn't considered what she must look like after four days of travel.

"Whit?"

"Mrs. Rhoades?"

She smiled.

He smiled back. His brown eyes sparked to life, causing relief and attraction to course through her.

"Please, call me Carrie."

He looked like he was experiencing the same thoughts at the sight of her. "I'd be happy to."

Carrie stared at him, not sure how to proceed. She barely remembered the nervous, gullible girl she'd been back when she met Johnny Rhoades. She had no other experience with men. Should she shake his hand? Dip her head? Curtsy? Whit seemed equally unsure. He suddenly looked past her as if realizing something was missing.

"Where are the children? Didn't they come?"

Was that hope in his voice? "No. I mean yes. They're here. They're with the minister—Preach. His wife made a cake. And punch, he said."

Whit chuckled, dispersing any hopefulness she thought she saw in his eyes. "Sounds like Marla. You'll have to watch her. She'll feed you within an inch of your life if you let her."

More relief flooded through Carrie. She liked a man with a sense of humor—or, she always suspected she would, should she ever meet one. "Thanks for the warning. I don't think she'll have to worry about the children. They're always hungry."

His jaw tensed momentarily. Did he worry they would eat him out of house and home if he chose to pursue a relationship with her? It was a possibility. Growing children *were* always hungry. They were also constantly growing, requiring new shoes and pants, and sometimes even medical treatment. She pushed the thoughts out of her head. Whit had invited her to come, knowing she had children. He was a bachelor who may never have considered the cost of a family. The concerns over their support were in her head, not his.

Whit stuffed the rag into his back pocket. "We haven't had little ones around here for years. Marla's been nearly beside herself at the thought of it. Can't talk about anything else. You know how women are." He realized what he said and smiled in apology.

Carrie smiled at the faux pas. "Yes, I know how they are."

He stared at her a moment, seemingly as awkward and uncomfortable as she felt. "Would you, um, like a cup of coffee? I have a couple loaves of fresh bread and honey."

"Do you bake?"

"Sometimes, though I'm not sure what comes out of my kitchen is fit for anyone but me. You don't need to worry, though. The bread I bought from Marla. She sells baked goods once a week at the trading post. I wanted to have something tastier than what I might've rustled up for when you arrived."

"Coffee and bread sound fine for later, but right now I wouldn't mind taking a walk. I'd love to breath some fresh air after traveling so long." She also wanted a chance to freshen up before sitting across a table from him, though she wouldn't confess that.

"Yes, of course. I can show you around the mill, but you're probably more interested in seeing the house and the property before it gets dark."

"I'd love to see anything you want to show me. It's a relief to be off the stage and stretch my legs." She winced again. Her legs were not a topic suitable for mentioning to a man she wasn't yet married to.

Whit didn't seem to notice. "Are you warm enough?" He glanced at her coat and gloved hands.

"Oh, yes, quite." In fact, in his proximity, she was surprisingly warm.

"All right then." He glanced down at her, looking awkward and unsure again as if deciding if he should take her hand or arm. Carrie answered the question for him by turning toward the door. He pushed down his shirt sleeves, shrugged into his coat, and set his hat on his head. At the large door Carrie had just entered, he reached past her to push it open. Carrie used the opportunity to take a deep breath and collect herself. Whit seemed polite. He was handsome, and his situation looked secure. She could certainly do worse in a husband. She *had* done worse. She could only hope Whit was as satisfied with the situation as she was. If things didn't work out between them, his life would continue on as it always had. Hers would be completely upended.

Chapter Four

Whit never dreamed she'd be so pretty. He wasn't the type to put much stock in a person's looks, but he sure was pleased by the fine figure Carrie cut. While exchanging letters back and forth with her, he had created a vague image of her in his head. He pictured a kind smile, bright, intelligent eyes, and a gentle spirit. When he first saw her lithe frame gliding across the floor toward him, his eyes had nearly bugged out of his head. This beauty couldn't possibly be here for *him*. Her golden hair looked thick and lustrous piled on her head under a dusky blue hat. Her skin was smooth and creamy white, seeming to beckon for him to reach out and touch it.

The most striking thing about her, though, was those wide-set cornflower blue eyes—looking sharp and intelligent and kind all at the same time. He was glad she wasn't a girl. He had wanted a woman close to his own age. She looked about ten years younger than himself, so that was close enough.

They'd only exchanged a few letters. After he sent his introductory letter, Carrie had written back an equally short descriptive letter. She described herself as small in stature, blue eyes, blond hair. Crimeny, had she undersold herself on that!

When Whit found out she had two children, he nearly told Rase he wanted someone else. Children cost money. They ate too much. They outgrew their shoes. When he put out money to raise children, he wanted them to be his own.

But something about Carrie Rhoades in that first brief letter spoke to Whit's heart and dispelled his concerns over supporting a family right off. In those few lines, he sensed everything missing from his own life. How much more would a couple of kids cost anyway? With a wife, he could easily triple the size of his garden. The children wouldn't need shoes and clothes the first day. At least he hoped not.

When he caught sight of Carrie crossing the room toward him, the loneliness and emptiness in his heart hit him like a hammer on an anvil. He grew up in a big, noisy family in the mountains of North Carolina. Except for his brother Henry, he had felt different than the rest. Like he was invisible, like he didn't fit. He had wanted someone to take the time to get to know him, to ask him what he really thought about things. Instead, he felt like he was always in someone's way. He knew his parents resented having so many mouths to feed. As soon as he was able, he left home. No one tried awfully hard to get him to change his mind.

When he opened the door for Carrie to go out ahead of him, her slim frame brushed against his arm holding the door. It jolted him almost as much as the time a calf kicked him during a roping session when he was in his teens. He resisted the temptation to put his hand on her back as he ushered her into the pale afternoon sunlight. He didn't have a right to touch her. Not yet.

He sure hoped that would change soon.

He wouldn't have many lonely empty moments in his life if Carrie married him and moved with her two children into his house. Pretty soon, there'd be more if the Good Lord saw fit to bless them that way. Whit hadn't thrown up his hand to request a bride without first giving it some serious consideration. Now with her next to him, panic sat down hard on his chest. Had he been impetuous? Had his loneliness forced the common sense clean out of his head? Could he provide for her and her children and give her everything she wanted while keeping them out of the poorhouse?

The gristmill did a good business, but Cowboy Creek was small. It provided just enough income to keep him operational. It wasn't like he had much savings. Most of the money he made went back into the business. The garden and livestock were enough to support one man. But a family? He'd done some calculating since Christmas. It worked on paper, but what if he had a bad year? What if a drought dried up the grain, and none of the surrounding farms had anything to run through the mill? What if a flood washed away the building and he had to start over? What if lightning struck the house and burned it to the ground?

Starting over would be hard enough for one man, but a man with a family. It was unthinkable.

Whit gave his head a small shake to bring his tumbling thoughts under control. Carrie had stopped walking and turned to look at him, a quizzical expression on her pretty face. Out in the sunshine, he saw she was even prettier than his first impression. She had the beginning of tiny wrinkles around her eyes and mouth. That was all right. It meant she smiled often. Warmth shone from her sparkling blue eyes. The eyes of a woman he wanted to know better.

He gestured to his right. "If you want to walk up this way, you can see the outside of the mill and how it operates."

"All right."

Her soft, sweet voice made him think of warm honey on a winter's day. He shook his head again. *Knock it off, Whit,* he inwardly scolded. *You haven't heard a woman's voice in so long, you're thinking jibberish..*

They walked along the side of the building so close their elbows bumped together a time or two. Whit tucked his hands into his belt to keep from taking her arm.

Did she expect him to take it, or was it too presumptuous?

He didn't have much experience with women. Pretty near close to none. He'd always been half afraid of them, which was probably the reason he detected something lacking in his life.

He needed to say something. They'd never get to know each other if he just kept moving forward until they walked into the river. "Did you have a—"

"How long have you—" Carrie started at the same moment.

They stopped walking and laughed. Whit swallowed. This was harder than he thought. He'd been talking his whole life. Why had his tongue suddenly seemed to forget how to form words now that he was looking into those eyes as vivid as a summer sky?

"I'm sorry. Go ahead."

"No, you first," she insisted. She smiled up at him, making his earlier thoughts fly out of his head.

After an agonizing moment, he remembered what he had been about to say. "I was just going to ask if you had a pleasant trip from Cincinnati."

A dumb question, he knew. The trip was bumpy and long and smelly and uncomfortable, but he couldn't think of anything else. He certainly couldn't ask the true question on his mind. How could a woman who looked like her have lived in a city as big as Cincinnati and still need to come to Cowboy Creek to find a husband?

She exhaled, looking equally relieved. "It wasn't bad. Long, but uneventful, so that's always a good thing."

They began walking again. Slowly. Ambling. Like they had all day. Whit liked it. He liked her small presence beside him. He was already getting comfortable with the idea of this woman living here, sharing his life. Watching the river levels and fretting when it got too high or too low. Studying his ledgers. Fixing his supper. Reminding him to relax and enjoy the sunsets. Giving him a reason to get out of bed in the morning. And a reason to get into bed at night.

"The trip was harder on the children," she said. "They got so tired. And cranky. We had to make several stops along the way, which meant more waiting. And there's always the worry that someone would get lost and we'd miss the next train."

She stopped talking and looked at him as if she wanted to say more. Or she was waiting for him to respond.

Whit wasn't sure what he could add to the conversation. He'd never traveled much and certainly not with children. If he had his druthers, he never would.

"I have to admit I never thought of that," he said. "The only time I traveled was on horseback by myself. I started when it suited me and stopped when it suited me."

She laughed a soft, musical laugh that warmed him from the top of his head to soles of his boots. He liked hearing it. Everything about her he liked. The shale path gave way to grass as they reached the creek. Her foot slipped in the grass. He grabbed her arm to steady her, though she hadn't come close to stumbling. He kept his hand in place. It felt natural there.

"There's a waterfall on up that way." He pointed with his free hand. "It's small, but it's nice. Someday after it warms up a bit, I could show it to you and the children."

Her eyes searched his. He wasn't sure what she was looking for, but he could tell by the look on her face he'd said the right thing.

"Thank you, Whit. They would love that."

He silently congratulated himself and turned her back onto the path. "How old are they? You wrote a little about them in the letter. The girl's older than the boy, right?"

"Yes, Candace just turned twelve. John Thomas is eight and Annie is close to five, as far as I can tell."

His brow furrowed. "Wait, what? That makes three. You wrote you only have two children."

She glanced away, but when she looked back, her blue eyes glittered with determination. "Yes, I did. I mean, I do. Candace and John Thomas are my children, like I wrote in my letters. But I couldn't leave Annie there. She had nobody, Whit. Oh, it was a tragedy. Her poor mother died a month or so ago, and her pa, well, he dumped her on the street without a care about how the little thing would get along. She had nothing to eat. Nowhere to go. I'm sorry I didn't tell you but there was no time. I only found out about her right before we left. I tried to turn her over to the authorities, but they were absolutely useless. I just couldn't leave her."

Whit's jaw tightened. He didn't want to lose his temper, but he felt it bubbling up inside him. Three children to feed and clothe and raise, and not a one of them his own.

He couldn't be a crumb like the girl's pa and refuse to take her in. But it grated on him all the same. Three children. He had grown up in a family with more mouths to feed than money. Never enough wood in the stove or blankets on the beds. Hand-me-down clothes and newspaper soles in the bottoms of his shoes. Whit always swore he wouldn't go back to that. He wanted to provide better for his family than what he had coming up. When he imagined his life, he thought of a wife and two or three children. No more. Now he had three, and he hadn't even kissed Carrie yet.

He'd been duped. Taken advantage of. Somewhere in Cincinnati, that little girl's pappy was living an easy, carefree life while Whit would have to tighten his own belt so the kid would have a roof over her head.

There was really nothing he could do about it. Carrie was right; she couldn't have left the child alone in the city to fend for herself.

Still, Whit felt like someone was having a big old laugh at his expense.

Chapter Five

She shouldn't have told him. Not like this. She shouldn't have sprung it on him with no lead-up at all. They had been getting along so well until she spilled the beans about Annie. Like a dark cloud over a picnic, the atmosphere changed, and Carrie prepared for a storm.

She hadn't lied. There hadn't been time to tell him she had practically kidnapped a child off the street and brought her along. She was tempted to plead her case a little more. Explain Annie's pa. How he didn't work regularly. How he was quick with his fists. How Annie's ma had taken the brunt of the man's volatile outbursts, protecting her daughter from the worst of it. How tossing Annie out of the house was maybe the only kind thing the man had ever done for her.

Carrie resisted, believing sometimes the more a person talked, the worse things became. She had nothing to explain anyway. Annie needed a safe place to sleep and food in her stomach. A mama. Protection from the cold, cruel world. If Whit couldn't understand that, well, she was better off knowing now. She didn't know how she would survive on the frontier without a husband, but she didn't want a man without an ounce of compassion in his soul.

"Would you like to see the house?" Whit asked.

Whit stood a good head over Carrie's petite five-feet and one-inch of height. She tilted her head to look into his deep brown eyes. His smile was gentle. Understanding. The dark cloud she thought she saw over him had dissipated. She sighed inwardly. She needed to extend a little patience to the man. No matter how compassionate, it would be a hard thing for a man accustomed to bachelorhood to discover he would be responsible for a wife and *three* children the moment he signed a marriage certificate.

"I would love that," she said.

The path sloped gently upward from the creek. The ground under their feet was wet and uneven and lined with tiny rocks from the creekbank. Whit slid his hand down her arm and took her hand. Carrie's heart lurched at the contact. It had been a long time since a man held her hand. In fact, she couldn't remember the last time. Johnny had never been one for romantic gestures. At least not with her.

She trusted the sound of rushing water to drown out the pounding of her heart. She looked around as they climbed the slope, breathing in the cool, crisp air. She still hadn't acclimated to the quiet serenity away from the city. She had almost forgotten how to walk a straight line without dodging wagons or impatient riders or skirting piles left behind by horses.

"This area is lovely," she commented. "I can see why you chose to stay after the mines played out."

He glanced past her to the creek. "I wouldn't have left, even if I was the only fella who stayed. The water puts me to sleep every night. Nature's lullaby. Sometimes the water's quiet, but most times it's like today. Loud and rushing, which is good for business. There was only a dilapidated mill when I arrived. No longer functional, but I knew I could make something of it. My grandpappy operated a mill back in North Carolina. I learned everything from him. There wasn't a house either back then. That didn't bother me none. I slept in the mill the first year while I filed for the deed with the territory since the property had been abandoned. I've been here longer than most everyone except Preach and Marla."

"How did you ever find this place?"

"Wasn't easy." Laughter played in his brown eyes, then faded abruptly. "I left home when I was young like most everybody else who strikes out west. I worked my way across the country, saving money doing any job I could find. I ended up in St. Joe, Missouri. That place was too crowded for me, I'll tell you that. I met a man there, though, who'd heard of this corner of Colorado. I was intrigued so I set out to see if I could find it. When I spotted the mill, I figured it was divine providence. My search for a place to belong was over."

"A place to belong? Didn't you belong with your family in North Carolina?"

Whit flinched. Carrie got the feeling he hadn't meant to say that part out loud. "Yeah, well, a man likes to have a place of his own."

She wondered what else he wasn't saying. "Were you nervous about building a business in such a remote place?"

They reached the top of the incline. Whit released her hand. Carrie immediately missed the warmth. "I wasn't worried about not earning much. My needs have always been simple."

Carrie wondered if she should point out that would change dramatically if they married. They reached the big house with the windows she wanted to peek into earlier. Whit stepped ahead of her to open the door. He smiled proudly. "Welcome to my home."

For a man with simple needs, he sure built himself a nice house, Carrie thought. The front door opened into a large airy room with high ceilings. She wouldn't exactly call it a parlor since it was wide open and sparsely furnished with only a padded sofa and a small table. No pictures on the wall. No bric-a-brac. She supposed men on the frontier didn't put much stock in ornamentation. A braided rug, much too small for the space, in front of the sofa was the only floor covering. To be fair, the pine board floor that matched the simple walls was polished smooth and didn't need adornment. Whit either swept this morning—even the corners—or no dust existed in Cowboy Creek.

A smaller room was next—what her family referred to as a middle room. A large window faced downhill toward the trading post. If the town grew, it would provide a pretty view of the main street. For now, the view consisted of mostly trees and a muddy path. Carrie envisioned a piano in front of the window surrounded by padded chairs and a comfortable settee where the family could gather in the evenings and sing and have devotional time. Her Grandmother Hopkins had owned a piano, and taught Carrie enough chords that she could lead her family in song. She was sure the skill would come back to her once she got her fingers on a set of keys.

Now the room was empty except for two empty wooden crates in the corner. The kitchen was last. It was obviously where Whit did most of his living. The window over the sink was the only one she'd seen that sported curtains. She gasped in pleasure.

Whit jerked his head around to look at her. She hurried to the sink and put her hand on the smooth pump handle. "An indoor pump!" she enthused.

He smiled at her delight.

She nearly told him she would marry him this minute if it meant she never had to walk to a well again on a frigid winter morning. She swallowed the words just in time. She didn't want him to get the wrong idea.

"I put that in last spring," he explained. "My experience operating a mill and having a blacksmith next door made the job a piece of cake. We got a lot of snow last year, and everyone was snowbound most of the winter. I got tired of making so many trips outside. Being this close to the water source, the pump wasn't much work. The most inconvenient step was waiting for the supplies from Good Hope."

"I would imagine so." She gazed around the large room. He had put the most effort into this room, as many frontier people did. The table was small and only had two chairs. Two open front cupboards stood on either side of the sink. Another had been hung on the wall for easy access to ingredients and supplies while cooking. The best thing about the room was that it was clean, which said more about Whit than anything else.

He went to the stove and opened the door. He poked at the coals and stirred it to life. He added a chunk of wood and set the kettle over the hotplate. He took a golden loaf of bread out of the larder and set it on a cutting board on the counter. Carrie wasn't used to anyone waiting on her. She wasn't sure what to do with herself.

"I'm sorry the place isn't more…comfortable," he said as he worked. "We bachelors never had much time to think on things that make a house a home. We rely on Marla when we need something stitched or fixed." He chuckled. "She's had her hands full the last few years. I don't know what she'll do with herself once all the brides get here and put her out of work."

He turned with the plate in his hands and gave her a measuring look. Carrie pursed her lips. How did a person know if they could spend their life with someone they'd only just met? Whit was obviously a hard worker. Ambitious. Motivated. Self-sufficient—everything her husband Johnny Rhoades had not been. From the look of things, he could provide for her and the children, especially if Cowboy Creek grew and the mill became more prosperous. Could she love him someday? She didn't want to marry a man she didn't love. She'd done it before with disastrous consequences.

"I'll get the plates." Without waiting for a reply, she moved past him to the cupboard and found two small plates. Everything organized and clean. The plates had tiny lines in the porcelain but no cracks or chips. He took care of things. She liked that.

She set the plates next to him on the counter. He put two slices of bread on each one. As he wiped the crumbs off the knife, Carrie carried the plates to the table and added the butter crock and honey. She wondered how the children were getting on with Preach and his wife. She hoped John Thomas and Annie didn't break anything and that Candace managed to rein in her horrid attitude. Carrie didn't want her host and hostess to think she'd raised an incorrigible brat, though she supposed she had.

Whit joined her at the table. Carrie focused on him. Nothing could be accomplished by worrying about the children in this moment.

"I expect Preach pointed out the mining camp on your way in."

"Yes, it was an interesting story. The children were quite intrigued, especially the younger ones."

"There are a lot of things here to interest a youngster."

They ate a few moments in silence. There was plenty Carrie wanted to know about the area. About this man. What was his life like growing up? Did he stay in contact with his mother? How severe were the winters here? Had any real wealth been mined out of the river? Was he lonely for companionship the way she was? Was it presumptuous to ask since they'd just met? If she was going to marry him, she supposed she needed to start the conversation somewhere.

"Did you have any success mining for gold?"

He snorted. "I wasn't a miner. Like Preach and Marla, I realized it was more lucrative to serve the needs of the miners than get my own hands dirty. They needed shovels and pans, and they needed bread."

"I doubt miners raised much grain that required a mill."

"No, but there were farmers farther out that knew we had hungry families here. We all did pretty well until everyone moved on."

"I know you said your needs are minimal, but after they left did you worry about supporting yourself so far from any type of industry?"

"Not really. I became skilled at several trades while I worked my way across the country. I worked for the railroads, which is what helped me save enough to get this place up and running. My pa was a woodworker," he glanced at the walls and floors, "so I know enough to parlay that into income if necessary. What about you? Have you always lived in the city?"

The bread went dry in her mouth. She knew questions about herself would eventually come. Maybe if she went back far enough, he would forget to ask about her husband.

"I was born in eastern Ohio across the river from Pennsylvania. My father decided work had to be easier in the factories in Cincinnati than trying to scratch a living out of the soil. I'm not sure if he was right. I was ten when we packed up and moved down the river. I was the oldest. I have three sisters and a little brother. We children were very excited about the move. My ma took it the worst. She knew she'd never see her parents again. She didn't."

Whit spooned a large blob of jam on his second slice of bread. "I'm sure it's harder on women to pull up stakes than men." He gave her a penetrating look. "It must be hard on you to know you'll probably never see your kin again."

"There's no one left," she said sadly. "By the time I was grown Mama and Papa had passed on. My little brother died of the pleurisy. My sisters married and scattered. I write to two of them occasionally. My youngest sister, Florinda, married a soap salesman and moved west. I don't know where she ended up. I don't know if she's even…"

The words trailed off. She didn't allow herself to think on all the things that could've gone wrong in Florinda's life. Sickness. A difficult childbirth. Accidents. An unhappy union with her salesman. Maybe Carrie was better off not knowing. Life was too fragile. If she thought on it much, she might never have the strength to face a new day.

Whit stayed quiet, seeming to understand where her mind had gone. She drizzled a little honey on her bread. "This bread if just right. My compliments to Mrs. Dodds."

"She'll like hearing it. Her baking doesn't always warrant compliments."

Carrie cocked her head at him.

Whit grinned. "I'm sorry. I should've waited and let you draw your own conclusions."

Carrie bit back a smile. "I'm sure it isn't that bad."

"Not really. Her soups and stews keep us all from wasting away during long winters."

"I hope the winters aren't that long."

"Not usually. Mostly just lonely." He gave her another measuring look.

Loneliness. A universal condition. Should she tell him she was lonely, too, even living in the middle of a bustling city?

She brushed the breadcrumbs off the table into her hand and tossed them into the stove. "I should be getting back. The children have probably driven Mr. and Mrs. Dodds to distraction with all their questions." She thought of Candace and nearly grimaced. Had her daughter insulted them with her attitude, or not spoken at all?

Whit pushed out his chair. "May I walk you back to the trading post?"

She saw nervousness in his eyes. He didn't seem to have much experience with women. It was endearing, however she'd rather walk back on her own in case the children had been awful and needed reprimanded. She also needed to think for a while. "Thank you but no. I've already kept you from your work, and the children will need my attention. Oh, I nearly forgot. Preach told me to tell you Mrs. Dodds is making supper for all of us. That includes you. They're eating at six. He told me to remind you when Mrs. Dodds extends an invitation, you can't refuse."

He laughed. "He wasn't kidding. Tell them I'll be there at six sharp."

Carrie knew without consulting the watch on her bodice there was only had an hour or two to unpack their things and freshen up herself and the children. She wasn't as tired as she had been when she first climbed out of the wagon. She could only attribute it to a good meeting with Whit. She had gotten over her first hurdle of telling him about Annie. Hopefully her other secret would be as easy to tell and as easy to forgive. If she put some thought into it, maybe she could come up with a way to keep from telling him at all.

Chapter Six

"**I** could marry her right now. Tonight after dinner if she was agreeable."

Whit looked at his reflection in the mirror and chuckled. Talking to himself. He guessed that was proof he was smitten already. He straightened the collar of his shirt and smoothed down the tails of his black tie. He hadn't put on a tie since Jacob Campbell married Rennie back in January. Tonight seemed to call for it.

On Sundays, most of the cowboys put on their best shirts and washed their trousers. They shaved or trimmed their beards and cut the hair hanging over their collars as best they could. Ties were reserved for funerals and weddings—not that there'd been a funeral in these parts in some time. He wondered if the next time he put this tie around his neck would be for his own wedding. Even with three kids he hadn't expected, he wanted to marry Carrie.

She was pretty and interesting and compassionate. He didn't know much about her, but he'd have a lifetime to learn the other stuff.

She needn't worry about him proposing tonight, no matter how confident he felt with only his reflection to talk to. It would be a long time before he worked up the nerve to say the words to her. He suspected she knew he didn't have much experience with women. He had even less experience with being part of a loving, well-functioning family—something he'd always wanted but had no idea how to make it happen.

Maybe he should've told Carrie more about his upbringing and why he left North Carolina. A bride had the right to know her husband's ugly beginnings that could influence the way he raised his own children and treated his wife. But how could he tell a gentle soul like Carrie about Pa's affinity to the strap? She didn't need to know he'd nearly beaten Whit to death the night before he left when he accused Whit of leaving the barn door open. When Whit told Pa he was the last one out of the barn and if the door wasn't secure, it was Pa's doing, the thrashing intensified. Whit knew better than to point out Pa's failing, but he was sixteen and tired of taking the blame for things he didn't do. After the fourth or fifth whack with the handle of a buggy whip, Whit yanked it out of the old man's hands and threw it on the ground. He stopped at the house long enough for his sister Grace to stitch up the gash on his head and the one above his eye that bled so heavily poor Grace thought Whit's eye had been knocked out, grabbed the only change of clothes he owned, and rode out of the barnyard stiff and sore from the beating.

Twenty-two years after that night, Whit liked to remember that he had been tough and strong and ready to face the world. In truth, he was terrified. He had grown up with nothing. He was used to that. But he had never been completely alone. Even though his home life was less than nurturing, he had others to share his misery. He doubted he could admit to Carrie the fear and despair that nearly crippled him the first two years he moved around the country, trying to find a place to belong.

He shook his head at his reflection and smoothed down the tie one last time. There was no need to tell Carrie ugly things that couldn't be changed and that a woman who'd probably never told a lie in her life would understand.

Just before six, Whit saddled his horse and rode down the street to the trading post. The blacksmith's house was tucked behind the smithy. A soft light glowed from the back corner of the little house. Lonnie Fanshaw was the oldest bachelor and a loner. Whit didn't know anything about Lonnie's life before he came to Cowboy Creek. It was probably by design. Most men had good reasons for leaving their former lives behind and had no desire to relive them. Like Whit himself. He wondered if Lonnie hoped for a bride. He had joined in the conversation back in December, but he hadn't been specific about what he wanted. Lonnie wasn't exactly a handsome picture of a man, and he might fear no woman would take him.

Light ahead cast flickering golden squares on the street in front of the trading post. The barn door was open, as Whit knew it would be. He rode his mount inside. Preach, always the gracious host, had a manger of hay prepared for Whit's horse. After securing the horse at the manger, he took off his hat and smoothed down his hair. He didn't own any of that pine-smelling pomade barbers used the handful of times he paid for a real haircut. With his stubborn cowlick, and the marching band raising a ruckus in his stomach, Whit wished he knew more about how a man prepared to dine with a pretty woman he hoped to marry. And her children.

He hurried down the alley between the barn and the trading post. Before he even raised his fist to knock, the door swung open and Preach smiled out at him. As Preach greeted him and took his coat, Whit looked past him to the crowded room. Their small parlor was always crammed with furnishings and overflow from the trading post. Tonight it was practically bursting at the seams with people.

Little people.

His gaze swept over a fair-haired young girl, the spitting image of her mama, a pale, skinny boy with two front teeth growing in crooked, and a dark-haired little girl with the widest brown eyes he'd ever seen on a face so small. Carrie stood at the back of the crowd waiting, a look of hopeful trepidation on her face. Earlier when she came to the mill, he found her pretty, but tonight she was downright stunning. The sides of her golden hair were braided into some sort of knot at the back of her head with the length of it spilling down her back. In the flickering lamplight, it reminded Whit of honey pouring out of a bee's nest. He imagined getting his hands caught in it. She wore an inky blue dress with vertical lighter blue stripes and a white bodice that emphasized her feminine curves and brought out the blue in those mesmerizing eyes.

She stepped forward. "Good evening, Whit."

It took Whit a moment to blink and catch up with what was happening.

"This is my daughter Candace."

The older girl glared at him from under a fringe of blond hair that had come loose from her braids. "This is John Thomas." The boy studied a spot on the rug and barely glanced up. "And this is Annie."

At the sound of her name, the little girl turned and buried her face in Carrie's skirt. Carrie smoothed her hand over the child's head and looking apologizingly at Whit. He thought of the child's pa in Cincinnati and wondered if he ever thought of her or wondered why he hadn't seen her around in a while. If Whit had the time to spare, he'd hop on the next train to Cincinnati and beat the living daylights out of the man.

He nodded a greeting to the older children. Candace's scowl deepened while bright red spots of embarrassment appeared on her brother's cheeks. Whit had not known what to expect. At least they kept their discomfort quiet. No crying. No hollering for attention. He appreciated that since he wouldn't have a clue how to handle such a situation. His parents had no patience for whining or what they perceived as disrespect. Whit knew firsthand how their volatile brand of discipline only bred resentment and hurt and never fixed the problem.

Preach placed a gnarled hand in the center of Whit's back and pushed him into the center of the room. "Marla's in the kitchen putting the finishing touches on dinner."

Carrie looked away from Whit for the first time. "I should go help." She spun away from the little girl and disappeared into the kitchen, leaving Whit in the middle of the room circled by the children. Candace gazed defiantly at him. John Thomas continued to stare a hole into the floor, though occasionally he glanced at Whit from under crooked bangs. Annie's chin trembled, but she sniffed mightily to hold back her tears. She stepped closer to the older girl and took her hand.

Whit remembered what he carried in his pocket. He reached in and drew out a slim hollow tube and held it toward the boy. "D'you know what this is?"

John Thomas shook his head without looking Whit in the eye, though curiosity edged him a little closer.

Whit smiled. He raised the tube to his lips and blew gently. A squeal pierced the air. Annie and John Thomas started, then smiles split their faces. Candace's cornflower eyes went wide, and her lips quirked upward in spite of herself.

Whit silently congratulated himself. "It blows a lot louder than that, but I figured the women wouldn't appreciate us raising a ruckus indoors." He held it out to John Thomas.

The boy looked from the whistle to Whit and back again, clearly wanting to accept the gift but suspecting a trap. Whit motioned with his hand. "Here. It's for you. I made it myself. When your ma wrote that she had a boy, I knew you needed a whistle. Who knows what sort of varmint you'll come across in these woods that you'll need to scare off."

The younger children's eyes widened and looked toward the door. Candace sniffed dismissively.

"A whistle's great for scaring birds out of the trees, and it'll help your ma keep track of you."

John Thomas reached a skinny arm out for the whistle. When he took hold of it, Whit didn't let go but turned the whistle between his finger and thumb. "See these lines. That's how I put it together and sanded it down. Inside's a little bead that makes the noise. I'll show you how to make one yourself. I expect your sisters will need their own."

Annie seemed to forget her fear of him. She nodded, her eyes gleaming. Even Candace looked interested. He let go of the whistle. John Thomas turned it in his fingers, admiring the smooth feel and the grain of the wood. He put the whistle between his lips and blew softly. The whistle made a soft trill.

"See there," Whit said. "You can make a soft call like a bird or really have a go at it and scare the bejeebers out of your sisters."

John Thomas's mouth dropped open at the suggestion. The two smiled conspiratorially.

"Do...do you know how to make a yo-yo?"

Whit rocked back on his heels and stroked his chin. "Well now, that's something my brothers and I used to make when we were kids. Weren't too good at it. Didn't have the proper tools or material so they didn't work so well. But you know, I wager if I could make a whistle, I could find some little pieces of scrap wood for a yo-yo." He looked at Annie. "I suspect you'll want one too."

She nodded eagerly.

"And you?" He turned to Candace.

She straightened her slim shoulders. "I had one once," she said in a clear voice that exuded an innocence her hard exterior tried to disguise. "It broke and I never got another one."

Whit suspected her angry expression was becoming too a heavy weight to hold in place forever. He'd see what he could do to help her let go of it.

He clapped his hands together. "Well, then, it looks like we'll have to go up to the mill someday and find good lightweight pine for three yo-yos. You know, I might just make one for myself. We can see who's better at it."

"We'll have a competition," John Thomas said.

"I'll win," Candace said. "I already know how to do it."

Whit nudged John Thomas's skinny shoulder. "Sounds like a challenge to me. We'll have to see who's better, boys or girls."

His reward was a huge grin from the boy who stood a little taller than he had when Whit walked in. The three children clustered around the whistle in John Thomas's hand, admiring it and making plans.

Whit looked at Preach and exhaled. Preach clapped him on the back. "Good job," he said under his breath. "Doesn't take much to make friends with a young'un. All they ever really want is for you to like 'em. Too bad we forget that once we grow up." He raised his voice. "Supper sure smells good in there. How 'bout we join the ladies in the kitchen."

They moved in a cluster through the crowded parlor into the kitchen. Heavy, mismatched plates and cups sat around the table, laden with food. It was a beautiful sight to Whit who ate most of his dinners standing against the counter while thinking of all the chores still waiting for him before he could turn in for the night.

Over the sight of the well-laid table and delicious aroma, the most appealing thing in the room was Carrie on the other side of the table. She looked up at him and smiled. Wavy tendrils of bright blond hair cascaded around her face. Her cheeks were flushed from the heat of the stove. From the shine in her blue eyes, he wondered if the blush was something else—if it had anything to do with him.

Marla's gaze swept the table, making sure everything was in place. "Everyone, have a seat so we can eat before it gets cold."

Annie rushed around the table and jumped into Carrie's arms. Carrie pulled a chair back from the table and set the little girl in it.

"Here you go, Whit." Preach said, indicating a chair he had pulled out.

The next few minutes were filled with blessings over the food by Preach and then the passing of plates. Carrie spooned out food for the children and chopped Annie's food into small bites before dropping into the empty chair between Whit and Annie. Whit watched the frenzied activity in bewilderment and wonder. Though the children only spoke when spoken to, the meal was still louder and more enjoyable than any meal he had experienced in a long time. The little girl leaned against Carrie through most of the meal. It had been a long, trying few days for all of them. Even Carrie looked pale and worn under her smiles. Despite her apparent fatigue, she managed to feed the child, feed herself, and join the conversation at the same time.

John Thomas kept his free hand on the whistle next to his plate and watched Whit as if half-expecting him to change his mind and take it back. Whit's heart ached for the boy. He probably hadn't spent much time around men since he lost his own pa so young. What interactions he had with men may have been unfavorable. Whit tried to include him in conversation as he and Preach talked about the snow and jobs left to do as they prepared for Spring.

The older girl didn't speak at all. She barely grunted in response when someone spoke to her. Carrie gave her a pointed glare or reprimand when she didn't reply in a suitable manner to one of the adults, but for the most part, she was ignored. The other adults didn't seem perturbed by the girl's attitude. Whit figured it was normal behavior for a twelve-year old girl snatched from the life she knew. In her shoes, he wouldn't be the life of the party either.

He couldn't keep from stealing admiring glances at Carrie. Every time he did so, Marla gave him a knowing smile. He didn't mind. There was no point in trying to hide the fact he had already fallen for Carrie. He wasn't in love, but that would come soon enough if he had his way. What he didn't know was how she felt. Women were a lot more complicated than men to his determination. Since leaving home, his life hadn't been easy, but it had been simple. Work hard. Save money. Survive. Adding a wife and three children to it would surely complicate things. Sitting here at this crowded table, complications suddenly didn't seem so bad.

Chapter Seven

Carrie recognized smitten when she saw it, and it was written all over Whit Whitamore's face.

She had to admit she was a little smitten herself. Her heart had lurched at the joy on her son's face when he showed her the whistle Whit made for him. It meant more to her than if Whit had given her a roomful of roses. She couldn't remember the last time John Thomas had been so delighted about anything. She had written in one of her letters to Whit that John Thomas was quiet and small for his age. She hadn't written that he was teased mercilessly by the bigger boys in their neighborhood, and he spent most of his time hiding out in their apartment instead of playing with the other children. Whit had put those pieces together with no prompting from her, thus endearing himself to Carrie more than anything else could've.

While Whit didn't talk much directly to her during the meal, she caught his glances of appreciation even while he talked to Preach about the equipment he'd worked on at the gristmill and the orders he received from a distant farm. She was glad she'd taken extra time with her hair and flattered that he noticed.

After dinner Preach got out his Bible and asked the children if they'd like to hear a Bible story. "Can you read us the one about the hand that wrote on the wall?" John Thomas asked.

"You know your Bible, young man. Not many people know about the king who threw a party and only Daniel could read the writing from the mysterious hand on the wall."

"He's my little scholar." Carrie didn't bother to restrain the pride in her voice. "He knows a lot of Old Testament stories and remembers them well."

Preach spread the Bible open on his lap and motioned with his hand for the children to gather around him. "If you girls have any requests, I'll read them after I finish with Daniel."

"Daniel. Daniel. Daniel," Annie chanted, bouncing up and down. Carrie laughed at the delight on the little girl's face. She had opened up more in the last few hours than she had in the past two weeks.

Preach laughed too. "Do you children know Daniel is my Christian name?"

"I thought it was Preach," John Thomas said.

Preach laughed again. "Nope. My mother loved Daniel's stories in the Bible, too. My two brothers were also named after Old Testament prophets."

Carrie glanced at Candace. The older girl looked rested after having taken a bath in the brides' house and combing out her hair, but her defiant scowl was still in place. Carrie didn't have the energy to reprimand her tonight. As long as Candace wasn't openly rude in Preach and Marla's house after their kindness, Carrie would give the girl time to get used to the new reality of her life.

Marla took Carrie's coat off the hook on the wall and pushed it into Carrie's arms. "While Daniel is finding the right passage, why don't you go out and help Whit saddle his horse?" The older woman's tone left no room for discussion.

Whit chuckled. "I guess that's my cue to leave."

"You know you're welcome to visit anytime, Whit. We hope to have you back soon. Now, go on. Take your time, Carrie."

Carrie buttoned her coat as Marla pushed her out the door. She and Whit laughed when the door clicked shut behind them.

"Is she always so subtle?" Carrie asked as she pulled her hat down over her ears.

"Usually. It's from spending too much time around us men. She doesn't have time for sugarcoating. She pretty much mothers us and we do as we're told."

"Then I guess I need to get busy helping you saddle your horse."

Whit turned in the direction of the barn. "Or you could keep me company while I do it."

"I like that idea better."

He offered his arm. Carrie hesitated only a moment before taking it. It was strange feeling a man's muscled arm under her hand but nice, too.

A thin layer of snow covered the ground. "Does it always snow this late in the season?" she asked.

He chuckled. "I've seen a foot of snow fall in May." At her gasp, he added quickly. "But this is fine snow, not the kind that piles up. As soon as the sun comes out tomorrow, it'll be gone."

Carrie's foot slipped on the spongy ground. She tightened her grip on his arm. Whit laid his hand over hers. "I didn't get a chance to tell you how lovely you look tonight," he said quietly.

Carrie was thankful Whit couldn't see her blush in the darkness. It had been years since she'd blushed. She had taken a bath in the brides' house after bathing the children and brushed out her best dress in preparation for dinner. She'd had the dress for years. She only wore it to church and on special occasions, yet it still showed its age. Before leaving Cincinnati, she thought about buying fabric for another dress. Then she found Annie. The expense of a new dress was out of the question. From Whit's reaction at seeing her when he walked into Marla's parlor, she hadn't needed a new dress anyway.

"Thank you," she murmured.

He smiled down at her. She flushed again. Tonight had been a grand success. While Marla may have been a little pushy, Carrie appreciated the chance to be alone with Whit to determine what he thought after spending time with her and meeting the children.

"I can't remember the last time I enjoyed supper so much," he said as if in response to her thoughts.

"I'm sorry you barely got a word in edgewise. After four days cooped up traveling, the children have so much energy to burn. They are very curious about this place and the people in it."

Whit laughed. He let go of her hand and opened the barn door. They both ducked inside. "Healthy curiosity is a good thing. They were very well behaved. Our family table was always crowded back home. When I saw the way Annie leaned against you during the meal, it reminded me of how I sometimes had to bounce a little one on my knee while I ate."

Carrie sighed. "She's barely let me out of her sight since I took her off the street. I wonder if she thinks I'll disappear from her life the way her ma did when she died. It did my heart good to see how she interacted with Marla and Preach. And you, too. I pray she's becoming secure with the way things are now."

"The whistle helped. I promised to make them yo-yos. She'll enjoy that."

"Oh, you don't need to worry about giving the children toys."

"I'm not worried about it. It's something I'd like to do."

They stopped in front of his horse. He turned to face her. Carrie's breath caught in her throat at the intensity of his gaze. The neckline of her dress suddenly felt too tight. She hadn't stood this close to a man on purpose in a long time. His raw masculinity made her feel small and vulnerable, but at the same time, safe. She noticed a loose button on his coat and nearly reached out to touch it.

"I, um, I should go back inside with the children. They're tired and probably getting cranky. I don't want them to get out of hand for Preach and Marla."

"Carrie."

She stopped talking and fixed her gaze on his. "It was nice meeting you today. I'm glad you came."

She studied the sharp planes of his face and the lines around his dark eyes. He'd had a hard life, and it had made him a hard man. A strong man. A good man.

"I'm glad too."

She was.

"Could I—could I come back and talk with you tomorrow?"

She nearly smiled at the uncertainty in his voice. "I'd like that, Whit."

His gaze dropped to her lips for an instant. Did he want to kiss her? Did she want him to? She wasn't sure, but the notion wasn't displeasing at all.

He settled his hat on his head and stepped back. "It's cold. You can go on inside. I'll take care of the horse myself."

They stared at each other another moment. "Thank you, Whit." She wasn't sure what she was thinking him for. "I'll see you—tomorrow."

She heard him whistling as she left the barn.

The children were still seated on the floor in front of Preach while he read quietly. Annie's head rested on Candace's knee. John Thomas looked nearly about to nod off too. Candace had lost the hold on the sullen expression on her face. None of them had gotten a full night's sleep since they left Cincinnati. Carrie whispered her thanks to her hosts and took Annie in her arms. The little girl snuggled in close without waking as if she'd been doing it all her life. John Thomas put his hand in Carrie's and leaned against her. He hadn't questioned bringing Annie along with them to Cowboy Creek, but Carrie knew he wondered what his place was now that Annie demanded so much of her attention. She had always shared a special closeness with John Thomas and wanted to maintain it despite all the changes happening so rapidly around them.

If only she could figure out how to get close to Candace again.

Even though the older girl behaved like Carrie was the last person she wanted anything from, Carrie knew she was hurting and needed the reassurance of her mother's love. Behind Candace's unrepentant wall, she wasn't a girl who threw rocks at an old man or tolerated stealing from shops. Carrie prayed that deep down Candace wanted to go back to the girl she was before she participated in those things but wasn't sure how.

Carrie longed to reach out and touch her daughter's cheek and brush the hair away from her face, but she didn't have a free hand. All she could do was offer a warm smile. It was not returned.

She thanked Marla and Preach again for the supper, the ride from Good Hope, and everything else they'd done for her and the children. She turned down Preach's offer to walk them to the brides' house.

Marla handed Candace a lantern. "I'll have biscuits and gravy in the morning for whenever you're ready for breakfast."

The past few weeks caught up with Carrie like a runaway locomotive. She wished she could rest her head on Marla's shoulder the way Annie was doing to her and cry a little.

Instead, she mustered a weak smile. "Thank you so much, Marla, but I'm afraid we'll probably sleep till noon."

Marla laid a gentle hand on her cheek. "You just do that, sweetheart. Then you can have biscuits and gravy for lunch."

Carrie ushered her brood into the night. The light snow from earlier was falling in earnest. She hoped Whit was right and it would melt off once the sun came out tomorrow. It wasn't a long walk to the brides' house, but by the time they got inside, they were all shivering. Carrie slid a sleeping Annie between the covers on the small bed near the stove and stirred the fire to life.

"Is that man going to be our new papa?" John Thomas asked.

Carrie braced herself. She knew this moment would come. Before they left Cincinnati, she had told John Thomas and Candace about Nan and the cowboys in Cowboy Creek who needed brides. She had explained they were coming west to build a new life where they would all be healthy and safe. She didn't say much about Whit in case things didn't work out between them. Now that they were here, it wouldn't take long for the children to arrive at their own conclusions.

John Thomas gazed up at her, his tired, smudged eyes bright with anticipation. Candace glared at them, no anticipation on her face.

"What do you think of Whit?" Carrie asked him in lieu of an answer.

"He's mighty nice. He made me this whistle." He pulled the whistle out of his pocket and held it out as if she'd forgotten it. "I like him. I like Cowboy Creek too. I'd like to live here. Preach is really nice. He told us a lot more about that hand that wrote on the wall in the Bible than you ever did."

Carrie laughed. "I suppose that's because he knows the Scriptures better than me. But it isn't proper for you to call him Preach."

"You call him that. Mr. Whit does too."

"Well, Whit and I are adults. Adults are allowed to be less formal with one another. He's Mr. Dodds to you, and Marla is Mrs. Dodds."

"Yes, ma'am."

Carrie wished she hadn't spoken to quickly. She rested her hand on his shoulder. "I'm glad you liked them."

Annie stirred and sat up in the bed. "I liked them too. Mrs. Dodds let us eat the whole sponge cake she baked." She rubbed her stomach. "It was so good."

"She's baking two more for dinner after church on Sunday," John Thomas said. "The whole town is having a dinner just for us. Did you know that?"

"Yes, I did."

"Well, I think that's mighty nice. Everyone here is so nice."

"I think so too." Carrie said.

She looked at Candace who was slouched in a worn stuffed chair. She stared at a spot on the floor as if she hadn't heard the discussion. "What do you think of Cowboy Creek, Candace?"

The answer was a lift of Candace's thin shoulders.

"I hope there's other children at the dinner," John Thomas said.

Instantly wide awake, Annie bounded out of the bed. "Yeah! Yeah!"

"Well, there's not!" Candace snapped.

The younger children stopped bouncing and cheering to stare at her.

"We're the only ones," she said glumly. "There are no other children for miles and miles and miles. No school. No stores. No one but us and a bunch of old men

who want to get married. None of them asked for kids."
She glared at her mother.

Weariness dropped onto Carrie's shoulders again
like a heavy buffalo blanket in the middle of July. "I'm
sorry for that, Candace. I know it'll be hard for a while.
On you, most of all. Maybe another family will move to
the area or another woman will come with children. It'll
work out. You'll see. Just give it a chance."

"Like I have a choice."

Carrie's patience snapped. "You're right. You
didn't have a choice in the matter. We're here and we're
staying for the foreseeable future, so we might as well
make the best of it. We're also tired and need to be in bed,
so let's go there."

Candace jumped to her feet with an energy Carrie
didn't personally possess and stomped into the only other
room to the bed she would share with Carrie. John
Thomas and Annie turned their faces to Carrie, their eyes
wide and fearful. She cupped both their chins.
"Everything's all right. We'll all feel better after we get a
good night's sleep."

She seriously doubted a good night's sleep would
alter Candace's attitude.

With an exaggerated stretch, she swayed her hips
from side to side, working out the kinks in her back. The
children laughed. "Let's say our prayers and thank God
for our full tummies and the new friends we've made and
big warm beds to stretch out in."

She glanced toward the other room where she heard
Candace rummaging through the trunk for her
nightclothes. Her daughter needed patience and
understanding, but Carrie was too tired to muster much of
either. She helped the younger children dress for bed, and

then saw to her own toilette. She thought of Whit Whitamore and wondered what he was thinking. Candace was probably right. She doubted the men of Cowboy Creek expected their brides to bring children. Whit seemed to get along with hers well enough, considering he didn't have much experience doing so. But chatting with them over supper was a far cry from accepting them as his own.

What if he never did accept them? What if Candace's insolence drove him away or he grew tired of John Thomas's shyness and Annie's clinginess? Carrie already liked him. If he didn't want her *and* her children, she wouldn't choose another groom among the men here. It would be too humiliating after one had cast her aside.

It was too late in the day to fret over things she couldn't change. Like she told Candace, they were here now, and they'd just have to make things work. After snuggling into the bed with Candace, she took her own advice and thanked God for bringing them this far. She gave Him her worries and doubts and fell fast asleep.

Chapter Eight

From Christmas until Easter Whit often had little work to do and no money coming in with which to do it. The first few years of operating the mill, the situation caused many sleepless nights. Even though he had money in the bank in Good Hope with plenty more stashed around the house, as well as a stock of feed for his animals and himself, he never stopped worrying over how easily one bad season or one unforeseen tragedy could thrust him right back into the desperation and poverty of his upbringing.

He vividly remembered those nights when he was a kid, the rumbling in his empty belly and the bellies of his brothers with whom he shared the bed, lulling him into a restless sleep. Many nights he laid in bed between his brothers under blankets inadequate against the cold and vowed that when he grew up and he was the one in charge, he would never go to sleep hungry. He wouldn't gamble away his money, leaving his children without food. He wouldn't idle away his working hours so that when a moment of calamity struck, he was caught unprepared. He wouldn't take out his frustrations for his poor decisions on a wife unable to fight back. He'd work hard and plan and make good choices in the first place. His wife could hold her head high when she walked into a store and bought what her family needed without begging for extended credit. His family would never know the fear of a man at the bank telling them they couldn't live in their house anymore.

So far, he had managed all of it. He worked hard from the moment he left his parents' house to accumulate money and provide security for himself. Lean times didn't worry him the way they once had. He'd never had a family to support either. It would take a lot more savings and security to keep a wife and three children through a long winter when there was no mill to grind or work to be had.

After supper with Carrie and the children, he went home with a light heart. The moment his head hit the pillow, though, the worrying and wondering started. Could he keep all those promises he'd made in his head as a boy? His doubts nearly made him jump out of bed and run down the hill to the brides' house to tell Carrie he couldn't become a husband and father to three children on the same day. It was too much. He needed time to think. To save. To plan.

Then the thought of her sweet face, ruby red lips, and cornflower blue eyes reminded him he had no choice. Whit Whitamore was no coward. It was time he took a chance. The decision to ask her to marry him filled with a sense of peace. It was like God was in the room with him telling him He had used Whit's growing up years to equip him to become a good husband to Carrie and father to those three children who God knew even back then would need him.

He bounded out of bed before daylight and hurried through his morning chores. After a quick breakfast of oatmeal, he saddled his horse and rode the half mile to the trading post to meet Preach before the minister could make plans for the day as he often did in service to the other men of Cowboy Creek.

Whit hoped it was early enough that Carrie and the children—and hopefully Marla—would be otherwise occupied so he could talk to Preach alone.

A lantern glowed inside the big barn between the brides' house and the trading post. Whit rode his horse through the open door and dismounted. Preach turned from a large feed barrel. He smiled knowingly, apparently expecting Whit after last night's success. "You're up early. I just got in here myself."

Whit closed the barn door, as much for privacy as to keep out the wind. "I wanted to talk to you. About Carrie."

Preach turned back to the barrel and drew out a scoop of feed to dump in the manger. "What about her?"

Whit swallowed a sigh. Preach knew good and well what about her, but the older man was going to make him say it out loud.

"I want to marry her."

Preach kept scooping grain. He merely nodded.

"Did you hear me? I'm going to ask her today. If she's agreeable, I'd be much obliged for you to conduct the ceremony Sunday afternoon after meeting."

Preach dropped the scoop into the barrel, hammered down the lid with the heel of his hand, and dusted off his hands on the seat of his pants. He finally gave Whit his full attention. "It's mighty quick, but you're not the first man to do it this way. Adam married Eliza the day she rode into town. You and Carrie aren't kids. You especially," he added with a grin. "You're both old enough to know what you want. You appear well-suited and those kids need a pa. I can't think of a reason to delay."

Whit heaved a sigh of relief. "Me either. I'll go talk to her now."

Preach grabbed his sleeve. "Do you know what time it is? I imagine she's still asleep. Even if she isn't, I doubt she'd appreciate visitors at this hour."

Whit felt like a dummy. "Oh, yeah. Right. I guess I'll…" He looked helplessly at the door.

"I guess you ought to rein in your enthusiasm for a few hours."

Whit chuckled. "You're right. I have things to do this morning anyway. I'll come back around lunchtime. Do you suppose Marla would be willing to bake a cake for me on Sunday? A special one—big with icing. Maybe little curlicues or something that would please the children. Does she know how to do that? I can pay her for her trouble, of course, and I'd really like to keep it a surprise from Carrie if at all possible."

Preach's smile widened. "I believe she can handle that."

Whit clapped his gloved hands together, unable to contain his excitement. "All right, then. I'll be back around noon. And thank you, Preach—for everything."

❀ ❀ ❀

It didn't take long for Whit to finish the work he had for the day. He couldn't stop looking at the clock. At noon, he fried up some ham for a sandwich and gulped it down with strong coffee. He cleaned himself up, taking extra care with his shirt and hair. He thought for a moment about putting the tie back on but decided that would be too much.

As nervous as a schoolboy working up his nerve to talk to a girl for the first time, he rode back down the road to the trading post. He had been right about the snow. A warm, late-winter sun hung in the clear blue sky. All that remained of last night's snow were a few lacy fringes clinging to shaded outcroppings. Whit took off his hat and let the soft breeze dry the tracks in his hair left from his wet comb. Candace sat alone on the stoop in front of the brides' house. Her head was drooped between her shoulders as her fingers absently picked bits of balled fabric off her stockings. She heard the horse at nearly the same time Whit spotted her. She jumped to her feet. She glanced at the door behind her as if planning to run inside. Whit replaced his hat and picked up his pace.

"Candace," he called before she could make a decision. Was she afraid of him or just so miserable she didn't want to talk to anyone?

She scowled. "Mama's not here. She took John Thomas and Annie to the creek."

Whit dismounted and looped the horse's reins through the hitching ring on the side of the house. "Sure is a pretty day, isn't it?"

She reached for the door handle.

Whit would rather think she was mad than afraid. Either way, he wanted the girl to feel welcome here. "Would you like to walk down to the creek with me to find them?"

She hesitated, her gaze taking in his clean suit of clothes and earnest look. Though she was young, she had probably figured out why he was here. Carrie wrote in her letters her husband had been gone for years, but Candace may have memories of him and didn't want a stranger trying to fill those shoes. Whit understood why she hadn't taken to him as easily as the other two.

"No." her voice was firm and eyes hard, but Whit saw it took effort.

She pursed her lips. "But thank you—Mr. Whit."

It was the first time he had heard her speak his name. She went inside without looking back.

Whit patted his horse's flank on his way past, his thoughts on Candace. She was just a kid, but she'd been through so much. Lost so much. He remembered his own fear and uncertainty as a child when he walked into the house one day to see Ma packing and Pa scowling with a drink in his hand. They never told the children why they had to leave another house or where they were going. It was always the fault of a stingy landowner or crooked bank man or hateful boss. Pa never accepted responsibility for anything as he loaded his family into a broken-down buckboard and pulled up stakes. Whit understood better than anyone the chip on Candace's shoulder, though she did have a loving mother who had probably tried to explain everything that was happening and why.

He circled the barn in the direction of the creek. He was less than halfway down the worn trail when he heard children's voices laughing and squealing. He smiled. It had been a long time since such a sound had come out of Cowboy Creek.

If the Lord willed, this would be the rest of his life. Children laughing. Running, Playing. Fighting.

Soon he and the other men would have to do something about a school. With all the other work Carrie would have to do once she accepted his proposal—if she did—she wouldn't have time to teach little Annie her letters and numbers and keep the other two up on their studies. Once they had their own children…

Whit crested a small ridge, and the creek came into view. Below him, the children played at the water's edge. Annie was throwing rocks into the water. John Thomas was jabbing at something with a stick. Carrie stood close by. Whit stopped walking to watch her. A breeze played with the tail of her skirt. Blond tendrils had escaped the twist of hair at the back of her head and played around her face. She reached up to brush them away. The fabric of her dress pressed tight against her form, accentuating her soft curves. Whit's heart stood still.

The dress had once been white with dark green flowers and paisley dancing across the fabric. Now the white was a dingy yellowish color and the flowers and paisley were faded. Even from fifty feet away, he could see the hem, sleeves, and neckline were worn and frayed. When was the last time she had a new dress? He had never considered how she supported herself and the children in the city without a man. Her quiet strength and the condition of her hands were a testament that she worked hard at something.

He thought of his own history of poverty and desperation. Carrie had probably grown up in a similar manner, though the fear and anxiety from lack didn't seem to have made her cynical or suspicious or tight-fisted. She knew how to relax and smile and love her children even without material possessions. He could learn a lot from her.

Annie spotted Whit first on the ridge above the water. She dropped the rock in her hand and pointed. Carrie turned. A gentle smile curved her lips. John Thomas threw down his stick and ran up the hill toward him. Annie followed, her dark eyes glowing.

John Thomas grabbed the tail of Whit's coat. "Mr. Whit, come see what I found. Come see. It's a frog, a great big'un. Deader'n a doornail. Frozen solid."

Annie skidded to a stop in front of them. "It's is-custing." Her pert little nose wrinkled, then she blushed realizing she had spoken out loud to someone she still considered a stranger.

Whit laughed. "Is-custing, is it?"

She chewed at her bottom lip and managed a bashful nod.

"Dis-gusting," John Thomas clarified. "I want to keep it, but Mama says no."

Whit laughed again. "That's probably a good idea. It won't stay frozen forever. Then it'll smell powerful bad."

John Thomas looked doubtfully over his shoulder to where he had dropped the stick.

"Is-custing," Annie repeated. She reached out and took hold of two of Whit's fingers. His heart did a strange lurch in his chest. The timid little thing had accepted him into her world. Maybe there was hope for Candace as well.

They started down the hill to where Carrie waited. She hadn't moved except for her smile, which had gotten wider. Whit stopped in front of her and they watched each other. Annie let go of his fingers. She and John Thomas ran back to the creek where John Thomas found his stick and went back to poking the frog.

"Did you—have a nice rest last night?" Whit asked.

She sighed audibly. "I feel so much better. It was impossible to sleep on the train and on the stage."

"I can imagine," Whit said, though he couldn't. He could sleep anywhere if he was tired enough. He'd fallen dead asleep on horseback before and rode for miles without falling out of the saddle. "Especially trying to make three children comfortable."

They continued to stare at each other. Whit knew what he wanted to say, he just had no idea how or if she'd want to hear it.

"Mr. Whit, come see," John Thomas called. "He's dead."

"Nuh-uh," Annie disputed. "He's just frozen. He's gonna wake up and be so mad."

Whit and Carrie walked over to the children to look at the discovery. A fat bullfrog had been melded into the shape of the rocks surrounding it. John Thomas was right; it was deader than a doornail. Whit made the appropriate sounds of approval while Carrie gasped in mock terror as mamas were supposed to do.

Annie found a stick of her own, and she and John Thomas began turning over more rocks in search of other interesting secrets of the creek. Carrie and Whit stepped away from the water and watched.

"It's a beautiful day," Whit said after a few moments of searching his brain for an intelligent comment. When all else fails, talk about the weather.

Carrie turned her pretty face to the sky and closed her eyes. "It's such a blessing." She opened her eyes and looked at him. "I'm so thankful for Marla and Preach and their hospitality. They've been so kind and patient with the children."

Whit steeled himself. "Maybe you won't need to rely on their generosity much longer."

Her blue eyes turned questioning.

Whit couldn't keep from smiling. "I was thinking— I'm really glad you came to Cowboy Creek."

"I'm glad too." Her voice was as soft as warm honey.

"I think we've hit it off pretty well," he said carefully, gathering his nerve.

"Yes, we have."

"We both know what brought you here."

He turned so he was facing her head-on. He took her hands. She didn't tense or pull away. Hope rose in his chest. "I don't know what either of us expect from this, and I can't tell you what the future might bring. But if you would like the same thing I do, I hope we can find out together. I want to marry you, Carrie. I know we don't know each other very well. I know this isn't what you planned for your life."

"Yes, Whit."

"I want to give you as a good life as I can. I want the children to become my children. I already talked to Preach. He said—"

"I said, yes, Whit."

He blinked. "You said yes?"

She giggled and nodded. A flush crept up her porcelain cheeks. He glanced at her lips, red and full. He wanted to kiss her. Was it permissible? They barely knew each other, but now that the thought was in his head, he couldn't think of anything else.

Annie shrieked and John Thomas yelled a retort back at her. Whit dropped Carrie's hands. She stepped away to take care of whatever dispute had erupted. Whit smiled and wondered how many kisses a married man could steal in a world dominated by the needs of children.

Chapter Nine

Life before Nan Canfield told her about the men in Cowboy Creek already felt like a distant memory. Carrie's trouble with Candace, worry over what to do with Annie, and concern for John Thomas growing up without a man's influence—all of it faded into the background as thoughts of Whit crowded in.

They had stayed at the water for nearly an hour after his proposal, playing with the children. He talked with them, making them laugh. He taught them how to skip rocks and make a boat out of a stick and dried leaves. While they played and asked him a thousand questions, he kept looking at Carrie. Every time he smiled that secret smile at her, she fought the urge to burst into tears. She couldn't believe from this moment forward her entire life would be different from what she'd known thus far. Once she married Whit, her family would become part of

Cowboy Creek, far removed from the betrayal and loneliness she'd known in Cincinnati.

Whenever Johnny Rhoades flitted back into her life, she let herself believe this time would be different. He was a charmer; she had to give him that. He would waltz into the house with smiles and warm kisses and promises he had given up the bottle for good this time. He found a good job, and he'd do whatever it took to keep it. He had realized family was the only thing that mattered. He missed her and wanted to be a papa to his children.

Carrie longed to believe every word out of his mouth, and he knew just which ones to say. When John Thomas was born, Johnny had never been happier. She had done her job right and given him a son. His chest puffed out so far, he barely fit through the door. There were many laughs and tears and hope on Carrie's part. Little Candace loved to sit on her papa's lap and search his pockets for goodies. She would rest her head on his chest. Johnny would laugh a deep rumbling laugh and Candace would giggle at the vibration.

Though Carrie prayed for sincerity from her husband, the grandiose boasting worried her more and more. John Thomas was only a few months old when she could no longer deny the signs. Johnny Rhoades wasn't made for bouncing babies on his lap and going to a regular job every day, only to come home and hand over his earnings to a wife and the landlord.

His absences started again and grew longer and longer. Carrie suspected another woman. Or several. Johnny's head had always been turned by a pretty face. A marriage license hadn't changed it.

Carrie held out hope. What choice did she have? Life was hard for a woman without a husband, and she honored her marriage vows even if Johnny didn't. She couldn't just up and leave. Where would she go? No, the cards were in his hand. All she could do was pray he would wake up one morning out of whatever stupor he was in and decide to be the man his family needed.

Eventually, he did, only he chose a different family.

Johnny Rhoades was a mistake Carrie never should've made. Yet she was reminded of his smile and his eyes every time she looked into the faces of her children. She couldn't hate Johnny. He had given her the greatest gifts she would ever have. She could only hope her mistake didn't follow her to Cowboy Creek.

Whit told them about the mines. He told them about a little island past the bend in the creek. "It's under water this time of year, but in the summer we can wade across the creek to get to it. On the other side of it is a little swimming hole. It sure is refreshing after a hot day of work."

"We don't know how to swim," John Thomas said.

"Well, that can be remedied easy enough, if it's all right with your mama, that is."

All three faces turned to look at her, the children imploring, Whit smiling gently.

Carrie's heart had melted. From the moment Nan Canfield told her of the opportunity to become a mail-order bride, she worried over how a man would treat her children. She didn't expect him to love them and care for them like a real father ought. She only hoped he would treat them kindly and with respect. It appeared she had been wrong. A man who wasn't kin to them *could* love them, and it looked like Whit Whitamore was that man.

"We'll see when the time comes," she answered.

Her gaze slid to Whit. Her stomach fluttered. Surely she didn't love him already. Not simply because he was kind to her children and looked at her the right way. And not because he was filling a desperate need by marrying her. She wanted their life together to be built on more than that. She prayed it would become so as they got to know each other.

Not long after, they climbed the hill to the trading post where they found Marla and Candace in the kitchen. Both were covered with flour. Marla was giving Candace instructions on how to roll out egg noodles and Candace was—smiling. Carrie nearly fainted from shock. She hadn't seen a genuine smile on her daughter's face in months.

As soon as Candace saw them, her expression went flat, but not before Carrie breathed a prayer of thanks. Her baby girl would be all right.

She reached for an apron on the hook on the wall. It was the middle of the afternoon, and she had spent the whole day outside with the children. She couldn't expect Marla to take over her duties after everything else she and Preach had done. "What do you need me to do? I can peel the potatoes while you…"

"What I need you to do is get out from underfoot," Marla scolded playfully. "Candace and I have everything under control in here, and you'd only be in the way. Daniel found some puzzle books while he was going through an old trunk in the trading post. He thought the little ones might like to look through them."

Marla was the only one who called Preach by his given name, so it took Carrie a moment to realize who she was talking about.

"Oh, Marla, I appreciate it, but I can't let you cook for all of us. It isn't right."

Marla waved away her words with a potholder. "Now, you heard me. This kitchen is too small for three women. You go on in the parlor and show the children those puzzle books. They're on the little table by Daniel's chair. There's a can of colored pencils too. They can color in the books as much as they want."

John Thomas and Annie gasped in anticipation.

"As for you two…" Marla put a dust-covered hand on Carrie's shoulder and the other on Whit's and turned them toward the door. "…You go on back outside and enjoy this beautiful day. Take a walk. Let Whit show you how the mill operates. Anything. Just get out of my kitchen. It's crowded enough. If I need you, I'll holler."

She pushed them into the parlor and went back to the counter with Candace.

Carrie laughed. "Well, I suppose she doesn't need my help."

"It appears that way." Whit found the stack of puzzle books on the table and leafed through one. Carrie saw coloring pages as well as puzzles and mazes, so there would be plenty for Annie to do too since she couldn't yet read. She positioned the children on their stomachs on the floor and handed over the books and can of pencils. After a reprimand to behave and share and not pester Marla, she and Whit stepped outside.

Though it was still early evening, the sun wasn't as warm as it had been an hour ago. Clouds edged closer, and the breeze carried the promise of rain. She tightened her shawl around her shoulders. Whit reached out and straightened a fold of fabric around her neck. His fingers skimmed her bare skin.

"Preach said he could perform the wedding ceremony on Sunday after meeting. If you have anything in your trunks you won't need until then, I can get the wagon and we can haul it to the house and unpack it there."

"That would save me so much work."

They untied his horse from where it waited in front of the trading post and walked it up the hill to his house. Carrie focused on the leisurely pace and the man beside her. The sound of the rushing stream was nearly the only sound breaking the peaceful quiet of the day.

Neither spoke during the ten-minute walk. The quiet companionship was something Carrie could get used to. After a while the house came into view. It was smaller than many of the German influenced houses she was used to in Cincinnati. But for the frontier, it was sprawling.

"You've built a lovely house, Whit. Much more than I would expect out here."

"Wasn't only me. I built it in stages while waiting for supplies to come in. Some of the men helped a lot, including a few who have since moved on."

"The only thing missing is a front porch," she said wistfully. "I always dreamed of a house with large porch across the front. What a treat to sit on it after a long day and listen to the water while we share our day."

He didn't speak right away. "You dreamed of that, did you?"

She was surprised to see he wasn't smiling. He looked as if the thought had never occurred to him to add a porch. "I expect most young girls do."

He stared at the house for a moment, as if contemplating its lack.

"I'm sorry, Whit. I didn't mean to disparage your house. It's beautiful. I envision many happy years with us and the children here."

He continued to stare at the house, his jaw hard. Oh, why had she gone and said the first thing that popped into her head? But she had no idea it would offend him. It was a fine house. Solid. Functional. It just lacked...warmth. Character. She couldn't very well tell him that. Especially now.

"Let's go inside," he said brusquely.

Trepidation rose in Carrie's stomach as they walked through the door. She was afraid to comment on anything and risk hurting his feelings again. Asking what she'd said wrong didn't seem like a good idea either.

The interior of the house was like the outside. Comfortable and solidly built but plain. Colorless. It looked so stark and lonely as if Whit had never finished moving in. The main room was large and open with only a few pieces of furniture. She counted right away there weren't enough chairs for everyone to sit down at the same time. A small braided rug that had seen better days lay on the floor in front of the fireplace. No curtains covered any of the windows. Curtains and rugs were an easy fix, but it would take miles of fabric to make the large house warm and cozy.

Upstairs was a large landing and two bedrooms. Candace and Annie could share the smaller one. The landing would make a suitable bedroom for John Thomas for the time being. Once babies came, Carrie would want them on the landing so they'd be close at hand. Other arrangements would have to be made for John Thomas.

Whit studied the layout as if working out the logistics of what to do with everyone as well. "I'm sorry I didn't think about the extra beds we'd need until now. Race and I can probably find a couple old bedframes in the miners' cabins. Or I can build a couple. I'm sure we'll find enough dry straw to fill mattress ticking for the children."

"The children can sleep on pallets on the floor for a few days if they have to."

"I don't want them to do that. The weather's been cooperative the last few days, but it can still get mighty cold at night over the next couple months."

Carrie nodded in agreement. She didn't want anyone to get sick. She walked to the far end of the landing where a small square window faced the mountains. "We could put a bed here for John Thomas. Eventually he'll need a separate room of his own that everyone else doesn't pass through on their way up and down the stairs. We could put a wall up here and a door." She motioned into the air with her hand. "Maybe build him some shelves for books and things."

Whit's face hardened. "What do you mean? Do you think we need to build onto the house?"

"Well, no. Not right away. But eventually, we'll need to think about other solutions."

Like where to put babies, she thought, hoping he would realize it on his own. John Thomas would not appreciate sharing the landing with a crying infant.

"Several of the men around here live in two-room cabin and they make do." His jaw was tight and his brown eyes dark and cold.

Carrie swallowed her impatience. Whit had gotten used to having this big house all to himself. She would have to give him time to acclimate to a ready-made family.

"I realize that. I grew up with five children in a two-room cabin and then spent the rest of my life in a small apartment. I didn't mean I couldn't make do with this house just as it is. I was just thinking of the future and how we might need more privacy as the family grows."

Whit exhaled and made a visible effort to calm himself. "I understand. You just caught me off guard. I thought I had a nice house to offer you. Now I see it isn't enough for a wife with three children."

Carrie caught hold of his shirtsleeve. She felt terrible. Everything she said was coming out wrong "Oh, Whit, that isn't what I meant at all. I just…I was thinking of babies. If we should be so blessed. We'll make do for now however we need to. But I thought—I didn't think…"

She stopped talking. How could she tell him she thought he was prosperous? She didn't think building a simple divider and a door to give John Thomas separate sleeping quarters was that big of a deal for a man who had built a house and a mill practically single-handedly. She didn't think it was beyond his means.

To be fair, this was all new to him. He had no children of his own. He'd never had to support a family. He had no concept of the cost of family and growing children and expanding walls to accommodate them.

He glanced at her hand on his arm. When he looked back at her, his frustration seemed to have evaporated. "No, Carrie, it's my fault. It's just a lot to take in all at once. I want our home to be comfortable for all of us."

"Thank you, Whit." She squeezed his arm and dropped her hand.

His eyes scanned her face before settling on her lips again. His eyes darkened but not in the way they had before. She knew he was thinking of kissing her. Should she make a move to show him it would be welcome, or would he think her too forward?

He took a deep breath and stepped away, taking the decision out of her hands. "I know you're having supper with Marla and Preach tonight, but I thought tomorrow, if it isn't too inconvenient, you might want to cook supper for everyone here. To thank them for their hospitality toward you and the children. I'm sure it would be much easier for you to prepare meals here than in the brides' house."

"That's a wonderful idea, Whit. It's what I'll be doing from now on after Sunday anyway."

His smile widened, and her insides warmed at the sight of it.

Everything was going to work out fine.

Chapter Ten

"Give me that handsaw there, would you, J.T?"

"What'd you call me?"

Whit looked down at the little boy, as skinny and skittish as a young deer but eager to please. Hopeful to be liked and accepted into Whit's world. "J.T. That's your name, ain't it?"

"No, my name's John Thomas."

"That's what I said. J.T. is short for John Thomas. It's the same thing."

Yesterday Preach and Whit had moved Carrie's trunks into the house. This morning they scoured what remained of the miners' cabins for bedframes and anything else they could use for Whit's rapidly expanding family. He took as little as possible, not wanting to use everything since there were other brides coming and other men would need furniture as badly as he did. Whit would need to take Carrie to Good Hope soon—possibly all the way to Ruby City—to procure proper furniture, bedding, and shoes for the youngsters.

Marla and Carrie were at the trading post going through piles of fabric and household utensils they had found in the cabins to take for their immediate needs, while sorting and labeling items for future brides. When Whit began putting the largest bedframe together upstairs on the landing for the girls to share, he invited John Thomas along. Though barely more than a tyke, it was past time the boy learn to help with men's work.

John Thomas jutted out his chin. Whit barely suppressed a smile at the look of confusion and indignation on the lad's face. "Nobody's ever called me J.T. before."

Whit pointed at the handsaw he needed in the canvas bag and waited for the boy to hand it to him. Then he sat back on his haunches. "I didn't mean to offend you. That's just what fellas do. They give each other nicknames."

He rested his hands on his thighs and regarded the child. "It's like when you call a tall man Stretch or a red-haired fella Red. Preach's name's not really Preach. That's just what we call him because he's the one who preaches to us every Sunday. If your last name's Smith, well, you can sure bet all your pals'll call you Smitty. Your mama might call you by your Christian name, and your gal, too, but every man you ever know will call you Smitty."

The little boy stared in rapt attention.

Whit sawed off a bit of length from the crosstie of the frame and jammed it into the notch of the bed leg. "Here, hold this steady." He didn't really need the boy's help. The leg wasn't going anywhere while he worked on the opposite end of the frame, but teaching always began with little things?

After the tie was secured to the front and back legs, he stood and brushed his hands together. John Thomas mimicked his moves.

"Just like me," Whit said. "I barely remember the name my ma gave me." He scratched his chin as if in thought. "I think it's Philip, but I could be wrong. Everybody's called me Whit since I was in short britches. That's just what fellas do when they like you. Now, when they don't like you, they'll call you all sorts of names not so nice. That's when you got trouble."

The little boy's eyes grew large. Whit winked, and they both laughed.

"You must know everything, Mr. Whit. I never heard none'a that stuff before."

Whit's heart ached at the earnestness on his face. He hadn't heard it because he'd never been around men before. "If you don't like it, I'll go back to calling you John Thomas."

"No, that's all right. I'm a man now. I reckon the other men will call me J.T. too."

"I expect they will." Whit turned away so the boy wouldn't see him smile. His worries and fears about raising a family and affording three children had faded with each passing hour. They were working things out, making room, putting together mismatched furniture to create a home for all of them. He was falling in love with this whole family. Not just Carrie. It may be ready-made, but it was quickly becoming his.

The front door opened below them. "Yoohoo, where are you?" Carrie called. "We brought lunch."

John Thomas went to the railing and peered over the side to the parlor below. "We're here, Mama. We're working."

"Well, hurry up and finish. Candace helped Marla make chicken and dumplings and I can't wait to try them."

John Thomas looked over his shoulder at Whit. "Are we finished, Mr. Whit?"

"As soon as you fetch the broom and sweep up all these woodchips and sawdust."

"Yes, sir."

John Thomas whooped and ran down the stairs. Whit went to the stair railing and watched as John Thomas skidded past his sisters and mother to get the broom from the kitchen. Candace had her arms wrapped around a large kettle. She wore a contented expression on her face. Whit still hadn't heard her say more than a few words when asked a direct question. Before long he was sure she'd be smiling and chattering like the rest of them. Carrie smiled up at him. He marveled again at just how pretty she was. It nearly took his breath away. He returned the smile. What was he worried about? He could make this work.

It was nice cooking and baking on a stove instead of relying on Marla and Preach for everything. Carrie easily found her way around Whit's kitchen. Even though they would be married in a few days and the kitchen would be her domain, it still seemed odd rearranging the cupboards and larder to suit her. There were several things she would do differently once the house was hers to cut down on steps and make the process of cooking and cleaning more efficient and convenient.

Since Whit had several butchered chickens in the icehouse, she decided to bake a shepherd's pie for supper. She loved making the dish and hoped Preach and Marla would like it as well. She had just begun cubing the raw chicken when she heard footsteps on the porch.

"Come in," she called to the knock at the door. She didn't want to stop and clean her hands. It was probably Marla anyway or one of the children who had gone outside to play.

"Hello?" came a feminine voice she hadn't heard before. Carrie grabbed the dishtowel tucked into her apron sash and dried her hands as footsteps headed her way. A pretty dark-eyed woman appeared in the doorway, her dark, almost black hair tied into a fat braid hanging down her back.

"I'm sorry," Carrie said. "I thought you were Marla or one of the children."

"You don't have to stop with your work on my account. I didn't mean to interrupt you. I'm Rennie Campbell. I have dinner to fix at home myself, but I was ahead of schedule, and it's such a pretty day—finally, no wind or rain," she added with a laugh.

Her exuberance was as refreshing as the day outside. She looked like no more than a girl with her dancing brown eyes and smooth ivory skin.

"I wanted to ride into town and introduce myself," she continued. "It's wonderful to have another woman in the area. I went to the trading post and Marla told me you were here. I hope I wasn't presumptuous to stop by unannounced."

Rennie finally stopped talking. Carrie resisted the urge to laugh. Even though she was newly married, and by all appearances, very happy, she was apparently lonely for female companionship.

"Please don't worry about that," Carrie said. "I doubt social conformity carries much weight around here. I'm glad you stopped in. I've heard so much about you. All good, I assure you. You were the first bride to come to Cowboy Creek, right?"

Rennie nodded. "I worked for Nan Canfield, Rase's aunt, back in the city as well as for some of her friends. That's how I heard the men here wanted brides."

Carrie quickly finished cubing the chicken and dumped it into a pot to cook. She poured hot water over her hands in the sink to wash them properly. "We have that in common," she said as she worked. "I know Nan from my church. She's been a blessing to so many people, me especially. Please, sit down. Let me make you some tea."

Rennie glanced at the stove. "You don't need to bother."

"It's no bother. I can keep an eye on the meat while we get to know each other a little."

Rennie pulled out a chair. "Especially since we're going to be neighbors." She raised her eyebrows in question.

Carrie laughed. "Yes, it looks like we will be." She had made shortbread cookies this morning and set two on a saucer in front of Rennie.

"So, are you and Whit..." Rennie took one of the cookies but didn't bite into it.

Carrie knew what she wanted to know. She took a seat in the chair across the table from Rennie while she waited for the tea to steep. "Whit proposed yesterday."

A flush warmed her own cheeks. At her age, she thought she was too old to be a blushing bride, but maybe one was never too old for that. "That's why I'm here today. I'm fixing supper to share with Marla and Preach. Why don't you and your husband join us?"

Rennie quickly shook her head. "We couldn't do that. I'm sure as time goes on, we'll have plenty of chances to share meals together. What do you and the children think of Cowboy Creek?"

Candace's pouting face flashed across Carrie's mind, but she pushed it aside. The girl was at a stage where she hated nearly anything her mother liked, so Carrie wouldn't let Candace's attitude sour her own enthusiasm. "It's so peaceful. I was happy to get out of the city. The younger children are having such fun exploring. I am a little concerned about their education. I can teach them some, but I would like to see them go to school. Good Hope is so far away, I'm not sure how that's going to work."

Rennie nibbled a cookie. "I suppose that will be a concern for all of us eventually. Hopefully, someday, there will be enough of us to hire a teacher or make some kind of arrangement."

Carrie uncovered the tea and set a pitcher of milk near her guest. "Preach and Marla have been wonderful. Marla is giving my oldest daughter cooking lessons, which is a good thing since the girl doesn't want me to teach her anything."

Rennie chuckled. "Preach and Marla were so kind to me when I got here. I lived in the brides' house for over a month before I married Jacob."

"So, you're the one I have to thank for the lovely curtains and slipcovers."

"I needed something to do to fill my time."

The women talked for several minutes over their tea and cookies. Rennie looked around the kitchen. "This is a beautiful cabin. I've never been here before. Jacob and I only have two rooms. We built a lean-to on the side. Eventually we'll need more space. I'm surprised this is so nice given Whit's reputation for frugality."

"Frugality?"

Rennie's cheeks colored. "I'm sorry. I shouldn't have said that. All I meant was some of the men were surprised to hear you had children. Whit was—cautious, I guess is a good word—about the idea of spending so much money to send for brides. He came around almost immediately, though, and I'm sure he's thrilled to have you all here." She looked away, as if wishing she hadn't opened her mouth. "Have you thought about putting out a garden yet? I started turning over ground yesterday. I'm still deciding exactly what to plant besides the usual staples."

While Rennie talked about gardens, Carrie offered half-hearted input as she thought of Whit's reaction when she mentioned the front porch and making sleeping arrangements for John Thomas. Would his aversion to spending money—or frugality, as Rennie put it—be a hindrance down the road? Carrie had three children. She hoped to have more with Whit. She didn't want to spend her life squabbling over money every time she needed new fabric for dresses or books for the children's education.

After Rennie left, the rest of the afternoon sped by. Carrie glanced out the window a few times and watched Whit showing John Thomas how to handle a shovel. Annie followed behind and tried to do her part. Mostly she picked up and examined rocks and sticks and dried leaves. Carrie's heart filled with warmth at the scene. Her children finally had a man of character to influence them. She wouldn't worry another moment over Whit being tight with a dollar, if he truly was. It was a trait to be admired, not loathed. Heaven knew Johnny Rhoades didn't know the first thing about managing money, and look where it had gotten them.

Marla drove the wagon into the yard an hour before supper was supposed to go on the table with a box of plates and silverware and four extra chairs. Whit only owned three. Even if the children sat on upturned boxes, there wasn't enough seating in the house for company. It looked like chairs would be the first order of business after the wedding.

By the time Whit, Preach, and the younger children came inside, cleaned up and hungry, the table was set and loaded with food. As Preach blessed the food, Carrie couldn't keep tears of gratitude from filling her eyes. She finally had everything she prayed for all her life.

Even Candace smiled and gave more than two-word responses when asked a question, though she mostly limited her interactions to Marla. Carrie figured the girl would come around when she was ready. Carrie needed to be the adult in the situation. She wouldn't expect more from her daughter than the girl was mature enough to give.

Conversation was light and fun. When Whit told them how he and John Thomas unknotted a tangle of baling twine, he included Annie in the story though she had done more getting in the way than helping. It reminded Preach of a story from his childhood and had everyone at the table laughing. Even Candace.

Soon it was time for dessert—Apple Brown Betty that couldn't have turned out better. Carrie cut generous servings for everyone and passed the plates around the table. "John Thomas, pass this to Mr. Dodds, please."

"Mama, it's okay if you want to call me John Thomas cause that's what mamas do, but from now on my name's J.T."

She stopped, the plate suspended between them. "Excuse me."

"My name's not John Thomas anymore. That's for little kids. I'm a man now. My name's J.T. Ain't that right, Mr. Whit?"

Whit winked at Carrie. "That's right, partner."

"I didn't realize," Carrie said with a lump in her throat.

John Thomas took the plate and passed it on as Carrie recovered. The adults at the table watched her. Marla's eyes glistened with tears. Carrie's heart melted at the swelling in her son's chest. This was what the influence of a man had on a little boy. Her son was growing up. She was thankful he'd have Whit to guide him there. Whatever rumors Rennie had heard about his aversion to spending money were instantly forgotten.

Chapter Eleven

Whit stepped out of the mill into the sunshine. It had been a busy morning, the kind he liked. Sawyer Jamison had come with a big order. Sawyer was his best customer in Cowboy Creek. He raised hogs and always needed feed. He bought his winter grain from a farmer near Good Hope and hauled it to Whit for milling. Sawyer was also a man of few words, so thankfully for Whit, he didn't ask a lot of questions about Carrie. Word had gotten around that Carrie was here, along with the news they were getting married tomorrow after having known each other in person for only five days. Whit could already feel the slaps on the back and hear the congratulations that would come his way. With Carrie and the three children, he hoped all the attention in the room would be directed at them, which suited him just fine.

He threw up his hand in a wave as Sawyer's loaded-down buckboard rattled off down the road. With his step lighter than he remembered it being before, he headed across the yard to the house. Last night after supper, Carrie told him she had too many things to do today in preparation for tomorrow, so she thought it better if they didn't have supper together tonight. Whit couldn't think of a thing he needed to do to prepare for getting hitched. Carrie had cleaned his house, rearranged a few things, and moved much of her things in. Besides a bath and a shave, which would take all of thirty minutes if he tarried in front of the mirror, Whit's schedule was wide open.

He smiled at the thought of all the mysterious things women went through to prepare for a man. He'd find out soon enough just why it took a woman half a day to get ready for an event when a man could be ready to walk out the door in twenty minutes. Of course, she also had three children's clothes to lay out, shoes to polish, as well as helping Marla prepare food for the dinner the community shared after Sunday meetings. Tomorrow's meal would be extra special. He hoped Marla could keep the cake he had requested out of sight from Carrie. He wasn't sure how she'd pull it off in her tiny living quarters, but Marla could be quite sneaky when the occasion called for it.

As he came around the side of the house, he paused mid-step when he saw the front door open a crack. He was sure he'd closed it securely behind him to keep an unexpected rain shower or curious critter outside. But there it was, open. He got closer and heard shuffling inside. Carrie must've changed her mind about coming today. His heart lurched at the thought of seeing her, though he'd seen her just last night. She wasn't in the parlor. He followed the sound of movement through the house to the pantry. Marla may have run out of something they needed and sent Preach or one of the children to get it. Preach would've stopped and asked him first, and the children wouldn't know where to find anything.

No, Whit's guess was Carrie. She was the only one who'd be rummaging around his pantry. He softened his steps to sneak up on her. He imagined wrapping his hands around her tiny waist and spinning her around. Oh, she'd get a scare all right, but if he was smooth enough, he could pull her right into a kiss.

Their first kiss they'd remember forever.

He didn't have a chance to sneak up on anyone. As he entered the kitchen, Candace stepped out of the small pantry, her hands empty. She stopped short at the sight of him. Her blue eyes went wide. He saw more than surprise in her eyes. Fear?

Whit swallowed his disappointment at missing out on a kiss from Carrie. "Candace? Did you need something?" He knew the girl didn't like him. Probably didn't trust him either. The only way to build trust, especially with someone in her situation, was with patience and kindness.

For a moment she looked like she would bolt without answering, then her usual defiance darkened her gaze.

"If your ma or Marla need something, maybe I can help you find it."

She pursed her lips—either building her nerve or deciding how much to tell him. "I was looking for ink. I couldn't find any at the brides' house and I didn't want to ask Mama or Marla."

Sympathy rose in Whit at the girl's plight. He couldn't begin to imagine the isolation and loneliness she felt so far away from her friends. He hated to tell her, but even after she wrote the letter, it might be months before she got back a reply. If ever. "The only ink I have is in my office in the mill. Do you need paper, too?"

"No, I brought some with me." Her voice softened but hard distrust remained in her wide-set blue eyes.

Whit wagged his head toward the front of the house. "Come with me and I'll show you where it is."

She shook her head. "No, thank you. I'll get it later."

Ah, she wanted privacy. He understood that. "It's right on top of my desk. Just be sure to tighten the lid back when you're done so it doesn't spill on anything."

"Yes, sir," she murmured.

"Are you writing a letter to one of your friends?" he asked, hoping she might open up to him.

She crossed her arms in front of her. Her eyes narrowed. "I'm writing a letter to my papa. As soon as I figure out how to get it to him, he'll come get me and take me home."

Whit barely heard any of the words she said past *Papa*. "Your papa?"

She lifted her narrow chin. "Yes. I hate it here. I never wanted to come, but Mama didn't give us a choice. I miss my friends. I want to go home."

Whit still couldn't understand what she was saying. "But your papa? What do you mean? I thought he was— dead."

Candace's pale brows slid together. "My papa's not dead. He lives in Cincinnati. As soon as he gets my letter, I know he'll come for me. I'm leaving and never coming back. Then Mama will be sorry. I hate it here and I hate you."

She ducked her head and ran past him out of the house. Whit barely got out of her way in time to keep her from treading on his foot. He stared after her, still trying to make sense of what she'd said.

A papa, alive and well in Cincinnati?

Carrie wasn't a widow. That meant she had either sneaked away from her husband. Or she was divorced. Either way, it was adultery. With a living husband, even a divorced one, was it legal to marry her? Did Whit want to? If she lied about being a widow, who knew what other lies she'd told.

Carrie had just finished cleaning up the remnants of the children's lunch when she heard a horse ride up. She knew without looking it was Whit. No other visitor would've ridden up so fast. Her heart leaped in her chest. Last night had been wonderful. It solidified in her heart that she had done the right thing for herself and the children by coming to Cowboy Creek. It would be hard on all of them without a school nearby or accessible medical treatment, but they would figure it out as they went along. The younger children already loved their new home. Annie had simply blossomed in the last five days. She was talking more and revealing more of her silly, happy, vivacious personality. John Thomas—or J.T. as he preferred now—held his head higher and was acting more like the boy Carrie always knew was inside him.

The only fly in the ointment was Candace. Carrie emitted a heavy sigh. Poor Candace. Stuck between little girl and bigger girl. Carrie saw in her eyes that she wanted to run and play and explore with the other children, but she had wrapped a protective cocoon around herself and wouldn't let any of them in.

Carrie hadn't seen her all morning. Right after breakfast the girl grabbed her tablet and slipped outside. It was just as well. Carrie figured it was best to leave her to her thoughts for a while. She was a good girl. Just going through a rough patch and searching for who she was in the world. Carrie would probably find her at Marla's later, struggling to learn knitting stitches or listening to Marla's stories. Marla seemed to know just what to say to soothe twelve-year-old angst.

She whispered a quick prayer for the Lord to touch the girl's wounded heart. As she took off her apron and hung it on the hook next to the stove, she prayed for some of the gentleness and compassion for herself that Marla had in abundance. She wasn't expecting Whit. She told him last night she had too much to do today. He must've decided on a quick visit anyway. She didn't mind. She was eager to see him too.

She smoothed her hair into place and walked as sedately as she could manage to the door. It wouldn't do for Whit to hear her bounding across the floor like a giddy schoolgirl though that's how she felt on the inside.

She opened the door and smiled out at him. He stood in the dirt at the bottom of the steps. His lips were set in a hard line, his dark eyes hooded. Carrie's heart stilled. He looked—angry. That couldn't be. She closed the door and hurried down the steps to him. John Thomas and Annie weren't in sight. They had probably gone next door to shadow Preach or accept bread and jam Marla always had on hand. By the look on Whit's face, she didn't want them to hear whatever news he came to bring.

"Whit, what's wrong? Has something happened?"

"Do you lie about everything?"

Carrie drew back at the venom in his voice. It took a moment to find her voice. "What are you talking about?" she hissed in case the children were closer than she thought.

Whit made no effort to keep his voice down. "I'm talking about how you told me you had two kids, then you showed up with three."

That again?

Her temper flared. Maybe he was a skinflint like Rennie suggested.

"I explained why I had to bring Annie. I told you—"

"Now I find out you're not even a widow," he bit out. "You have a husband."

She recoiled at the word. How did he—?

She took a fortifying breath. The *how* didn't matter at this point. She should've told him the whole story in her very first letter. But how could she explain Johnny Rhoades in a few pages? How could she tell him she'd been so young and gullible and desperate when she married Johnny, she hadn't recognized the snake that he was? How could she have written in a letter about his cheating and lying and the violence...

She shook away the thoughts. She didn't want to think about those early years, let alone explain them to someone.

"So, who's lying to me? You or Candace? Are you still married or aren't you?"

She flinched again. Stung. She wanted to lash out. Tell him she wasn't a liar. Neither was Candace. She swallowed her anger. He had every right to be mad. And hurt. She had lied—sort of.

"No, Whit, I'm not married and he's not dead. We're...I'm divorced."

"Divorced?" He spat out the word as if it were detestable. She supposed it was.

She squared her shoulders. "Yes, divorced."

"Why didn't you tell me?"

"Because I don't think of myself as divorced. If not for my children, I wouldn't think of myself as ever being married. I haven't for a very long time."

That was only part of the reason. The easy part. How could she explain the rest when she didn't completely understand it herself? She glanced around to make sure the children weren't around to hear. Especially Candace. She never spoke ill of their father. She had always made excuses for his behavior, so they wouldn't think any of it was their fault. Maybe her omission had been the same as a lie to them too.

She lowered her voice, even though no one else was in sight. "It's hard to explain to every person I meet how I was stupid enough to marry the most worthless example of manhood who ever walked the earth. It was embarrassing. Not only did I make a terrible decision, he couldn't stick around to be a papa to our kids. I left the city to give my children a better life than the one they had. I needed a husband. They needed a father. A good one who wouldn't take off if a prettier face or better opportunity came along. It was too much to explain in a letter."

Whit's face didn't soften. "No, it wasn't, Carrie. It's everything about who you are. I left home because every decision that ever affected me was made by someone else, and they were always bad ones. You didn't give me a chance to make up my own mind."

She crossed her arms in front of her. "So, I'm a bad decision, huh? You wouldn't have given me a chance if you knew I was divorced, but that's not why I didn't tell you. I didn't tell you because I didn't want you to know. I didn't want Preach and Marla to know and look down on my children because that's not who we are anymore."

"*I* had the right to know. This affects me. It wasn't fair to keep it from me."

Carrie felt like the ground was crumbling under her feet. "It doesn't affect you, Whit. It doesn't change anything. I was young and stupid when I married him. You're not marrying the naïve girl I was back then. That part of my life is over. I was hurt and beat down by that man. We barely ever lived together as man and wife. As far as I'm concerned, I *am* a widow."

"Just because you feel like something doesn't make it fact. You aren't a widow. The man, as horrible as he may have been, is still alive, right?"

"Yes."

"Then according to the Bible, you aren't released from the marriage covenant."

"You don't know everything, Whit. You're making assumptions without knowing the whole story. If you'll calm down—"

"Don't tell me to calm down," he nearly shouted. He glanced at the door behind her. When he spoke again, his voice was lowered but the anger was still evident. "I want to know what else you've lied about. How much more is there?"

Carrie's jaw tightened. "I never lied to you, Whit. I didn't lie to you about Annie, and I didn't lie about Johnny Rhoades. I just hadn't told you the whole story. It must be nice not to have any big mistakes in your life you wish you could undo. Or ones you don't let yourself think about it."

He snorted. "How can you not think about it every time you look at those kids?" He hooked his thumbs onto his belt. "I'm sorry, Carrie, but I don't know if I can marry someone who keeps things from me."

Heat flamed on her cheeks. "And I don't know if I want to marry someone who makes up his mind without listening to the whole story."

He threw his hands in the air. "I would've listened if you'd told me anything. Instead you come into my house with a laundry list of changes you want to make. A front porch. More bedrooms. Do you have any idea how much that'll cost?"

"Yes, it'll cost some of your precious money. I didn't come to you with a laundry list of demands that needed filled. I mentioned things that will make all our lives better and more convenient. If you don't want to let go of a nickel, you never should've sent for a wife. Even a young wife with no children would need dresses and shoes and food. I won't be made to feel bad because my children need beds to sleep in and John Thomas can't sleep in the same room as his sisters forever. As for a porch, I only mentioned that I always imagined sitting on one at the end of the day and watching the sun go down. I never dreamed it would send you to the poorhouse."

His shoulders sagged. "I'm sorry. I shouldn't have mentioned the porch. I always intended to put one on. I just never got around to it."

"You meant it, so it's just as well that you said it. I want to know how you truly feel."

"And I want to know if there's anything else you haven't told me. If we're going to get married—"

"If?" she cried, tears threatening. "What does that mean?"

"I guess it means I better go before I say something I'll really regret."

"Oh, I think it's too late for that."

Without another word, Whit whirled around and stomped to his horse tied at the corner of the house. Carrie fought down the urge to run after him. She wasn't through. She wanted to hurl a lot more words at him. She had married a man once who resented her and made her feel like a burden. She sure didn't plan to do it again. She wouldn't saddle herself with a man who begrudged every morsel of food that went into her children's mouths.

When he was out of sight, she gave into the tears and let them spill unbidden down her cheeks. She had been on her own for most of her life. She could do it again. They would survive without Whit. She just didn't want to. She loved him, blast her treacherous heart.

Whit wasn't ready to go home. He had some frustration to pound out on the rough roads. He cut across the field between the meetinghouse and one of the abandoned buildings with no destination in mind. Carrie lied. She was married—or had been—and lied about it. Worse, she didn't even have the decency to apologize like he expected her to. If she had at least shown a little remorse, they might've been able to talk the situation out. Instead, she acted like the whole thing was his fault.

He shouldn't have mentioned the porch or the extra bedroom. He'd figure out where to get the money to build her a castle if she wanted one. But the way he said it made him sound like a complete jerk.

He slapped his leg with his hat. He knew everyone in Cowboy Creek thought he was stingy. Stinginess had nothing to do with it. He was afraid of going back to those terrible years he'd had growing up. He tried to trust the Lord with his money concerns, but even the Good Book said; A man who didn't work shouldn't eat. The book of Proverbs made it clear what God thought about slovenliness. A man's livelihood depended on his own sweat and grit, not faith that the Lord would provide for a foolish man.

He didn't look up when he heard hoofbeats approaching. It was probably Preach riding after him to find out why he told Carrie he wasn't sure he could marry her. It wasn't likely Carrie had tattled on him, but Preach may have overheard part of the conversation. Whit didn't feel like talking. He spurred his horse faster, hoping Preach would take the hint. The horse behind him picked up its speed too. It couldn't be Preach on the animal. He slowed and turned in his saddle

Rase Canfield rode up alongside him. He took off his hat and wiped his brow with the back of his arm. "Land sakes, Whit. Where you off to like a house afire?"

"Nowhere. Just letting off some steam."

Rase looked at him warily. "I'd'a thought you'd be back there making moon eyes at your lady. I hear you two are getting hitched tomorrow."

Whit bit back his impatience. "Word sure gets around."

"Ain't nothing else of interest going on. Didn't think it was a secret anyhow." He leaned forward in the saddle to get a better look at Whit's face under the shade of his ten-gallon hat. "How's that pretty little filly of yours anyway?"

"Is that why you chased me down? To put your nose in my business?"

The easy-going smile slid off Rase's features. "You know that wasn't what I was doing. If you got a problem with me or anybody else, this ain't the way to settle it."

Whit exhaled and waited a moment to speak. "I'm sorry, Rase. It isn't fair to take my aggravation out on you."

"What have you got to be aggravated about? You're getting married tomorrow. Pretty near every other fella in Cowboy Creek would give his eye teeth to be in your boots. Preach said the two of you go together like bread and butter."

Whit wasn't ready to have this conversation. He wanted to get off by himself and think about everything he'd just learned. He didn't want Rase or anyone else to know he'd fallen for Carrie's lies.

"I don't know so much about that anymore."

The horses walked slowly across the uneven meadow. Rase took a toothpick out of his shirt pocket and stuck it between his teeth. He slumped loosely in his saddle as if he had all day to talk. Whit figured his thinking over the matter might work itself out faster he if spoke the thoughts out loud.

"She isn't who I thought she was, Rase."

"Who did you think she was?"

"A widow with two kids. Turns out she's neither."

"I don't follow."

"She turns up here with three kids instead of two, and she's not a widow. She's divorced."

Rase sucked air between his teeth. "Ah, I see."

"Yeah, divorced. I never met a divorced woman in my life."

Rase didn't say as much, but Whit figured he hadn't either.

"It's not just that she's divorced. She's lied to me since her very first letter. She brought another kid with her, one that wasn't even hers. You know that means I'll have to support her. As soon as I asked Carrie to marry me, she started talking about improvements to make on my house. I didn't grow up in a house half the size of what I've got now, and there were ten of us. We boys were thankful to find a spot of dry hay in the barn to lay our heads."

"Is that what you want for those kids?" Rase said, jerking his chin back the way they'd come.

"Well, no. I want a nice house for them. But how nice does she expect? When will she be satisfied?"

"Probably never." Rase laughed. He sobered when he saw Whit wasn't laughing with him. "Listen, women like nice things for themselves and the little ones. It's why we have civilization. If it were left up to us men, we'd still be writing on cave walls."

Whit wished Rase would take the matter seriously. "She didn't ask nothing about my financial situation. She just assumed I could afford to do whatever she wanted."

"You can."

"This year. What if we have a bad season? What if there's a drought or a flood that washes all your farms out of the valley and nobody brings me business? How will we support our own children if something like that happens? Here we are, starting out with three."

Rase looked off into the distance as they rode a little farther. Whit wanted to complain some more. It looked like the valid points he brought up weren't getting through, just like they hadn't gotten through to Carrie.

No, he'd shut up. Nobody liked a whiner.

After riding a few more yards, Rase turned to study him. "Whit, what will you do if Carrie gives you five more children? Or ten? You'll love every last one of them, that's what, and you'll do whatever it takes to support them. We can't predict droughts or floods or poor growing seasons. God's in charge of all that. All we can do is trust Him to see us through when it happens."

"Easy for you to say," Whit growled. "I didn't see you raising your hand to take a wife."

"No, I didn't," Rase agreed, "but it had nothing to do with money. I'm not the marrying kind." They reached a line of trees in the meadow and stopped just outside of the shade. The day was cool, and the sun felt good on their backs. "It won't cost much to add a couple rooms onto the back of your house. You'll need the space eventually anyhow. What's the difference if you do it now or later? We all have building material to spare. You know the rest of us will do whatever we can to help."

"I don't need a handout," Whit grumbled.

The anger had seeped out of him. Every word Rase said was true. Terrible things happened everywhere, whether to a man alone or one with a house full of children.

Rase clapped a hand on his shoulder. "I'm not offering a handout. You know we all help each other around here as the need arises. Before you go getting all het up again, I want to ask you something. Did Carrie actually write in her letter that she was a widow or did you assume it?"

"I don't see how that matters."

"It does matter. You said she wasn't who you thought. Sounds to me like the problem lies with you. You assumed something before she told it. I know divorce is a terrible thing, but there are conditions for it, even in the Bible. Did you ask her how it came about?"

"I don't see what difference it makes. She should've made sure there was no room for misunderstanding."

He thought of her comment about how nice it must be that he'd never made a mistake. Oh, he'd made plenty. He may have just made another one.

"Listen, Whit, don't go off half-cocked and ruin a good thing. You probably don't want to hear this, but I'm going to say it anyway. It almost sounds like you're looking for an excuse not to get married. You've realized what a family costs, and it scares the socks off you."

Whit gripped the reins between his fingers. "You don't know anything about what I'm thinking."

Rase held up both hands in surrender. "Maybe not, but I know you had a rough time growing up, and it's affected you mightily. You got a good woman back there who for some reason has agreed to marry your sorry hide. I don't want to see you let fear keep you from it."

"I ain't afraid of nothing."

"Oh, come on, Whit. We're all afraid of something. Look at me. I'm afraid of women altogether. That's why I didn't raise my hand at Christmas."

Both men chuckled.

"I know you don't like it that she's divorced. Whether widowed or divorced, the situation is usually outside the woman's control. If her husband died or abandoned her and those children, it doesn't really matter. It's the same result. She was left alone and needs a good man. And Heaven knows you need a good woman.

Tomorrow's your wedding day. You better get this worked out or she'll be on the next stage back to the city."

"Maybe that's the best thing."

They turned the horses back toward the settlement. "Maybe. You've lived alone most of your life. You've done pretty well for yourself. Built up a nice business out here where most men would've given up. Maybe that's enough for you. It's enough for me. But I think you want a family. I think you want the love and warmth you never had coming up. Over the last few days, you've seen what it's like to have a woman and children in your life. Might be hard to go back to nothing but your business, your empty house, and that bucketful of coins hidden in your well."

"Okay, okay, I get your point."

Neither man spoke again until they were within a stone's throw of the back of the meetinghouse. They brought their mounts to a stop. "I appreciate you listening to me rant," Whit said.

Rase smiled. "Anytime. We all need to let off steam sometimes. I'll pray for you about tomorrow. You've got a lot of life left to live with whatever decision you make. The rest of us will miss Carrie if she leaves, and Cowboy Creek will be the worse off without those children. But you're the one who has to marry her. To vow before God you'll honor and cherish her and love her until the day you die. And sometimes to forgive." He turned the horse toward his own property.

"Hey, Rase, wait a minute." When Rase turned in the saddle, Whit asked, "How'd you know about the bucket of coins in my well?"

Rase laughed. "Oh, Whit, everybody knows about that."

Chapter Twelve

Carrie dried her face on her apron and pulled herself together. It wouldn't do for the children to find her a teary mess. She needed to get her mind off Whit for a while. Maybe she'd take a nap. Or a bath. She didn't know what would happen tomorrow. It wasn't likely she was getting married. She thought of the few dollars stashed in her reticule. It wasn't enough to get her anywhere. Nan had told her if marriage was impossible, the men of Cowboy Creek would pay her trip back to Cincinnati or wherever she chose to go. She didn't want that to happen. She wouldn't become a charity case. She had always pulled her own weight, and she supposed she could do it now. The problem was she didn't want to. She wanted to stay here. She wanted to marry Whit and build a beautiful life together. She cared too much for him to leave. She might even love him. Stubborn faults and all.

Just as she opened the door to go inside, John Thomas and Annie came running up behind her. "Where have you been?" she cried. "It's too cold to stay away from the house for so long. Look at your clothes. You've got mud all over your pants."

John Thomas looked down at his legs. His lower lip trembled. "I'm sorry, Mama. We was just...playing."

"We're sorry," Annie repeated.

Carrie exhaled and struggled to rein in her ire. It wasn't their fault she'd had a row with Whit. They were just being children. If she'd ignored her own embarrassment and fear and told him the whole story in the beginning, he wouldn't feel like she lied to him.

"It's all right," she said. "Come inside and change into some dry clothes while I put those in the tub to soak."

The children scampered up the steps, eying her warily as they hurried past. Carrie tousled their hair to show them all was forgiven.

As she helped the children change, she took a few minutes to pray for peace. She asked for forgiveness for lying to Whit and prayed everything would work out between them however it was meant to.

She had just dunked their dirty clothes into a tub of hot water when the door opened. Candace came in, carrying her writing tablet. She glared at Carrie.

Carrie swallowed her impatience at the familiar look. "You missed lunch. Are you hungry?"

"I ate at Marla's."

Of course you did, Carrie thought.

She might say something to Marla about sending the girl home for meals instead of feeding her. Then again, Marla seemed to be the only person Candace was comfortable talking to. Carrie hated to take away her only friend after she'd lost everyone else.

"That's fine, just please tell me where you're going when you leave the house. Anything could happen to any one of you out there. There are wild animals and who knows what else."

Candace started past her. "You can't expect me to sit in this shack all day with those two crybabies."

Carrie grabbed her arm and pulled her to a stop. "Don't call your brother and sister names and don't disrespect the roof over your head the good Lord has provided. I don't care what you want to do, you tell me first where you're going and what you're doing."

Candace jerked her arm free. "You forced me to come here and live crowded up in this rundown—house. Now I'm not even allowed to go someplace quiet to think. To write letters home to people who care about me. That figures."

Carrie swallowed hard. John Thomas and Annie were hanging on every word. They were already upset. She didn't want to make matters worse by fighting with Candace.

"Candace, please. It's dangerous out there. Just like in the city, I need to know where you're going and when you plan to come back. That's all."

Scowling, Candace dropped into the stuffed chair. She clutched her tablet to her chest as if it contained all the world's secrets.

"You are right about that, though."

Candace looked up at her, puzzled.

Carrie looked from her to the younger children. "We have been in this musty house all day. Let's go for a walk."

"To Mr. Whit's?" Annie asked hopefully.

"No, not there. Remember the waterfall he told us about up the river? Let's walk that way and see if we can find it." It didn't hurt that the waterfall was in the opposite direction of the mill so she wouldn't have to worry about running into him.

John Thomas and Annie skipped across the floor for their coats and hats.

"How about it, Candace?" Carrie asked. "Come with us."

Candace didn't look up from her tablet. "No thanks."

Carrie thought about forcing her, but that would spoil the trip for everyone. If Candace wanted to stay inside and mope, Carrie would leave her to it. As she helped the younger children into their coats, she wondered if she'd ever get back inside her daughter's head or if that was the last place she wanted to go.

Carrie kept the children at the waterfall until the sun slid behind the trees. They spent the afternoon laughing and running and having a wonderful time. She tried to fit in a few science lessons by pointing out budding trees and different varieties of birds. The children needed to be in school. If she stayed here with Whit, any education they received would come from her. At least for the time being. She needed to talk to Marla. If she and Whit couldn't make amends, she would have to leave. There were six other bachelors in Cowboy Creek, including Rase Canfield who claimed he wasn't in the market for a wife. She was sure one of them would be happy to take her as a bride. She couldn't bear the thought of staying here, though, and seeing Whit all the time. Especially if he sent for another bride. One who wasn't divorced with three children.

As she and the children entered the yard, the back door of Marla's house opened, and Candace ran out and past the barn toward the brides' house. What was that about? She sent the children to the brides' house after Candace and tapped on Marla's door before letting herself in.

"Did something happen with Candace?"

Marla shook her head. "Not really. She's a good girl. Just as a hard age, and this really hard thing has happened to her. Her whole world's been upended. Please, don't be discouraged. I've already seen a change in her."

The only change Carrie had seen was more attitude.

Marla motioned Carrie into a chair and set a cup of tea in front of her. "She misses home, but she's more worried about you."

"About me?" Carrie snorted. "I didn't think she realized I'm alive except when I annoy her about something."

"She wants you to be happy. But she also misses the life she left behind, which she knows didn't make you happy. So she feels pulled in opposite directions. More than anything, she wants a family. She thinks she can find it in Cincinnati with her papa."

Carrie's heart ached. "Whatever gave her that idea? She hasn't laid eyes on him since she was three years old."

Marla clicked her tongue. "Yes, she told me all about him. I'm sure that's where most of the problem lies.

Children need to know they're loved by their parents. Both parents. Even when the parents do absolutely nothing to deserve their love and adoration. She's always going to want her papa's acceptance, even though he's given her no reason to expect it. It has to be hard for her to accept that he wants nothing to do with her."

Tears pricked Carrie's eyes. "I didn't realize she thinks of her papa for one minute. She never talks about him. Oh, Marla, I've made such a mess of things. Not only did I move Candace away from her friends, I moved her away from her pa. She must think if I hadn't brought her here, he might wake up one day and decide to be the father she needs. Now that we're here, she knows that'll never happen and it's all my fault. What have I done?"

Marla edged the steaming cup of tea closer. "You haven't done anything. Just keep loving her and giving her time and she'll come around."

"I don't know. I may have ruined everything with Whit, too. We may have to leave again. Then she'll never stop hating me."

Marla ducked her head to look into Carrie's lowered eyes. "How have you ruined everything with Whit? He's over the moon for you."

"He was. Now he thinks he can't trust me. We may just be too different to get along."

"I don't think so. There's nothing that could've happened you can't work out."

Carrie exhaled. "If only it were that easy."

"Do you love him, Carrie?"

"I don't know. I think so. I haven't had time to get to know him that well."

Marla waved her hand. "Oh, pooh. Look at all those couples in the Bible who married because the man thought the woman was beautiful. You two are a good match, I can tell. You're getting married tomorrow. I don't want to hear another word about being too different to get along. Different is good. It makes life interesting."

Carrie took a sip of her tea and then pushed away from the table. "Thank you, Marla. I would be lost without you and Preach. But I really must go. I should see what the children are into. And I need to think about Whit."

Marla got up and hugged her. "Think long and hard, Carrie. I don't want you and those children to leave. But more than what I want, I know Whit doesn't want you to either."

Carrie wasn't so sure, but she didn't say so. She smiled her gratitude and left. Her footsteps slowed as she crossed the yard. What would tomorrow bring? It was supposed to be her wedding day. How would she bridge the gap between her and Whit?

A cold wind blew down the hill, lifting grit and dirt off the street into the air. The last few days had been temperate, but it looked like some late winter weather was blowing in. Her steps faltered in surprise at the sight of Candace sitting on the bottom step in front of the brides' house.

When Candace saw her, she jumped up and ran to her. "Mama, I'm sorry. I ruined everything. I was rude to Mr. Whit. Now, we'll have to leave."

Carrie felt like a rock that had just been skipped across a pond, her thoughts ricocheting around Candace's words and what she'd seen from the girl the last few weeks. She pulled her into her arms and patted her back. She couldn't remember the last time she'd held Candace or the last time Candace let herself be comforted.

"Hush, child. It's all right. What do you mean? You didn't ruin anything."

"Yes, I did," Candace mumbled against Carrie's shoulder. She sniffed and pulled herself together. "I told Mr. Whit I was going to write a letter to Papa and have him come get me. I told him I wanted to go home. But I don't, Mama. I don't know why I said that. I said I hated Cowboy Creek. I said I hated him."

"Oh, Candace." Carrie pulled her close again. "It's all right."

"I don't hate him. I just hate...I don't know. Sometimes I want to go home. Other times, I'm afraid Whit will get tired of the way I act and send all of us away. I miss my friends, and sometimes I get mad. But I like it here. It's so...quiet. No one pressures me into doing things I know are wrong. Like when Millie stole those earbobs. I knew she was going to do it. I wanted to tell her not to. I liked Mr. Steiner. But the other girls said it was nothing. They do it all the time. They said I'm a baby. I'm not, Mama. I just don't want to be like them. I didn't like how the little kids in the neighborhood were afraid of us and the older people didn't like me anymore. But those girls are my friends. I think. I wanted them to like me."

"I know, baby."

"I heard you and Mr. Whit arguing. At first, I was glad. I knew we would get to go home. But then I thought of how I'd never see Mr. and Mrs. Dodds again. I thought of how I'd have to make friends all over again. The good girls wouldn't like me because I'm not like them. The bad girls would try to make me be like them, and I don't want that either."

"I don't want that for you either, Candace. I don't want it for any of us."

"What'll we do? Are you going to marry Mr. Whit? Will we be able to stay?"

Carrie still couldn't believe the questions were coming out of Candace's mouth. "I don't know, sweetheart. I think I want to. I guess I need to learn to see things from his point of view. He's had a rough life." She thought of how she'd jumped off the handle at him. She should've tried harder to explain about Johnny. Now it could be too late.

"I really love it here. Mr. Dodds and Marla are so nice. I know you don't think I should call her that, but she said I could. She's teaching me all sorts of things, and she has the best stories. I want you to be happy. And Mr. Whit. I think he needs you, Mama. He's so lonely. He needs all of us. I want him to be our papa."

Carrie hugged her. "Oh, sweetheart."

"I shouldn't have told him I was going to write a letter to Papa." She lowered her eyes.

"It's all right, Candace. I don't want you to ever hide what you really think or want because you think it will hurt one of us. I know you worry about your papa. You want to make sure he's all right. As soon as we get settled…" Whether in Cowboy Creek or somewhere else, she wasn't sure. "I will figure out how to contact him and tell him where you and John Thomas are and that you're well."

Candace's eyes brightened. "Oh, would you, Mama?"

"Of course."

"I love you, Mama. I'm sorry I've been terrible."

"Hush now. Whatever happens, we'll be all right. Marla said you helped her make beef and rice for supper. Let's get the little ones cleaned up and then we can eat."

Chapter Thirteen

Whit puttered around the mill all afternoon, checking belts and oiling gears—things that didn't need done. He didn't want to go in the house. Evidence of Carrie and the children was everywhere. She had measured the windows for curtains, pulled furniture away from the walls to clean, blacked the kitchen stove, and scrubbed all the woodwork. Rase was right; now that Whit had tasted life with a family, how would he go back to the dry, tasteless existence he'd had before? How could he send Annie back to poverty and abandonment? He'd already made an impact on J.T. Whether he wanted to admit it or not, the boy had made an impact on him as well.

And poor Candace. Believing her pa would come all the way out here to fetch her. If he wanted her that badly, he would've stopped Carrie from leaving Cincinnati. Unless Carrie sneaked off with the children in the middle of the night behind the man's back. She'd left town with one stranger's child. Maybe she did the same thing with her own children. Whit immediately dismissed the notion. If she had sneaked off from anyone, it was because she had no choice.

Whit went to the mill door and leaned against the doorjamb. From where he stood, he could see the tops of the trees surrounding the brides' house. The sun had dropped behind the horizon, and the temperature outside was rapidly cooling. He couldn't avoid going inside the house much longer.

Easter was a few weeks ago. His life had changed so much since Christmas Day when the men first heard Rase's plan. Whit had put up the biggest stink over the financial ramifications, though as soon as he heard the suggestion, he knew he wanted a bride. He wanted more to show at the end of his life than a gristmill in the middle of nowhere. He wanted a reason to walk into his house at the end of the day. He wanted to hear a woman moving around the house in the early morning and children laughing and chasing each other around the yard. He didn't want to go on with life as it had been. How could he now that he knew Carrie and those three little ones?

He thought of the borrowed chairs still pulled up to his table from the dinner Carrie fixed last night. His stomach lurched. He couldn't bear the thought of going back to one occupied chair at the table and eating nothing but his own overdone cooking. He hadn't given Carrie the chance to explain about her husband because he was afraid of the truth. Rase had been right about that, too. The last week had moved so fast, he hadn't had time to think about what he was getting into with a wife and three kids. It scared him. Maybe he was looking for an excuse to go back to the safe, comfortable life he knew with only his own needs to consider. No responsibilities but his own. No one dependent on him but him.

How was he any better than his old man? He might not have turned to the bottle to deprive his family of basic comfort, but the outcome was the same. Whit Whitamore was a coward—a slave to stinginess. Greed. He let fear keep him from grabbing onto the best thing God had put in front of him.

He gripped the doorjamb until his knuckles turned white. Even with all his frugal efforts to fill his storehouses like the foolish man in the Bible, he could still fail. A flood or sickness could wipe out his livelihood in one day. He could lose it all and have to start over again. But he'd have Carrie beside him. This was his chance at happiness. He was through being a coward and letting fear dictate his decisions. He slid the big mill door closed and headed down the hill. He didn't even take the time to saddle a horse. The walk would do him good.

Carrie has done all the cleaning and straightening she could in the tiny house. Annie and John Thomas quietly played a made-up game with marbles and pieces of wood Preach had found in a tin box. Candace was reading a book Marla had given her. She never knew either of her grandmothers. Carrie's parents had died before she moved to the city. If Johnny Rhoades had family, he never mentioned them.

Carrie's heart ached. She had friends at church in Cincinnati and friends among her neighbors. But this was the first time in her life she felt like part of a community.

An extended family beyond the three other people in this room. She went to the window and looked out. Days were getting longer but it was nearly dark outside. She wondered if she'd ever get used to the utter quiet and darkness with no streetlights or sounds of the city.

She turned to John Thomas and Annie. "Gather your things. It's time to get ready for bed."

It was a little early for bed, but they didn't complain. They returned the game pieces to the tin box. Candace looked up from her book. "Do you mind putting them to bed for me?" Carrie asked. "I think I'll go outside for a little while to get some air."

Candace dropped her legs out of the chair. "Do you want company, Mama?"

Carrie crossed the room and put her hand on her daughter's cheek. They had grown so distant over the last year. Was her sweet, carefree, laughing girl coming back to her?

"No, sweetheart, but thank you. I'm all right. I just want to think."

Candace nodded and set her book aside. Carrie wrapped her shawl around her shoulders and went outside. She circled the barn and stopped at the henhouse fence. All was quiet. The noisy chickens were asleep. Though she knew Preach had already done so, she went to the gate to make sure the latch was securely fastened. The peaceful rushing of water called to her. The sound was loud and comforting. Wherever she and the children ended up, she hoped they would be near water. She had lived within walking distance of the mighty Ohio River, but she barely noticed its presence over the noise of the city and demands of her life. In Cowboy Creek, this insignificant tributary was as important as the Ohio River was back home.

Her nose prickled with unshed tears. She sniffed them away. There was no point in crying over something outside her control. Maybe she shouldn't have come. Immediately, she recognized she hadn't had a choice. She had needed to get Candace out of the city. John Thomas and Annie too. John Thomas may eventually have turned into a bully to protect himself against those who bullied him. She wouldn't dwell on what may have become of nie if she had stayed with her drunken father or been forced into an orphanage.

Almost without thinking, her feet led her to the path around the barn. In one direction she could see the remains of the slue the miners had used to take gold from the river. The other direction looked upriver to the mill. A full moon reflected off the water, lighting her way. Here, she didn't have to worry about drunken men lurking in the shadows waiting to reach out and grab unsuspecting women. Many times she had walked home from work after dark and had to stay in the center of the street and keep ready to break into a run if someone got too close. She didn't have those worries in Cowboy Creek. There were dangers all right, like wolves or foxes or places she could fall and no one would know she was hurt until it was too late. Still, she felt protected by the community and God.

"I don't want to leave Cowboy Creek," she said aloud in prayer. "The air is so fresh, the water crystal clear. There are no other children yet, but mine are happy and healthy. This place is good for them. It's good for me too."

She walked to the rock outcropping where people used to watch the miners at work, though she couldn't see anything but deep shadows in the darkness. "I shouldn't have lied to Whit. I should've told him about Johnny Rhoades in my first letter no matter how uncomfortable it was. Whit is a hard man, but I know he has a gentle heart. J.T. needs a man like him." She laughed out loud. "I'm calling my little boy J.T. already. He'll probably never be my little John Thomas again."

She leaned heavily against the railing and stared into the darkness. In the distance she heard footsteps coming from the direction of the mill. She knew before she turned around who it was. In the moonlight she saw familiar long legs striding down the road. Her heart leapt in her chest. Whit. She loved him—a mature love, not the childish infatuation she once had for Johnny. But could they make their union work? Would he resent the money he spent on her and in turn cause her to resent him?

Whit was about to pass where she stood in the darkness. She stepped off the outcropping and walked up the incline to the road.

"Whit?"

He stopped and turned in the direction of her voice. She couldn't see his expression in the moonlight, which was maybe just as well.

"Carrie?"

"What are you doing out here?"

He didn't answer right away. He took a few steps toward her. She saw uncertainty in his expression. And doubt. "I could ask you the same thing."

He stopped a few feet from her. His closeness made the breath catch in her throat. She wanted him to take her hand like he'd done the last few days, the contact letting her know they were still connected. But she didn't know if she could live with this man. Why did her heart always pick men who couldn't love her and accept her the way she needed them to?

"I needed some air," she said. "That little house gets very crowded with all of us in it."

"I guess I needed air too."

"You came all the way down here to find it?" She half smiled, teasing, until she remembered she was mad at him. She couldn't let herself fall for the charms of a man who would hurt her. She'd done it before. She had been so desperate to believe Johnny loved her and would become the man she needed that she closed her eyes to the awful things he did.

Whit took a step closer. "The house seemed especially empty tonight."

Her heart leaped hopefully.

"I've been on my own since I was sixteen, Carrie. I have friends here, people who I know care about me, but I'm only responsible for myself. I've never had someone depend on me. Need me. I like it."

"Just not enough to sacrifice everything you have for another?" she bit out. Unfair maybe, but he needed to hear it.

Whit looked over her head toward the sound of the rushing water. Carrie shouldn't have spoken so forcefully, but she was still mad. She wanted to tell him everyone in Cowboy Creek knew how tight he was with a dollar. They talked about it behind his back. But she didn't want to hurt him. She understood it to a degree.

After a moment he brought his gaze back to her. "I'm sorry, Carrie. I guess I'm afraid."

She opened her mouth to ask him what a strong, ambitious man like him had to be afraid of, but she had a feeling she knew.

"Fear has always ruled me. Fear of going hungry. It's how I grew up. My parents were poor. Neither of them wanted to work very hard so we ended up doing without. I guess they were brought up the same way and didn't know how to break the cycle. If the weather cooperated and the crops were good, we did okay. Sometimes we'd have a good year with calves and pigs, and Pa would have extra to sell so we had shoes and coats for the winter. Other times, well, it didn't work out that way. I remember plenty of times sneaking into the neighbors' field with my brother Henry and digging potatoes out of the ground. We were so hungry we'd eat them right there, squatted among the plants."

Carrie made a little sound of sympathy in her throat. Whit shook his head. "I didn't tell you that to feel sorry for me, or even so you'd understand. It's just the way things were."

He sighed, his mind drifting into the past. "Henry and I would sit there in the field eating those stolen potatoes and talk about how things would be when we grew up. We'd live in a fine house with a bed for every person and blankets piled so high, we'd never feel the cold. There'd always be plenty to eat, and our kids would never have to worry about going to school with their toes sticking out of their shoes."

He looked hard at Carrie. "I swore I'd never go hungry and nobody I loved would either. When Pa beat me that last time, I knew my life would never change if I stayed. That's when I took off."

"What about Henry?" she asked gently

"He died when I was fourteen and he was thirteen. Never knew for sure why, but I expect it was from the malnutrition. We young'uns were often sickly because of it."

Tears blurred Carrie's vision. "Oh, Whit. I'm so sorry."

He jammed his fists into his pockets. "I know. I appreciate it. It's just that when you told me the other day you brought an extra child with you, that old fear reared its head at me again. I had gotten used to the idea of a wife and two children. Two aren't so many. I figured when we had our own, two or three more, I could keep that many fed and clothed. But when I found out about Annie, well, I felt like my choices had been taken from me again."

He rubbed his hand over his face. "God forgive me, Carrie. I resented Annie, and I resented you for bringing her. I understand why you did it. I know the situation she was handed wasn't her fault, but all I could think of was that hungry kid in the potato field, struggling to survive because of decisions made by someone else."

"I never meant to lie to you."

"I know. I'm sorry I blew up at you. You did what any decent person would've done. I was the one who behaved un-Christian-like. The Bible says to suffer not the little children. Annie's the same as an orphan, even though her pa's still breathing."

Tears stung Carrie's nose as she thought of everything Whit had gone through and what Annie would've gone through if she stayed in the city—either suffering with her abusive father or being dumped in one of the city's orphanages. Was she better off now? Carrie had no idea where they would end up if they left Cowboy

Creek. Life was hard enough with two children. How would she feed and raise and love three of them on her own?

"Thank you, Whit, for telling me about your childhood. I'm sorry I wasn't more patient and understanding. I grew up poor myself. There were many nights I went to bed hungry, but my parents always did their best for us kids. None of this is your fault. I couldn't get word to you about Annie before we arrived, but I have no excuse for not telling you about Johnny Rhoades."

She tightened the shawl around her shoulders and wrapped her arms around herself.

Whit unbuttoned his coat as if to give it to her. She held out her hand to stop him.

"I'm not cold. It's a nice night. I'm just..."

She took a deep breath. She looked across the road. Under the full moon, she could see the outline of the brides' house roof. She thought of Candace hoping they could stay in Cowboy Creek, and Annie and J.T. lying down to bed, not knowing what tomorrow would bring. She hated doing that to her children. She turned back to Whit.

"Johnny left me long ago. Well, he didn't actually leave—he just didn't come home. From the day I met him, he was in and out of my life. He'd come around when nothing else was working out and he needed somewhere to stay. I married him when I was seventeen. Before Candace was even born, I knew I had made a huge mistake. It was too late by then. I was married. A woman can't leave a man simply because he's lazy or gone for weeks on end or spends time with other women. Men have that right. Women are expected to sit around and wait for whatever happens."

She inhaled slowly, refusing to give in to the self-pity that always threatened if she thought about her ex-husband for more than two minutes.

"Then he disappeared for two years. I began to think of myself as a widow. People saw me with Candace. I was a respectable woman, so they assumed my husband was dead. Even I began to think he had died. Then he came back. He told me he was sorry and he had changed. I wanted so badly for it to be true. We moved to another neighborhood. He told me it was for work. It wasn't. It turned out there was some men looking for him for some sort of trouble he'd stirred up. Anyway, he was home and I thought we might have a regular life together. He only stayed long enough to—"

Heat rose in her cheeks. Shame and disgust at her own weakness nearly made her unable to go on. "After John Thomas was born, I thought having a son would make him stay."

She sighed. "Johnny left again within a few weeks. His absences grew longer until he was gone for good. I heard rumors he was living with another woman. He did that sometimes. Then Candace got sick. Really sick and I needed money for a doctor. I found out where he was living, and I went there. I knocked on the door, and a woman answered. It was like looking in a mirror. I saw the same tired, beat-down look on her face that I always wore. The same sad, rundown apartment with the falling apart furniture. And a baby crying."

Carrie looked past Whit's shoulder, unable to look him in the eye. "That poor baby. The woman stiffened her back and told me to get lost. Johnny was hers, she said. They were married. I don't know if it was true, but that's what she told me. I held onto Johnny and hoped he'd come to his senses because my children needed a papa. That woman's baby needed a papa too. If I tried to hold onto him and convince him to come back, I'd be committing adultery and taking another child's papa from him. That woman needed him more. I was strong, or so I told myself. That woman couldn't get by on her own. I was doing all right for myself.

"It took me nearly a year, but I saved enough money to hire a lawyer to write up a divorce for me. I was so ashamed. Everyone I knew already thought my husband was dead. I never told them otherwise. It's easier to be a widow people will pity than a divorcee everyone will judge. I took the coward's way. I didn't just lie to you, Whit. I lied to everyone."

He took her hand. She wrapped her fingers around his and reveled in the warmth and strength.

"I'm sorry for what I said." His voice was soft and husky. Comforting. "I let my insecurities color how I treated you. I couldn't make things better for my brothers and sisters. I couldn't help Henry. I was the oldest. I failed them. I don't want to fail you and those children."

She squeezed his hand. "Oh, Whit, you can never let us down."

He leaned forward and touched his lips to hers, gently at first, then stronger. Carrie fought to steady her knees. When he broke off the kiss, he smiled down at her. "I'm not an easy man to live with. Sometimes I might get stubborn, and you'll have to knock some sense into me."

"I could do that," she said with a teasing smile.

"Are you still willing to marry me tomorrow?"

"I don't want to do anything else."

He drew her into his arms and kissed her again. "I'm so glad you came. You and the children, all three of them. You're the family I always wanted."

"Mr. Whit. Mr. Whit."

They broke apart as John Thomas and Annie came running down the hill from the barn. Whit opened his arms to receive Annie as she propelled her little body at him.

"I thought you two were in bed," Carrie admonished.

"We heard Mr. Whit and wanted to say goodnight."

"We haven't seen Mr. Whit all day," John Thomas chimed in. "Mama took us to see the waterfall. You should've come with us, Mr. Whit."

Whit arched his eyebrows. "I don't want you calling me Mr. Whit."

Confusion colored John Thomas's pale face in the moonlight. "What? Oh. I...I'm sorry, sir.'

Whit rested his big hand on the boy's head and tousled his hair. "From now on, I want you to call me Papa."

John Thomas's blue eyes went wide. "You mean it? I will, Mr. Whit. I mean...Papa." He threw his arms around Whit's waist.

"Papa!" Annie squealed and hugged Whit's neck.

Whit reached over the boy and pulled Carrie against him, squeezing John Thomas between them. Annie giggled with delight. He kissed the tears off Carrie's eyelashes. "I love you," she whispered.

"And I love you. All of you."

The End

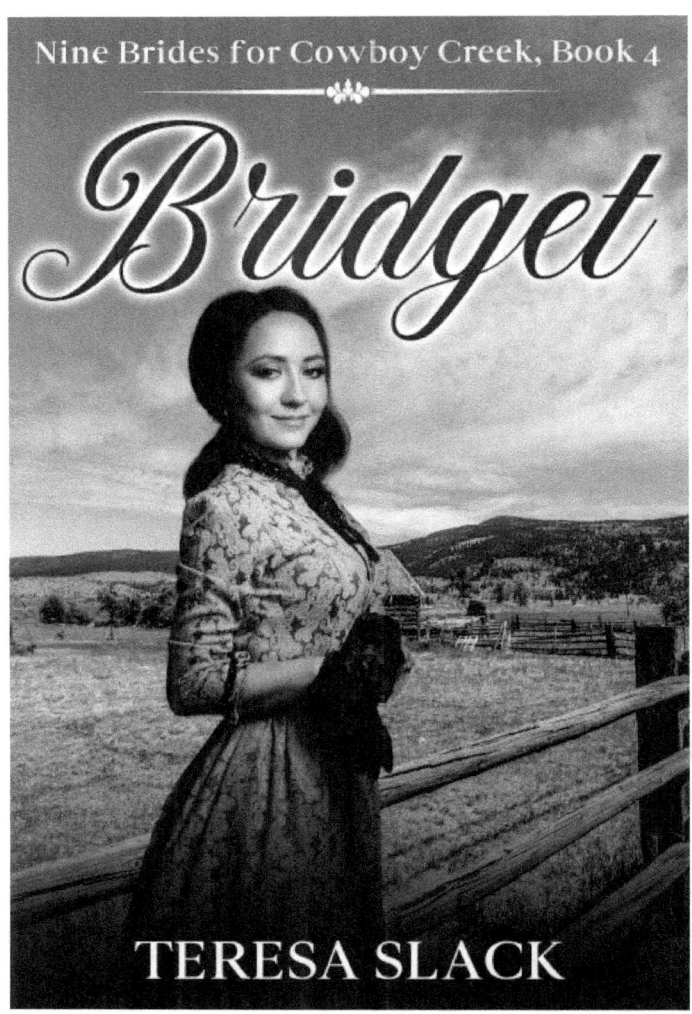

Nine Brides for Cowboy Creek, Book 4

Bridget

TERESA SLACK

Chapter One

Bridget Reidy took a deep breath to gather her courage. She already knew how the next few minutes would go. She'd heard this song so often she knew every verse. Yet it didn't make it any easier to sing.

She wouldn't apologize for what she was about to do either. She wasn't helpless or incompetent, and she mustn't let Charles and Ellen think she believed she was. She would take charge of the meeting the instant they walked through the door. This was her house, after all. Mother and Father left it to her in their will. Not Charles. He and Ellen would make a good argument. As male heir and the oldest, property would typically pass to him after a parent's death. This wasn't an ordinary situation.

She knew it, and Charles and Ellen knew it. She wouldn't let them make her feel guilty. Not this time.

She closed the heavy volume of poetry and clasped it to her chest. If only life were as simple and romantic as the lines she loved to read.

The front door opened. Charles's clear tenor voice reached her ears as the maid let him and Ellen in. Bridget pursed her lips and breathed a prayer for God's grace in the situation. "Help me be strong, Lord. And help Charles see reason."

She already knew he would use his bombastic personality to take over the meeting. She couldn't let that happen. She wasn't wrong.

With trembling fingers, she set the book on the table. Too close to the edge, it toppled to the floor. The flimsy side table wobbled at the change of balance, and a glass of water and potted succulent followed the book to the floor.

Bridget cried out at her carelessness. She leaped out of the chair and scooped the book off the floor and out of the way of the water and dirt from the plant. She blotted the water on the cover with her shirtsleeve. The dress could be replaced. The book was precious. She opened it and dabbed the water at the edge of the pages.

No serious damage. Thank goodness. Why couldn't she be more careful? Always in a hurry. Always with her nose buried in a book instead of paying attention to important matters. Shoulder-deep in her fantasy world with no idea how the real world worked. That's what Charles always said. That's why he would insist she had no business managing Mother and Father's estate.

With trembling fingers, she placed the book on the table. She uprighted the planter and grabbed a wastebasket.

"Bridget?"

She looked up, a handful of spilled dirt in her hand. Her brother and his wife stood in the doorway. Both looked at the mess at her feet. Disappointment and confusion wrinkled Charles's brow. Ellen's narrow lips pursed in disapproval—and barely concealed humor. She wanted to laugh. Who could blame her? What a spectacle Bridget always managed to make.

The maid rushed past them. "I'll do that, Miss Reidy." The household staff had referred to her as Miss Bridget until Mother's passing when she immediately became Miss Reidy to everyone under their roof. Bridget tried to tell them the title change wasn't necessary. They looked at her like she had horns on her head. After a few attempts, she stopped correcting them. She was forever Miss Reidy.

She backed out of the way as the maid cleaned up the worst of the mess. Without a word, the woman straightened and left the room. Bridget knew she would return momentarily with a broom and dustpan. She was used to tidying up the effects of Bridget's clumsiness.

Ellen left the doorway and took hold of Bridget's sleeve as if correcting one of her daughters. "Look what you've done. You've ruined your dress."

Bridget pulled away. The pale blue fabric was damp and smudged with dirt. An apology formed on her lips. She stopped herself just in time. She wasn't a child. She certainly wasn't Ellen's child. She would apologize to the maids later for giving them another avoidable chore, but she wouldn't apologize to her sister-in-law.

Charles looked as disapproving as ever. "Books again?" He glanced at the cover. His lips pressed together. Bridget knew what he was thinking. Reading anything other than newspapers, medical or financial journals—and the Bible if one had time leftover—was frivolous and unproductive.

"Now that Mother and Father are gone, you must learn to manage your time better. You knew we were coming. You know how valuable my time is."

More valuable than mine or anyone else's? Bridget wished she had the nerve to ask.

She may have the nerve not to apologize, but she couldn't stand up to her brother. She had never stood up to him, even when they were children. They looked so much alike. Both were tall and thin with sloping shoulders. They had Father's large brown eyes on a narrow face and Mother's thin lips and high cheekbones. Unlike Father's, Charles's eyes were shrewd and menacing. Bridget couldn't remember the last time she heard him laugh. She suspected it coincided with the time he met charmless Ellen.

She needed to take charge of the situation before it got completely out of hand. "I did know you were coming, Charles, and I have everything prepared."

She took Ellen's hand and turned her away from the scene of dirt and water on the floor. "Frances has set out sandwiches and cakes in the sunroom. I'll let her know we're ready for the tea. It's a beautiful day. We can watch the barges go by on the river."

Neither looked interested in watching freight barges, but they followed through the large house with its high ceilings and opulent furnishings. The sunroom was the only room Bridget really enjoyed in the big house. She, Mother, and Father used to sit there for hours on end discussing politics and books as they watched the sun set over the Ohio River. Now that her parents were gone, she found solace and communion in this room.

Charles and Ellen found seats without waiting for an invitation. Bridget couldn't fault them for that. Charles had grown up in this house, too. It would be odd if he looked to his little sister for direction. Still, Bridget wished they saw her as the authority figure in the situation since she had Mother and Father's wishes on her side. Sadly, she knew they never would.

She swiped at a smudge of dirt on her skirt as she sat in her favorite chair facing the river. The damage was more evident when she was seated. She should excuse herself and go upstairs to change. She couldn't, of course. This meeting wasn't about her anyway. The sooner she got it over with, the better.

"We've come to talk to you about the house?" Charles launched in without waiting for the ladies to get settled or for Bridget to offer the refreshments as a gentleman would in someone else's home.

"And the rest of the estate," Ellen added. She and Charles exchanged a look of communication.

I never thought for a moment you came to inquire about how I was doing, Bridget said to herself.

It was obvious they had discussed how to ambush her all the way here. Probably for the last week.

"This house is too big," Charles continued. "Maintaining it and the staff is a drain on the family resources. Business isn't what it once was."

Bridget cut him off. "You're right about that. Not without Father at the helm," she added intentionally. No need to point out Charles would never be the businessman Father was. It would be only by God's grace if the company Father had helped found would be in business in five years.

"I've already cut the household staff by half," she said instead. "I hated to let them go, but I don't need as much help living here alone. I'm also well aware of the household budget. Mother made sure of that from the time I was a girl. With her and Father's investments, I can manage the house just fine, as long as I live frugally."

"Or..." Ellen perched on the edge of Mother's favorite chair. She and Charles exchanged another look before she pinned Bridget with a patronizing smile. "Charles and I have discussed it, and we believe you'd be better off selling the house and moving in with us and the children. You will live lavishly the rest of your life without a care in the world."

Bridget resisted the urge to jerk her out of Mother's chair. How dare she sit there! She'd never had one kind word for Mother. Always so condescending because her family came from money and never had to build a thing from nothing.

"Without a... I'm not an invalid," Bridget reminded them. "I don't need you to take care of me. I have a house here. I can afford—"

For the first time Charles looked uncertain. "That's why we're here, Bridget. We realize you can afford it, quite well thanks to Father's wise business decisions. He made all this possible. But sometimes other matters need to be considered. Like the future of your nieces and nephew. Mother and Father's *grandchildren*."

Bridget looked from him to Ellen. "I don't understand," she said, though she was beginning to.

Charles glanced at Ellen as if for nerve. She nodded discreetly.

He glanced at his clasped hands between his knees. "I've made some poor investments of late. With an influx of capital, I know I can remedy everything and get us out of this hole. I talked to Mr. Fredricks at the company. He said with Father's good standing, there's no reason I can't ensure my own position, despite my past—lapses in judgment."

Bridget's mind whirled. She knew all about Charles's lapses in judgment. Mother and Father had been paying the price for them for years. The gambling. Long evenings at the gentlemen's club downtown where he liked to pretend he was more successful than he was.

"You...you talked to Mr. Fredricks about the situation? You should've discussed it with me first before you brought him into it."

"Now, Bridget, Mr. Fredricks isn't exactly an outsider."

"He doesn't need to know our private affairs. As for the influx of capital, just where do you plan to obtain it? I suppose you and Mr. Fredricks worked that out as well?"

Charles and Ellen exchanged another glance, giving her the answer she already knew.

When Charles didn't speak, Ellen gave him a withering look and took over. "There's no point in you living in this enormous house all alone. You don't have family except for Charles and me and the children. You'll never marry. Living in this house by yourself while our children—your nieces and nephew—have needs of all growing children is, well, I'm just going to say it—selfish. Charles and I believe it will be better for everyone if you sell the house and some of your parents' assets and move in with us."

Selfish! She had never been selfish a day in her life. How dare Ellen use her children to manipulate Bridget. Black dots swam in front of her eyes. She wasn't going to let it happen. "*My* assets! I inherited everything in this house. Mother and Father wanted—"

Ellen's face hardened. "Yes, well, we know all about that. As the firstborn *son*, Charles had the legal right to the inheritance. But that's neither here nor there. We have no interest in taking you to court for the whole city to see." She lifted her pointed nose as if doing Bridget a grand favor. "Your parents made their decisions for reasons known only to them."

The reasons were known to anyone with half a brain, Bridget thought, but there was no point in beating that dead horse again. Charles had received a fair inheritance from Mother and Father, but they had known anything given to him beyond that would be quickly squandered.

"What's important now is moving forward. Moving in with us will save the estate a fortune. You won't be giving up anything. The funds will be used to help Charles build the business and his standing in the city. It will be an investment for both of you. You'll receive your funds back with interest as Charles continues to invest and make money."

Bridget took a deep breath. She knew the heat in her face was giving away her true thoughts. Her panic. She needed time to think. "I don't..."

How could she tell her brother—her only surviving relative—she didn't trust him or his grasping, conniving wife? Mother and Father hadn't trusted him either. That was the reason they cut him off and gave Bridget nearly the entirety of their estate.

"We have a family," Ellen pointed out nastily. "Children to think of. You never will. I'm sure you agree they deserve a good education. All the things this lifestyle can afford. You'll never benefit from it. You're perfectly satisfied here with your…" She threw her arm into the air, gesturing to the bookshelves which lined three of the room's walls. "…fantasy world."

Bridget wanted to scream. She wanted to throw the sanctimonious Ellen out of *her* house. She couldn't. She had been raised better than that.

"Mother and Father left the house and their business holdings to me," she said around a tight throat. "I won't disrespect what they worked for by selling this house and—"

"It isn't disrespectful to their memory for you to help me out of this spot, Bridget," Charles put in, more gently than his wife. "It isn't fair for you to keep the house and their wealth all to yourself when Ellen and I suffer. Our debt could destroy everything I've worked for. You know Mother and Father would want you to help me."

She didn't know that at all.

"I have children to support, Bridget. You don't. You don't need much. We'll give you all you need in our house. We have that nice little guestroom."

Which was no bigger than a broom closet, Bridget remembered.

"Charles can take over the dealings in your parents' investments." Ellen smiled as if she could already feel the money between her fingers. "He's been doing it his whole life. He has more experience with financial matters than you. The money will be safe as long as you live. You'll receive a substantial allowance, of course. You can travel as much as you like. Enjoy your books. You can spend more time with our children. You'll come to love them once you get to know them better."

Bridget directed her gaze at Charles since she knew she wouldn't get anywhere with Ellen. "Don't you trust Father and Mother's judgment, Charles? Don't you want to honor their wishes?"

"I think I know more about their wishes than you, Bridget," he bit out. "I'm their son. The eldest."

She flinched at his words. Charles had always resented the way their parents loved and trusted Bridget and worried about the lackadaisical path Charles had taken. She took a fortifying breath. Her parents knew this moment would come. They had done all they could to protect their assets from Charles, but they couldn't prevent Bridget from turning them over to him if he talked her into it. She loved her parents too much to do it.

"I won't be given an allowance out of my own money. This is my house, as are the investments. Mother and Father set aside trusts for your children they can access when they turn twenty-five. It's more than enough to give them a good start in life. They also gave you an inheritance, Charles. Why don't you use that for your infusion of capital?"

Charles looked away.

Bridget gasped. "Don't you have any of the money left? Mother only died four months ago."

"You'll never understand, Bridget, how much it takes to raise a family. My share of the inheritance wasn't enough to pay a fraction of my creditors. Ellen and I have big plans. You'll get every penny back with interest. If it's the allowance you're worried about, we can..." He glanced at Ellen as if asking permission. "We'll look more into that after the sale is settled."

Ellen's impatience took over. She stood and glared down at Bridget. "I've known you for a long time,

Bridget, and I never thought you were selfish or unreasonable. Once you've had time to think about it, you'll see this is best for everyone. With the sale of this house, we'll buy a bigger house of our own, so you can have a suite of rooms if that's what it will take to please you."

Her face softened into a congenial smile while her blue eyes remained frosty. "You must realize you can't live in this big old drafty house until you die alone. You must want more from your life than that. Just think about it. You'll see you're better off when surrounded by people who love you."

Bridget wanted to ask just who those people were and if she would meet them someday.

Ellen offered one last smile and turned away, without even acknowledging the sandwiches and cakes Frances had prepared for them. "Come along, Charles. We'll show ourselves out."

Bridgett stared unseeing across the crowded dining room. The planning meeting for the committee Mother had founded ten years ago to benefit local charities had just wrapped up. She could scarcely recall a topic they'd discussed. She hadn't seen Charles and Ellen for nearly a week, but she knew they'd be back. The thought of it made her sick to her stomach. She had thought and prayed about their *solution*, despite Mother and Father's wishes. It would certainly be easier in the short term to give in and let them have their way, but she felt no peace in putting them in charge of her property and assets.

If she moved into their home, she would be a second-class citizen. But once they had her money, at least they'd stop pestering her about it.

"Bridget, I don't believe you heard a word I said."

She blinked and focused on the kind woman across the table from her. With a start, she realized the other members of the committee had left. Only Nan Canfield remained at the table.

She didn't know Nan well. They served together on several charitable committees. Nan was strong-willed and determined and not afraid to get in on the actual work even though she was well into her fifties. She had a warm kind face and deep dark eyes that were always alight with warmth and intelligence.

"I'm sorry. I guess my mind wandered," she told Nan.

"I think it's been wandering all morning." Nan leaned closer and looked searchingly into Bridget's face. "Is something the matter, dear? You seem out of sorts."

Bridget nearly told her, no, everything was fine. She was just distracted. But she needed someone to talk to besides the household staff who already had their thoughts and opinions of Charles and Ellen.

But was it right to burden a virtual stranger?

She studied Nan's kind brown eyes. It wouldn't do any harm to get another person's perspective. Nan was thoughtful and compassionate. At their meetings, she never made a decision without hearing all sides of the matter. She might be just the person to take into Bridget's confidence.

"I have a financial situation taking place at home. It involves my brother and his wife. I'm afraid I don't know how to handle it."

"Oh dear," Nan said. "It would be inappropriate for me to offer financial advice, but I have a listening ear if you want to talk."

Bridget looked around the room. The only people who remained were a few patrons on the other side of the room and the staff cleaning up from the luncheon.

She had to talk to someone. The book of Proverbs said there was wisdom in a multitude of counselors. She could certainly use some wisdom and counsel now.

"It's not a financial matter as much as it is my brother and his wife trying to make my decisions for me."

Nan winced. "Oh, my, that is a sticky situation. One hates to offend family, but one must have the right to make her own decisions."

Bridget thought of Nan's own situation. From her position in the city and the boards she served on, she looked comfortably situated. Most everyone called her Miss Canfield, so Bridget assumed she was a spinster as well. She may have found herself in a similar predicament from well-meaning—or greedy—relatives. She smiled inwardly and silently thanked God for orchestrating this meeting with the older woman.

"My parents left me a substantial inheritance, including a house and investments. My brother and his wife have suggested I sell the family home and move in with them."

Nan's face softened. "Do you not wish to sell your house?"

Bridget looked down at the spot where her plate had been. A round indentation remained etched in the linen tablecloth. "My brother needs money. It looks like he's gotten into a bind. He and his wife want me to live with them so they'll have access to the money Mother and Father left me."

"Oh, dear," Nan repeated with more fervor this time.

Bridget bit her lip. "I don't know what to do. I don't want to disappoint my brother. He's the only family I have. If I don't do as he asks, it will ostracize him forever. Mother and Father were Charles's parents too. I suppose it is unfair of me to keep their inheritance to myself when Charles has a family to support and needs the money so desperately."

Nan didn't answer right away. "Do you know why your parents left their estate to you instead of your brother?"

It felt like a betrayal to say the words out loud to someone she barely knew. But how could Nan offer advice if she didn't know the whole story?

"Charles has always been...reckless with money. Mother and Father feared he would lose the inheritance in no time through careless spending and business decisions, leaving both of us with nothing. They wanted to make sure I was in a good situation for the rest of my life."

"And they believed Charles could take care of himself?"

Bridget pursed her lips as she thought of a charitable way to speak the truth. "I think their greatest hope was the circumstances would force him to grow up. They didn't want him to continue to rely on them the way he's always done."

Nan reached across the table and rested her hand on Bridget's. "They must've trusted and loved you very much."

Bridget's gaze turned misty. "Yes, ma'am, they did. They love Charles too. They just wanted him to face his responsibilities."

"All good parents do, dear heart. This is a hard situation for a young woman like you to find herself. But you're strong. You remind me of myself when I was young. I never married and I only had one brother. He was wonderful and supportive, but I never completely relied on him. He and my parents wouldn't allow it. They wanted to make sure I knew how to take care of myself.

"It sounds like your parents wanted the same thing for you. This is your money, but with it comes great responsibility. Your parents didn't want you to rely on an allowance and housing from a benevolent male relative. This isn't eighteenth century England."

"I don't want to hurt my brother."

"From where I'm sitting, it sounds like he isn't worried about hurting you. He's using guilt and family obligation to play on your sympathy and get what he wants."

"It isn't just about the money," Bridget assured her. "It's as though he and his wife are disregarding what Mother and Father wanted. Disrespecting them."

Nan gently patted Bridget's hand. "Do you think your parents would want you to give in to your brother and his wife because it's easier? They wanted you to have the money so you could have a good life for yourself. I don't think you will if you're living in someone else's home waiting for an allowance every month like a ward of your brother. I've seen how hard you work with our committees. You're a smart young woman, Bridget. A life like that would destroy you."

"What is money when you're alone?" Bridget implored. She leaned closer and lowered her voice. "I've been so lost since Mother and Father died. Rattling around in that big house with only the household staff for company. I spend most of my time in the sunroom reading. I don't want to move in with Charles and Ellen. I don't particularly look forward to growing old in that house with no one either."

Her nose stung with unshed tears. She tried to sniff them away.

Nan smiled gently. "Oh, dear heart, you're entitled to happiness." Her gaze turned thoughtful. "Tell me, what is it you want? What do you want more than anything in your heart of hearts?"

"Love. A family," Bridget burst out without censure.

She reigned in her enthusiasm. She had accepted long ago those things weren't meant for women like her.

She sighed, embarrassed. "I don't really mind the idea of selling the house. It's so big. Too big for just me. I don't think I could manage it alone, and I don't really want to. I suppose if I could have anything I want I'd be most content in a small cottage someplace where I could see great expanses of blue sky. I don't mean to be disrespectful of my parents' hard work. They've given me a good life. But sometimes I wish I could sit on a windswept hillside under an oak tree with a book on my lap and contemplate God and life and love. If I wanted to burst into song of praise, no one would hear me or think I was the odd spinster daughter of John and Adele Reidy."

Nan took her elbow. "You're not odd, Bridget."

Bridget laughed. "You don't know me very well." She sobered as she looked at the other woman. "I rather like being different than everyone else, but sometimes I think I embarrass those I love who don't understand me. I've wondered lately if this inheritance is God giving me a chance to truly begin my life. A chance for what I never had before. Romance."

Embarrassment warmed her cheeks. She looked at Nan through lowered lashes. She *was* odd. No point in denying it.

Nan didn't look judgmental. "You don't say."

"I know, it's silly."

"It's not silly. Do you think you'd someday want to marry?"

Bridget's face fell. "Oh, yes, I think of it a lot. I often wish I could have my own romance instead of reading one in a book. But look at me. I'm not a beautiful swan like the heroines in novels. I'm a plain barn swallow. You don't see paintings in museums of barn swallows. Just like me, no one knows they exist except when they need to shoo them away."

"Oh, dear heart, you're not plain. You're intelligent and interesting and warm."

"That's kind of you to say, Nan, but I have a mirror. Men don't pay attention to warm, interesting women who look like me."

"Bridget..."

She waved away her disagreement. "It's all right. I accepted it years ago. I'm too tall. Too skinny. My nose is too long and my lips too thin. And I'm odd. Men don't like odd."

"Stop," Nan said, her fervor surprising Bridget into silence. "I won't sit here and listen to you disparage what God created. You are a beautiful person, inside and out."

Bridget agreed it was wrong to dismiss God's blessings. She had two working arms and two strong legs, more than many people she passed on the streets. But she wasn't beautiful. She didn't resent it; she just knew what it took to get a man's attention and she didn't have it.

"With all due respect, men don't see what you see. They see the wrapping long before they take the time to look inside the box. My time for romance is past anyway. I'm twenty-six."

She sighed and the lightness dropped from her voice. "I suppose I'll do whatever Charles wants. He is my brother. I know he wants the best for me. Perhaps if I'm under his roof, I can influence him to make better financial decisions. I can get to know my nieces and nephew. They don't seem to like me much. Maybe if I live there, I can change that."

Nan pursed her lips. It looked like something was on her mind. Bridget's curiosity was piqued.

"You need to stop thinking about what's best for your brother and consider what's best for you. Have you ever heard of mail-order brides?"

"Mail-order... Do you mean those women who answer advertisements in the backs of magazines from men on the frontier looking for wives?"

"Yes, but the situation I'm thinking of isn't in a magazine. My nephew Rase lives in a lovely little hamlet called Cowboy Creek with great expanses of blue sky. I think you would love it there."

Chapter Two

Four weeks later

Dominic DeSantis. Bridget rolled the name around on her tongue.

Bridget DeSantis.

That's who she'd become if she married the man she would soon meet in Cowboy Creek, Colorado. She still couldn't believe there was a chance she would marry at all. What would Mother and Father think? They'd be so happy—so relieved to know she wouldn't die a spinster with only Charles and Ellen and their spoiled children to mourn her passing.

She smiled around a flutter of nerves in her stomach. Had she taken leave of her good sense? She knew practically nothing about this Dominic DeSantis. She had only read one letter from him, and it was barely three paragraphs long.

She hadn't personally received the letter. Nan had received it shortly after she and her nephew orchestrated the plan to find brides for the men of Cowboy Creek. They wanted the prospective brides to know a little about the men they were going west to meet. And for the men to know what to expect of the women.

"Your situation is unique from the brides who've proceeded you," Nan had explained. "It's unique from nearly every woman I know. Your financial situation allows you the freedom to go wherever you want in the world if you choose. That's why I think going to Cowboy Creek is a perfect opportunity for you. You have nothing to lose, except for some time, should you decide you don't want to stay. Think of the adventure. The chance to see some of the country and get to know people you would never meet in your neighborhood in the city. Hopefully, like the women before you, you will find true love."

Bridget had liked the sound of that. Adventure. New people. Escape from Charles and Ellen's disapproval. Maybe even true love.

After reading Mr. DeSantis's letter, she liked the idea even more. Dominic hadn't written much about himself except that he wanted a woman who would help him bring their children up in the fear and admonition of the Lord the way his parents had raised him. He wanted a wife who understood hard work but was anxious to enjoy the fruit of that work with him.

Instead of going straight home after discussing the matter with Nan, Bridget had gone to her solicitor's office to look into selling her house and settling her affairs. The pompous man suggested she come back with Charles because the legal wranglings might prove too much for her female brain. Bridget had nearly bopped him in the nose with the handle of her umbrella.

With the help of friends and her housekeeper Frances who she'd known since she was a girl, Bridget began selling furnishings and deciding what she couldn't live without while waiting for the house to sell.

With Nan's counsel, she decided that even if things didn't work out in Cowboy Creek, she wouldn't come back to the big house in Mt. Adams overlooking the Ohio River.

When Charles and Ellen found out what she was doing—thanks to the big-mouth solicitor—they came at her like a pack of hungry dogs. To appease them and get them out of her hair, she handed over several expensive pieces of furniture and artwork from the house. Charles claimed the pieces had sentimental value to him, and he couldn't bear to think of them on the walls of someone else's home. Bridget was sure he planned to sell them as soon as she turned her back. She didn't care. They were gifts. He could do whatever he wanted with them. She couldn't take everything with her to Cowboy Creek anyway, and she didn't have the time or desire to catalog each piece for the auctioneer.

She resisted their questioning as long as she could, but she had never been adept at standing up to interrogation. As soon as they found out she was going to Colorado—though she didn't tell them a man waited for her there—they ridiculed and mocked her and told her she'd be robbed and murdered before she got as far as Louisville. Charles even had the audacity to feign concern for her well-being. Bridget knew the only concern he and Ellen had was for her fat wallet.

By the time they left, she was determined to make the situation work, if nothing more than to spite them.

God forgive her.

Before the train even pulled out of the station in Cincinnati, Bridget realized traveling with money beat traveling without it any day of the week.

Most of her fellow travelers were dirty, smelly men or oily salesmen she trusted less than the rats the grounds man at home occasionally caught. A few poor families rode near the back of the train. Bridget rode with them to avoid the men. She quickly made friends with the women and bought the children candy and food. (They were always hungry no matter how much their mothers packed in wicker baskets and bags.)

The comfort of the train lasted as far as Breckenridge, Colorado where she transferred to a coach. There was little means of comfort on the stage and less women to talk to that made the trip more pleasant. In Ruby City she discovered the stage wasn't big enough to carry the rest of the belongings she had brought with her to the end of the line in Good Hope. Instead of taking the stage to Good Hope, she chose to travel with her belongings in a rented wagon since malingers lurked at every corner, ready to abscond with her belongings the minute they were out of sight—including a disreputable driver. However, by the time the oversized carriage's wheels made three rotations, Bridget couldn't decide if getting robbed was preferable to riding the slow, unforgiving conveyance all the way to Good Hope.

The wagon took an ugly bounce over a deep rut in the road. A cry escaped Bridget's clenched lips. Would they never get there?

"At least the rain's over," her driver said through several missing teeth and a tangled beard. "This time last week, I was up to the axels in mud. You'd'a had to got out and pushed."

He looked down at her traveling dress and snorted.

"Well, then, I'm glad it's not last week," she returned.

He sucked air around a brown, chipped tooth and turned his attention back to the road.

Just when Bridget thought her back couldn't take one more minute on the hard seat, the sound of civilization reached her ears a moment before she saw evidence of a small town through the budding trees. Good Hope. And beyond that, Cowboy Creek. She nearly cried out with relief.

Excitement fluttered in her stomach. She knew as little about Cowboy Creek as she knew about Dominic DeSantis. Rase Canfield, Nan's nephew, had chosen to settle there, so the place must have some redeeming qualities. She didn't know Rase either, but the fact he was related to Nan brought a measure of comfort.

She craned her neck to look around the dreary streets of Good Hope as they rode in. There wasn't much to see. Two narrow, rutted streets. A laundry. Two saloons. A mercantile with an American flag hanging limp against a gray sky, which indicated it also served as the village post office. A restaurant with rooms to let upstairs. A hardware store. A sawmill. A blacksmith shop and little else. Bridget swallowed her disappointment. If this was the end of the stage line, what must Cowboy Creek look like? She was on an adventure, she reminded herself. She didn't have to stay, but, oh, how she hoped she would want to.

The driver drew the carriage to a stop next to a large barn with curling unpainted boards. Deep ruts in the street indicated this was the stage stop. The daily stage had already departed, and the street around it was deserted. Bridget's stomach sank. Where was Dominic? Surely, he had received word she was arriving today. If not, she would rent a room for the night. And have a bath! The thought of sinking into a tub to soothe her aching body somewhat assuaged her disappointment at not seeing Dominic.

Without a word to her, the driver climbed down and went to the back of the wagon to lower the tailgate. Bridget turned in her seat. "Wait!" She looked around desperately. "You mustn't unload them yet. I'm taking them to Cowboy Creek. You need to wait—"

"I'm not waiting for nothing. I gotta get back on the road."

"But what if…what if no one is here to meet me? You can't just leave me in the middle of the street. I'll pay you to drive me the rest of the way."

He jerked his thumb toward the barn. "That there's the livery. Somebody'll haul your stuff inside out of the weather."

Bridget clenched her hands around her reticule. If he tried to drag the trunks off himself, he'd drop them into the dirt where they'd split wide open and ruin the precious cargo inside. Cargo that had taken her parents a lifetime to accumulate and would take Bridget another lifetime or two to replace.

"You can't do it alone. They're too—"

"Heavy? Yeah, I know. Who do you think helped load them?" He grabbed hold of the leather handle of one of the trunks and jerked it to the back of the wagon.

Bridget scrambled down from the wagon as fast as her skirts would allow. As half the trunk cleared the end of the bed, a tanned hand reached out to stop its progress.

"Easy there," came a deep drawl. "I can tell by the way you're straining, this here's too heavy to be moved half a dozen times. How about you back the wagon into the livery behind the station, and we'll stow the trunks there?"

Bridget's gaze traveled up the long arm clad in a black wool coat to its owner. Thick black hair curled out from under the man's hat. Dark eyes smoldered against his olive skin. Bridget was too worried about her belongings to notice more of the handsome newcomer. She set her hand on the other side of the trunk aware it was only inches from his. The man's piercing eyes, as dark as the night sky, drew her up short. For a heart-pounding moment she forgot what needed to be said. With a determined breath, she quickly recovered.

"We can't leave them in a livery. They're mine."

His obsidian eyes lit up in amusement. "I assumed as much, ma'am."

Her irritation piqued at the humor in his eyes. Yet another man who saw her as a flighty female fretting over something that didn't warrant it. "Then you should also know these trunks are filled with books, and they can't be stored in a musty old barn. Who knows what they'd be exposed to."

"Books," the driver said with a disdainful sniff.

"Yes, books. I'm taking them with me to Cowboy Creek. I'm waiting for my ride—"

"That'd be me, ma'am." The dark-headed stranger swept off his hat. "Dominic DeSantis. Miss Reidy, I reckon."

Warmth washed over her like hot oil, lighting the skin on her cheeks and through her limbs with prickly heat. Dominic. Her Dominic. Oh, dear. She had expected a grizzled rancher with poor grooming skills, a few missing teeth, and ill-fitting clothes, much like the driver between them. Not someone with a cleanshaven face, well-fitting clothes, and a confident bearing.

She thought of her own appearance. Plain on her best day, after four days transferring from train to stage, her indigo traveling dress was covered with a layer of silt and wrinkles. Her fine brown hair was weighed down with road dust and had become hopelessly disheveled during the bouncing and jarring of the carriage. She knew without the benefit of a mirror fatigue was evident in the slump of her narrow shoulders and listless brown eyes.

She thought of Father and what he told her when she was a child lamenting her lack of beauty. Instead of assuring her she was beautiful and would someday blossom into a rose, Father said true beauty came from inside a person, and he felt sorry for those who failed to see it.

She smiled warmly and extended her hand. "Yes, I'm Bridget Reidy. It's so nice to meet you, Mr. DeSantis."

"Dominic," he said. His soft drawl puddled her insides.

Warmth flooded her face again. Oh, dear. She wished he wouldn't look at her like that—as though he wasn't disappointed by her plain countenance.

"Then, please, call me Bridget."

He took hold of her fingertips and held onto them as he gazed into her eyes. The look lasted only a moment, but it felt to Bridget like what she always imagined the magnetic draw would be between the heroes and heroines in the novels she loved. His piercing dark eyes were nearly as black as the thick hair that brushed his coat collar.

"It's nice to meet you, Bridget." An easy smile warmed his features even further.

The driver pushed between them. "If you two are through gettin' to know each other, I don't got all day to stand around figurin' this out." He shoved the trunk back into the wagon.

Bridget hastily stepped out of the way, nearly stumbling over her too-large feet. The driver circled the wagon and jumped onboard. Dominic took Bridget's elbow and steered her out of the way as the driver turned the wagon in a tight circle and carefully backed it into the entrance of the livery.

She turned to Dominic. "I can't leave my books in a barn. They'll be damaged by the weather. I planned to take them along with my other things directly to Cowboy Creek."

"I'm sorry, but there's no room. I didn't bring a wagon big enough to haul them and I only have one horse hitched to my buggy."

Bridget bit back tears. She hadn't even thought of that. Would it insult Dominic if she offered to hire a wagon to take them the rest of the way? She didn't want to get off on the wrong foot with him by insulting his male pride. Nor did she want to leave her precious books in a damp, musty barn.

She hurried through the door where the driver was standing on the hard-packed earth next to a tall, bent man with a broad forehead and questioning blue gray eyes.

"Do you have someplace safe to keep them?" she asked the man. "They must be kept dry. I'll pay whatever it takes."

The stationmaster pulled a hand through his thin gray beard. "It'll just be for a couple of days, Dale," Dominic said. "Just until I get a few free hours to bring a couple horses back to retrieve them."

"All this fuss over a couple trunks 'a books," the driver Bridget had hired muttered under his breath. They all heard him easily enough. "Can't believe anybody'd pay good money to tote them all this way." He directed the comment to Dominic as he rolled his eyes.

Bridget drew in her breath. Her patience had worn to its breaking point, and now she'd have to leave her books behind. She was relieved Dominic had offered to come back for them as soon as he got the chance.

Dominic squared his wide shoulders. "Don't reckon it's any business of yours what she brought with her as long as you were paid for the job."

Bridget's spirits soared. She could scarcely believe it. Someone other than Mother or Father was defending her. Her own true-to-life hero!

The driver sucked air around his broken teeth. He arched his back and twisted to work out a kink. "Ain't no skin off'a my nose either way. She's your problem now."

The stationmaster opened the door of a stall lined with wooden shelves. He pointed to a wooden platform a few feet off the ground. "They'll slide right in here, ma'am. Keep 'em nice and dry until you come back to fetch 'em."

Bridget prayed it wouldn't be long and prayed it wouldn't rain a deluge and ruin the trunks' contents in the meantime. While she thanked the stationmaster and tried to pay him for the storage, which he adamantly refused, Dominic and the driver moved the trunks into the stall. The driver panted and grunted the whole way. Dominic showed no sign that he noticed the weight. Though Bridget tried to focus her concern on the two trunks, she couldn't help noticing the way the muscles of his back and shoulders strained against his coat.

Oh, my!

The driver had already been paid, but she tipped him handsomely despite his surly disposition. Mother always tipped generously. "It doesn't cost that much more to show a person how much they're worth in God's eyes, even if we don't always see it," she'd say.

A few minutes later, she and Dominic stepped out of the barn into the warm sunshine. Spring was all around her, heralding new growth and new beginnings. Tiny leaves unfurled on the trees, and tufts of grass stubbornly sought purchase amidst the wagon ruts crisscrossing the narrow street. The day seemed fitting. She hoped her future with Dominic bore the same promise.

The stationmaster remained inside. The driver had unhitched his team and took them somewhere for brushing and water. Without the activity of the last few minutes, discomfort washed over Bridget like an unexpected summer rain. She nervously straightened the seams on the fingers of her gloves. "I'm sorry about the books. I didn't think, I mean, it didn't occur to me I wouldn't have a way to take them to Cowboy Creek." She looked earnestly at Dominic. "I pared down my collection as best I could."

His obsidian eyes widened. "You mean there were more?"

"Oh, yes. Rooms and rooms of them. Mother and Father, they… We loved to read."

He arched a thick eyebrow. He glanced back at the open door of the livery and then at her. "We'll work something out."

"Thank you."

She wanted to say more, to explain. While he wasn't as perturbed as the driver, she could tell he couldn't understand why a woman would travel across the country with two trunks of books when books could be bought anywhere and hardly seemed worth the horseflesh it took to haul them. If he didn't yet find her odd, he would soon enough once he got to know her better.

She hoped he was willing to overlook her flaws—her plain looks and personality quirks and build a life with her. Now that she'd met Dominic in the flesh, she not only wanted the situation to work, she needed it to. She wouldn't go back to Cincinnati and face Charles and Ellen as a failure who had sold the property it took her parents a lifetime to amass. Nor did she want to. She glanced at Dominic from under the brim of her hat. Her life was here now. For better or for worse.

Chapter Three

Books. Dominic was nearly as flummoxed as the driver. He couldn't imagine anyone going to the trouble and expense of hauling two trunks of *books* halfway across the continent. Other than a Bible, he couldn't think of a single book he'd bother to stick in his saddlebag and tote a hundred yards.

Anyone who cared that much about books must be smart. A genius, he reckoned. He was half afraid to open his mouth. As soon as he spoke more than three words, the fancy lady in front of him would know he was about as far from genius as a person could get and still walk upright. She'd go running back to Cincinnati on the first thing with wheels and tell Nan there'd been a terrible mistake. She couldn't marry a fellow as dumb as Dominic DeSantis.

Before she had a chance to do just that, Dominic took her elbow and turned her toward the stage platform where the driver had left her other things—a smaller trunk, two valises, a satchel and two carpetbags he imagined contained things city ladies like her couldn't live without. How had she gotten this far toting all the clutter by herself? He reckoned a warm smile, a gentle word, and a coin or two, if warranted, got a woman pretty much anything she wanted.

Bridget Reidy wasn't what he envisioned last Christmas when he raised his hand to let the other men know he was interested in taking a bride. He had imagined someone with work-worn hands and a little desperation in her eyes indicating she was down to her last chance. Mentally and physically suited for the demands of frontier life. Nothing like this gal. Bridget didn't look like she'd worked awfully hard in her life. From her expensive travelling duds, she didn't look desperate either.

She was tall with long arms, narrow shoulders, and narrow hips to match. She had a keen look in her large, brown eyes. Curious, Dominic would call it, like she was trying to look in every direction at once, take in every detail around her. She was smart, all right. She looked better suited for a job as schoolmarm or librarian at one of those tall city libraries he'd heard about but never seen. She sure didn't look like she was ready for the rough, hardscrabble life she'd endure here if they proved suited for marriage.

His mouth quirked upward when he thought of how she'd handled the driver. She had refused to put up with the man's nonsense yet was thoughtful and considerate of him in the end. Even if she wasn't suited for frontier life and decided it wasn't for her, Dominic still looked forward to getting to know her for however long she stayed.

He regarded her from under the brim of his hat. Most men wouldn't call her beautiful, but she had a pleasing face. Besides her large expressive eyes that he couldn't look away from, she had a wide mouth that hadn't stopped smiling. She looked eager to express the thoughts behind those brown eyes. Her brows were high and straight and gave her a look of depth. He wondered again if anything he said would interest or intrigue her.

She reached for one of the bulging valises. Dominic grabbed it first. He slung the strap of a valise over each shoulder and grasped the small trunk with his hands. A grunt of exertion escaped his lips as he straightened.

"I'm so sorry," she said. "Should I fetch someone from the livery to help?"

Dominic grinned at the distress on her face. "No, ma'am, I got it. You can set those other bags on top of the trunk for me though." He motioned with his head to the bags at her feet.

Her brown eyes widened. "Oh no. That would be entirely too much. I'll get them." She looped her embroidered purse over her shoulder, tucked the satchel under her arm, then finagled the handles of the carpetbags until she could grip one in each hand.

Dominic bit back another smile. He nearly set down the trunk to help her, but he could see she wanted to do her part. Despite her pampered appearance, she obviously wasn't one to put the work on someone else. He maintained a slow pace as he led her to the wagon so she could keep up under her burden.

At the wagon, she slung the smaller bag into the back and let the heavier one land on the ground with a thud. "I'm sorry about the trunks," she said breathlessly, her cheeks pink. "Whenever I traveled with my parents, Father always teased Mother and me about bringing the entire house with us."

"It's no trouble," he assured her as he deposited her things into the carriage around the supplies he'd bought today.

"The books are part of my parents' collection," she explained as he worked. "Father kept a small office at home and every wall was lined with books. All through the rest of the house, you could find a shelf or table or cubby with a few books tucked inside. Books were very important to my parents. They knew they couldn't give my brother and me the world, so they strove to give us as much of it as they could through the books we read."

Books in every room of the house? She was well traveled as well. She was going to be in for a mighty big letdown when she saw the houses and cabins in Cowboy Creek—especially his. Dominic hoped she wouldn't be so disappointed she hightailed it back to civilization.

She blushed and her narrow face became almost beautiful in the moment. She sighed to come back from the place her heart had gone. "I'm sorry. That must make me sound very spoiled and pretentious."

"Not at all. How long have your folks been gone?"

She blinked and her eyelashes sparkled with unshed tears. "Father passed away a year ago next month. Mother died just before Christmas."

Dominic lost his own ma nearly two years ago. He hadn't seen Pa since he left home. The pain sat like a dull ache in his jaw that never went away even when he managed to set it aside for a time. He watched her for a moment, hoping to convey that he understood, and she could talk about it if she chose. Or not if that was easier. Keeping her eyes on him, she took a deep breath. Her brown eyes cleared.

He finished loading the trunk and her bags—a tight fit in the worn carriage he had borrowed from Preach and Marla. All he had at home was a buckboard. He figured she would be too tired from her long journey to ride in that.

"Do you need anything before we head out of town?"

He couldn't imagine a single thing she hadn't stowed in all those bags, but he was far from an expert in the physical needs of women. "There's a mercantile across the road that carries nearly anything you can think of. I'm afraid you won't find much once we leave Good Hope. The trading post in Cowboy Creek carries only the basics and very little of it. Marla and her husband Preach—I should say, Mr. and Mrs. Dodds—they own the place. Marla started stocking a few items women might find...useful. Bolts of cloth, soap, and the like. The prices are higher than you'll pay here so if you can think of anything..."

He let the words trail off, uncomfortable that he'd said so much. A couple weeks ago at the trading post when no one else was around, he had picked up a bar of soap from a metal bin Marla had set on the counter and took a deep whiff. The scent of gardenia filled his nose and reminded him of things soft and warm and gentle. Things he hadn't dwelled on in a long time. He dropped the soap back into the bin as if it were a hot coal, embarrassed by the thoughts it evoked in him. He carried the scent around in his nose for days.

He glanced down at Bridget's fancy duds. They appeared top quality. He couldn't imagine her finding anything comparable here or even in the bigger city of Ruby City where the residents of Cowboy Creek traded their harvest surplus every Fall.

"Thank you, but I think I brought everything I'll require for the time being."

Dominic didn't doubt that. "There's a café at the end of the street if you'd like to get something to eat before we go." It was still early afternoon. Now that the daylight hours lasted longer, they had plenty of time to sit a spell before getting on the road if she had a mind to.

"No, I'm fine. Unless you want to." She looked at him with eager eyes. "I'm quite anxious to get to Cowboy Creek."

Adventure and excitement sparked in her eyes. Dominic's heart swelled. Maybe she wouldn't be a fish out of water after all.

"All right then." He took her hand and assisted her into the carriage.

He hadn't touched a woman's hand on purpose since he told his ma goodbye when he left home. Even through her traveling gloves, Bridget's were about as soft as a goose feather. He doubted she possessed a callous or a blister. He should prepare her for Cowboy Creek. Warn her about the loneliness and long winters and two feet of snow that sometimes lasted until May. He didn't. He liked the eagerness in her inquisitive brown eyes and didn't want to be the one to dash it. That'd happen soon enough.

"I'm sorry you'll have to make an extra trip to collect my other trunks," she said after he settled into the seat next to her.

"No, it's my fault. I should've considered you might bring a lot with you and hitched the team. Don't worry. The trunks'll be fine where they are for a couple of days."

"Is your bookcase big enough to store them?"

Dominic caught himself before he laughed out loud. A bookcase was the last thing she'd find at his house.

His stomach sank as realization set in. Nan Canfield had made a huge mistake in matching Bridget with a blockhead like him. It wasn't anyone's fault but his own. The only man in Cowboy Creek who knew his secret was Rase, Nan's nephew, and even he didn't know the extent of it.

The only book in his cabin was a Bible a previous resident had given him before he rode out of Cowboy Creek. He carried the volume with him every Sunday to church. Sometimes just holding it brought comfort as he pondered what he heard at church. He recognized the words *Holy Bible* on the cover because that's what the others said they were. Beyond that, Dominic couldn't read a word of it.

He should tell her. This well-read, well-traveled woman needed to know before they traveled one more foot she would never find him suitable. Try as he might, he couldn't look at that gentle face and make himself say the words.

Bridget cocked her head. "Dominic?"

"I'm sorry. No, I don't have a… My cabin's pretty small. Only got two rooms. Ain't never seen a need for a bookcase."

"Oh." She snagged her bottom lip with pearly white teeth. "I…um…I guess it was impractical of me to assume, but I had an image in my head of bookshelves like I had at home."

He wouldn't say impractical. More like naïve. He'd let her figure that out on her own. "There might be some bookshelves at the brides' house. That's where you'll be staying until—well, until you're settled. We can store the books there after I fetch them from Good Hope. The little house is dry and warm. The brides before you fixed it up right nice. Leastways, that's what I hear."

She smiled in acknowledgement, but he could see she was still worried about her things. She was probably puzzling over how everything she brought would fit in a two-room cabin should they marry. Dominic was wondering the same thing.

"As soon as I get a chance to gather some spare lumber, I'll plane it down smooth and build you a proper bookcase."

She clasped her hands together. "Oh, thank you. I mean—I hate to put you to any bother."

He shook his head. He already liked that happy gleam in her eyes and didn't mind at all working to keep it there. "No trouble, a'tall. Just might not happen right away. This is the busy season for all of us."

"Oh, of course. I understand. I feel much better, Mr. DeSantis—Dominic."

He softened at the sound of his name on her lips.

Color warmed her cheeks as if she liked the sound of it too. "I presume you're Italian?"

"Ma and Pa immigrated from Italy when they first married. My oldest sister is the only one of us young'uns born there."

She blushed prettily, which softened her sharp features. She had written three letters in the last six weeks. From the length of them, Dominic figured she wanted them to know each other by the time she arrived.

Rase Canfield read the first one to him. That letter was two neatly written pages. As Rase read, Dominic committed every word to memory. Memorizing came easy for him, so not knowing how to read or write had never caused him much trouble. As he went about his work while waiting for her arrival, he replayed the words of her letter in his mind. In the evenings in front of the fire, he held all of them in his hands and caressed the words with his eyes, thinking about the woman who had written them and God's plan for their life together. He wondered what she'd think when she saw his simple cabin, when she experienced his way of life. Would she see herself as part of it?

Several times, he nearly swallowed his pride and asked Rase to read the other letters. He never did. It wasn't Rase's problem that he was an illiterate dummy.

It looked like it was about to become Bridget Reidy's problem.

She had come here with her trunks full of books and her head full of city school learning. What would she think of a groom who couldn't think of a thing to say that a lady like her might find interesting enough to hear?

"In my neighborhood in Cincinnati, everyone is either German, Welsh, or Scottish," she said, unaware of the simple thoughts crashing around in his head. "Reidy isn't nearly as lyrical on the tongue as your surname. I often wonder about the history of names. Imagine the journeys the people who bear them took to end up where they are. Do you ever wonder about things like that?"

Dominic wasn't sure what she just said. He had never spent a moment of his life wondering about the origin of a name or a flower or an animal scrambling up a rocky outcropping in front of him except to determine if it was within rifle range. Yes, this woman was too dang smart for him.

"I can't say that I have."

"Oh." She glanced at him before focusing her eyes on her lap. Instead of looking disappointed that he didn't ponder such deep thoughts, she looked embarrassed. Embarrassed that she'd confessed something another person might find odd.

"Does your brother still live in Cincinnati?" he asked, hoping a different topic would be easier on both of them.

She stiffened. Dominic inwardly kicked himself. She had probably written the answer in one of her letters, and now thought he was insensitive or rude or hadn't bothered to remember.

"My brother Charles lives nearby with his wife and their three children. We weren't close growing up. As I wrote in my letters, he's ten years older than me. Most of my memories of Charles are of him running in and out of the house on his way to school or out with friends."

She sighed and tilted her head to one side as she seemed to look to the past. "Oh my, I thought he was grand. So smart and handsome in his school uniforms. He was my hero. Maybe because he never slowed down long enough to talk to me," she ended wistfully.

Dominic could tell there was a lot more to that story she wasn't saying. Maybe she'd written it in her letters. He got the feeling she hadn't.

Her walnut brown eyes lit up again. "What about you? Are you originally from this area?"

"I don't think anyone is originally from here. I'm closer, though, than a lot of folks hereabouts. My parents lived in New York City for a year or two after they arrived from Italy, working to save enough money to move West. That was their dream. They lived in Pennsylvania for a few years. That's where I was born. Then we settled in Kansas where I did most of my growing up. I have six sisters and four brothers."

She gasped aloud. Her cheeks colored. Dominic smiled at her response. He was beginning to like the way she reacted to things with unadulterated delight. Her joy alone was worth taking this woman as his bride.

"Eleven children!" she exclaimed. "How fascinating. I always dreamed of being part of a big family."

Her blush deepened as she realized the implications of her words. Dominic doubted she knew how pretty she was when she smiled like that. He tried to rein in his own smile but couldn't help himself. He didn't mind the implication of her words. Eleven children sounded just fine to him, too. Was that what the Lord had in store? A noisy houseful of young'uns like the one he'd grown up in and this woman beside him?

"We children learned to work hard from the time we took our first steps," he told her. "Didn't really have much choice."

"I would imagine not." Admiration rang in her voice. She didn't seem to think less of him for working with his hands and not his head as her own papa and brother obviously had.

"When we were old enough, most of us moved out and started making our own way or stayed close by to help Mama and Papa run the farm."

"When is the last time you saw them?"

His shoulders slumped. "I've been on my own since I was sixteen. Never did make it back to the homeplace. I stayed down in Natchez with one of my brothers for a time before I headed up here. He sent word two winters ago Mama had passed away. Papa moved in with my sister Rosa and her family. I reckon he's all right."

"They don't write?" she asked gently after a respectful moment.

"No."

Nothing more needed said there. He couldn't read their letters even if they wrote, and he certainly couldn't write back.

"That must be hard. I know you're busy with all the work you have. If you have your sister's address, I can write a letter for you this week. Just tell me what you'd like to write. I'm sure you're worried about them. There must be lots of news to share from such a large family. Perhaps you'll have your own news to share soon."

Her eyes widened and her porcelain cheeks flushed in embarrassment. Dominic marveled again at how pretty she was once a fellow took the time to study her.

He pulled at the collar of his shirt. The afternoon sun had begun its descent. The day was warm and bright, reminding him of the chores waiting for him at home. "I don't have Rosa's address, but I can probably find a way to contact my brother in Natchez. If he's still there. Now that the spring rains have let up, I have a lot of planting to get into the ground besides my other work. And I'll have to get back to Good Hope to fetch your trunks."

"I'm afraid my impetuous actions have added to your workload. Father loved history. He instilled that love in me. Mother loved art and literature. There were just so many books I couldn't leave behind."

She wrinkled her long straight nose as if sniffing back tears. Dominic figured leaving behind the books had been like losing a big part of her family. He almost wished he could've helped her carry every single book she owned from Cincinnati.

"Don't fret over the trunks," he said gently. "We'll get them to Cowboy Creek as soon as possible. As for writing home, some evening after my work is through, I could tell you the things I'd like to ask my family and you could let them know what you think of Cowboy Creek."

She smiled. "I would like that."

They settled into companionable silence. Dominic already liked the feel of her beside him in the wagon. He wondered if she would think the same about him once she realized he didn't have much to offer.

Chapter Four

"There you are. We were beginning to wonder." A rounded older lady with faded brown eyes and a wide smile rushed forward and pulled Bridget into a warm embrace. "Weren't we, Daniel? I couldn't stop looking out the window."

Behind her, a thin man, only a few inches taller than his wife, smiled indulgently. He had a long thin nose, sharp blue eyes, and a ring of gray hair encircling his head. "I'm surprised she didn't wear a path in the rug. I told her not to worry; you'd get here when you got here."

The woman released her embrace but kept hold of Bridget's elbows. "Well, you got here safely. That's all that matters. It's a nice day for traveling. Oh, dear, I'm sorry." She let go of Bridget's and smoothed a hand over her thick pile of graying hair. "Where are my manners? You must be Miss Reidy. I'm Marla Dodds. This is my husband, Daniel. We run the trading post here as you can see. Danial also serves as the minister in Cowboy Creek. He and I host the brides until…" Her gaze swept past Bridget to Dominic. "Well, until you young folks have a chance to get to know each other."

Mr. Dodds stepped forward and took Bridget's hand. "Nice to meet you, Miss Reidy. I trust your trip wasn't too taxing."

"No, sir," Bridget answered. Her back and hips screamed in protest that, yes, it had been an exhausting trip. One she hoped she wouldn't have to make again.

"It's a pleasure to meet you, too. Please, call me Bridget." She directed her smile at both of them. She liked the couple instantly.

Mrs. Dodds tightened the shawl around her throat. Now that the sun had slid behind the tallest peaks of the nearer mountains, the temperatures had cooled significantly in just a few hours. It was nearly June but reminded Bridget of late March. She hadn't expected the Colorado weather to be much different from Ohio. Maybe Spring held on tight while it had the chance, or today was unique.

"Well, Dominic, don't just stand there. You and Daniel can unload Miss Reidy's—er, Bridget's—things into the brides' house and then come in for supper. I know you both must be starving."

When Dominic opened his mouth to protest, the older woman cut him off. "Now, I know you've been driving all day and you don't have anything prepared to eat at home."

"Nothing as good as Marla's venison stew," Daniel put in. "No point in arguing, Dominic. It's already decided and we men have little say in the matter." He clapped his hand on Dominic's shoulder and turned him toward the wagon.

Bridget watched them go. She wouldn't mind going with them to show them where she wanted everything placed in her quarters. She hoped there was a big window in the parlor where she could sit and read or write in her journal while looking out at the mountains. She wondered how many bedrooms were in the brides' house. Most likely one if the ramshackle buildings they passed on their way down the street were any indication. If there was a second one, she could store her books and other furnishings there until she and Dominic decided if they were well suited.

She thought of the shipment on its way down the river from Cincinnati. Where would she put everything? Dominic's house only had two rooms. Even if he doubled the size of his house by the time the shipment arrived, it would make for close quarters. Oh well. She had no choice but to put aside her worries until the time came.

While they got to know each other—as Mrs. Dodds put it—she'd be living under the good graces and hospitality of the Dodds. She was in no position to question the way they did things. The thought of venison stew—and hopefully warm biscuits with honey—sounded divine despite her anticipation at seeing the brides' house.

Marla looped her arm through Bridget's and turned her toward the door of a crude, unpainted building that appeared to be the main building in the little settlement. Bridget glanced left and right as she stepped onto the weathered porch. She had never seen such a tired, forlorn place. Besides the trading post, only one other building on the street showed signs of use, though she couldn't tell from the outside what that use might be.

The trading post didn't look much better inside than out. Shelves were fashioned from rough boards over wooden pegs driven into the walls. A counter stood alongside one wall crowded beyond imagination with buckets of nails and coils of rope and other implements Bridget couldn't immediately identify. At the end of the narrow passage between shelves and overflowing barrels of shovel and hoe handles, they came to a long table fashioned from a sheet of plywood over a pair of sawhorses. The wood bowed in the middle under the weight of a colorful selection of fabric and sewing notions, out of place in the dismal space. It appeared the Doddses had made an effort to appeal to the changing demographic of shoppers now that women were moving to the area.

Shopping. Would she ever shop in a real store again? She had completely left civilization behind.

Where would she find lace or embroidery thread or buttons to replace one lost or damaged? What about her toilette? Reticules? Intimate items? As she discarded one household item after another before her move, she assured herself she could replace whatever she couldn't live without once she got to Cowboy Creek. Now she realized her life would never resemble what she had lived with Mother and Father.

She didn't think of herself as materialistic, but now that she faced practically no physical possessions, she prayed she would find contentment in the change.

Marla led her through a cluttered parlor at the back of the trading post and into a slightly bigger kitchen where the smell of venison stew set Bridget's stomach to rumbling. She had only eaten venison a time or two in Cincinnati. It wasn't her favorite dish. Growing up in the

Queen City on the Ohio River, her palate was accustomed to pork, beef, and chicken. Wild game was not something she preferred.

She had followed the housekeeper Frances to the meat markets more times than she could count to buy strings of sausage as long as her leg and wedges of cheese wrapped in wax paper. She helped prepare many of the dishes for the family's table, but she wasn't sure what to do with venison or rabbit. Or squirrel. Her nose wrinkled in distaste at the thought. Weren't squirrels just rats with fluffy tails? How could she choke squirrel meat down her throat? She didn't consider herself sheltered from the realities of life, yet she never had to think how a squealing pig or somber cow ended up on her dinner plate either. She prayed again she was ready for what she'd gotten herself into.

She didn't have time to think of much else once Marla removed her shawl and tied her apron around her stomach. Bridget quickly set aside her own wrap and went to work while Marla bustled around the small space, talking a mile a minute. After four days of travel, it was wonderful to move around freely and talk to someone about matters other than the endless delays of a train schedule. Marla seemed to relish the female company. Bridget's excitement grew as Marla talked about the three brides who had preceded her to Cowboy Creek. They were also from Cincinnati. If they had made the adjustment to living in the rough foothills, Bridget was encouraged that she could too.

It wasn't long before the men's boots sounded at the back door. A strange flutter filled Bridget's stomach at the sound of Dominic's voice. Was it the romantic notion of marrying someone after resigning herself to a life of spinsterhood that sped up her pulse? Or had she already developed feelings for the man? She wasn't sure, but she couldn't ignore the excitement when he stepped through the door.

During dinner, she didn't learn much more about Dominic than she already knew. Daniel—or Preach, as he insisted everyone call him—asked questions about his farm and how the new calves were doing. Marla was more interested in learning what she could about Bridget and things in the city. She and Preach were anxious for news from the East. Bridget was well versed in politics and how decisions in Washington impacted the young nation's economy, so she held her audience in rapt attention. Dominic was quiet and only contributed to the conversation when Preach asked him a direct question. It appeared he wasn't as interested in politics or news from the city as the older couple.

After dinner, Marla pushed aside Bridget's offer to help clean the kitchen. "It's a lovely evening. You and Dominic go out on the porch and enjoy it while Daniel and I take care of what needs done in here."

Dominic looked as uncomfortable at the notion of spending time with Bridget on the porch as she was, even though they had ridden all this way from Good Hope. Neither could stand up to Marla, however, who seemed to know just how young people went about getting to know each other, so they did as they were told.

Two wooden chairs had been placed on the front porch of the trading post for passing the time, should one find himself in possession of any. Dominic led her to them. After she was seated, Dominic lit the lantern nailed to the side of the building next to the door and took the empty chair beside her. While there had been plenty to talk about inside with Marla and Preach, Bridget found herself hopelessly tongue-tied. She hunched her shoulders against the cold. She was glad she'd taken the time to put on her gloves. Dominic didn't seem to notice the cold. He was probably used to it.

Over the sound of the gurgling stream across the street, she heard a child call out. She jerked her head in that direction. She saw nothing through the thick foliage. "That must be the Whitamore children Marla told me about," she said. "I didn't realize they lived so close."

"They're at the top of the hill in the house next to the gristmill. You'll meet them at Sunday meeting if they don't come down here to meet your before then. Cowboy Creek's turning into a bona fide community."

"I'm glad I'll have neighbors. Does the community have a school?"

"No need for one at the moment. Not unless more families move to Cowboy Creek."

Or until we brides get to work and start making babies. Bridget's cheeks colored in the gathering darkness. She was glad Dominic couldn't see.

"Are there other neighbors in town?"

"Only Lonnie Fanshaw. He's our blacksmith. He has a place near the mill. The rest of us are scattered throughout the countryside. We don't see each other much except on Sundays when we come to town for meeting. No one misses that." He pointed at the building across the road that Bridget had noticed earlier. "That's our meetinghouse. After church, we have dinner together, inside in the winter, but outdoors now that the weather's getting warmer. That's pretty much the extent of our socializing. Work keeps us all busy, especially this time of year when planting and groundbreaking needs done."

Bridget knew what he was doing. Reminding her she wasn't in Cincinnati anymore. Whatever pampered life she had enjoyed there was over. People out here went days at a stretch without seeing another living soul, and they sure didn't have the luxury of sitting around discussing art or literature or politics.

"My place is about two miles northeast," he continued. "Jacob and Rennie Campbell are my closest neighbors. There's a steep ridge between us so I don't see them often. I'd like to take you out to my spread tomorrow. Around lunchtime if you'd be interested?"

Bridget clasped her hands in the fold of her skirt. She'd never gone anywhere alone with a man who wasn't related. Not ever. Riding with him from Good Hope was one thing, but this was different. This would be like courting. She nearly laughed out loud. Courting was exactly what they were doing. She just never thought she'd do it—an old maid of twenty-six. Would she know how to handle herself? She almost wished she could ask Marla to come along, but she already knew what Marla would say.

"I'd like that, Dominic."

"Do you ride? Or would you rather I bring the wagon?"

The thought of subjecting her backside to the springs in a rattly old buckboard nearly made her groan out loud. She'd rather walk. "I don't know how to ride," she confessed.

"That's no problem. I can teach you if you like. I have a gentle mare that's made for learning. I'll bring her with me. You'll be riding in no time. Everything around here is faster and easier on horseback, so you'll be needing to learn anyway." He set his hat on his head and got up.

Bridget stood quickly beside him.

"I should be getting on." He paused. His eyes scanned her face. Bridget's frosty breath caught in her throat. No man had ever looked at her as intently as Dominic was doing now. He didn't look disappointed that she was no beauty, but she wouldn't fool herself into thinking he wasn't at least a little bit so.

"I still have chores to look after when I get home," he said, regret heavy in his voice.

"Yes, of course. I…I appreciate you picking me up at the stage. And for moving my things to the brides' house."

"No trouble, Miss Reidy. Bridget." He adjusted his hat that didn't need adjusting. "It was a pleasure meeting you. And…"

His words drifted off. She imagined he didn't know anything more about this situation than she did. That made her feel a little better. "Thank you, Dominic. I look forward to tomorrow."

He nodded and stepped off the porch. Bridget wasn't sure if it was proper to stand in the shadows and watch him mount the horse he had left in the barn while he went to Good Hope to fetch her, but that's exactly what she did. He stared down at her for a moment, then tipped his hat, wheeled the horse, and rode away.

Bridget watched until his horse was swallowed up by the lengthening shadows. She wrapped her arms around herself in the cool night air and marveled at how different her life was from just a few weeks ago. What were Charles and Ellen thinking tonight? Once they realized they weren't getting more money from Mother and Father's estate, they probably bid her good riddance. She missed Frances. She had given the beloved housekeeper a hefty bonus before boarding the train and reduced the woman to tears. Bridget told her Mother and Father would not want her to be forced to seek a new position once she left the family's employ.

Besides Frances and the maids, there was no one in Cincinnati to miss her or that she would miss. She was on the precipice of a new life.

With Dominic?

Would they fall in love? Would they have children? Eleven of them! A shiver of nerves ran down her spine. She had never seen herself as a wife and mother, but this might be exactly what God had in store for her. Under all her uncertainty and nerves was peace. She was doing the right thing. She only hoped Dominic thought so too.

Chapter Five

"Easy there. Take it slow. Just like that." Bridget looked down from atop the horse, joy and wonder on her face. Dominic smiled back. He never thought teaching someone to ride a horse could be so much fun.

When he arrived this morning leading his mare Ginger behind his own mount, Preach showed him a sidesaddle he had unearthed in the storehouse. Dominic wasn't sure if he could teach someone to ride sidesaddle since he'd never sat on one himself. It turned out the mechanics were the same and it looked more comfortable for Bridget in her long skirts.

He walked alongside the horse, one hand ready to reach for the halter if need be. He'd bought Ginger from a family leaving Cowboy Creek who needed the money more than the expense of a horse too lazy to keep up with the others. She was slow-footed and best suited to the plow or cart. As expected, she made the perfect horse for a shy rider.

"You're doing fine. You weren't pulling my leg, were you, about not being a horsewoman?"

"Oh, no, I wouldn't do that." Bridget grinned when she realized he was teasing. She was breathless, and her cheeks shone with exertion and excitement. "Mother and I took carriages everywhere we went. There was never a reason to learn to ride."

"Well, she'd be mighty proud to see you now."

Bridget beamed down at him. "Ginger's just a good horse. Aren't you, girl?" She loosened her white-knuckled grip on the reins as he had reminded her a dozen times and carefully patted the horse's neck.

Dominic ducked his head so she wouldn't see the smile under his hat brim. What would she think if he asked her to marry him right now?

She had been waiting on the porch of the trading post when he rode into town an hour ago. Like yesterday, her chestnut brown hair had been rolled into a small knot at the nape of her neck. Dominic wondered what it looked like loose around her shoulders, then immediately chastened himself. He had no business thinking about her loose, flowing hair or the way her sage-colored dress accentuated her lithe figure.

Adam Waring had married his bride Eliza the very night she arrived in Cowboy Creek. Dominic didn't have the nerve to even suggest that. His cabin only had one bedroom. One bed. While the thought wasn't displeasing to him at all, he figured Bridget would need a little time to get used to the idea of marital relations.

He stepped away from the horse's side to give Ginger room to move forward instead of in the small circle she'd been moving. A little sound of surprise escaped Bridget's lips as the horse's pace increased, though she was still plodding along.

"Oh! Dominic, where are you?" she asked, too intent on the horse to turn her head to look for him.

He stepped into her field of vision but lengthened the space between him and the horse. "Don't worry about me. You're doing fine. Straighten in the saddle and relax your shoulders. Don't hold onto the saddle horn. Use the reins and your body. Ginger knows you're tense. Relax and both of you will enjoy the walk."

Bridget didn't reply, but she moved her hands from where they hovered over the pommel and visibly relaxed her shoulders and arms. The horse's rigid stride also relaxed, and it began to walk loosely and evenly.

A bubble of laughter escaped her lips. "I'm doing it. We're doing it, Ginger. Dominic, we're doing it."

"Take her up to the corner of that building and let her circle back." Dominic raised his voice as the distance increased.

"How do I do that?"

He laughed. "Just give her a little tension with the left rein like I showed you. She knows how to turn."

She laughed again. "Yes, I suppose she does."

Dominic watched them ride about fifty feet before the horse made a wide turn in the middle of the street and came back. "That was wonderful," she said, her face glowing. "Can we go for a ride now?"

Dominic laughed back, amazed at how lovely she was with her cheeks flushed and the brightness of discovery in her brown eyes. "If you're sure you're ready. It's a couple miles to my place." The trip would take all day at this plodding pace. Hopefully once she got used to the sidesaddle and the horse under her, they could move a little faster.

"Oh, I'm ready," she assured him, "and so is Ginger? Aren't you, girl?"

He mounted his horse, and they began the ride to the ranch. Within a quarter mile, Bridget had relaxed into the rhythm of the horse, and they enjoyed a pleasant walk. Maybe on the way back, he would suggest a trot, but he wouldn't push her if she wasn't ready.

Her eyes scanned the countryside. "I can't get over the difference in this place and home. I'm sure the sky is just as blue in Cincinnati, but it seems so vivid here. It feels like I can see forever."

Dominic followed her gaze. "It's part of what drew me to this country. Sometimes I almost think I can reach right out and touch Heaven."

She looked like she wanted to say something, but either couldn't find the words or didn't want to offend him. The moment passed and she said, "How did you learn about this place?"

"Same as everyone else. I was just riding through. Looking for a place to settle. I met Marla and Preach at the trading post. Weren't many folks left by that time. The mines had played out, and everybody with somewhere to go had done gone. They told me about a place where the river went narrow with good land that had never been turned. Said the previous tenants hadn't bothered to file a claim, and I could file with the land agent for a good price. They were right. The government wanted to settle the area and was willing to help with the lending. Only thing there the first time I rode up was a falling down shack and a shed barely wide enough for two horses to stand side by side."

He smiled at her expression. "Don't worry. It's better now. I tore down both structures and used what lumber I could salvage for the foundation of a proper barn. Then I built the cabin. Another couple of good crop years and it'll be all mine. Or…ours."

Bridget hastily looked away. Dominic hoped he hadn't spoken too soon. That wasn't how he meant to propose. They both knew why she was here. No point in dancing around the issue. He wanted to marry her. Why wait? She was interesting and smart, and he liked the sound of her laugh.

He hoped it was enough, considering how different they were in every other way. Her parents had means. His did not. She was book smart. He hadn't gone past the second year in grammar school. She rode trains and carriages wherever she needed to go. The only time he'd been on a train was when he hopped one in Louisiana, only to get tossed into a ditch when another boxcar rider took offense at something he'd said.

Not for the first time since leaving home, Dominic wished Papa was here. Or one of his brothers. He would like to ask what they thought about him marrying a woman he'd just met. God was only a prayer away, but he sure would feel better if someone would confirm he was doing the right thing, and he and Bridget could build a life and family, despite their differences.

They rode into the dooryard of a small simple cabin. Bridget looked around, marveling at how far they were from town. It was so quiet. No shouts from street hucksters. No noise on the river. No children playing in the streets. Last night in the tiny, cramped brides' house, which didn't have a parlor by the way, it was so quiet she had heard an owl capture a field mouse and take flight, its huge wings disconcerting in the otherwise silent night. She had been so busy over the last month with packing and selling off her family's furnishings and things Charles didn't want, she hadn't considered the little things she'd never hear or see again or realized how much she'd miss them.

Dominic dismounted and secured his horse to the post of a narrow front porch. He lifted his arms to her. Awkwardly and as modestly as possible, Bridget shifted her legs in the saddle and slid into his arms. Her back had grown stiff during the long ride and one leg was nearly asleep. If she was going to spend much time in a saddle, it was probably more prudent to learn to ride astride. She hoped it wouldn't scandalize her parents' memory too terribly.

She shook the needles out of her legs. "It's so quiet," she said in a near whisper.

Dominic looked around as if he hadn't noticed. "You think so? I hear all sorts of things."

Bridget cocked her head and listened. She became aware of the wind rustling the tall grass, a horse in the paddock, and farther away, rushing water from the creek.

"Growing up, my life was always noisy," he explained. "Out here, without the confusion and press of people, I'm able to focus on creation. I've heard things I never heard before. There are always sounds. Voices in the trees. On the wind. Life. I think that's why I can't imagine living anywhere else."

She stared at him, nearly as enthralled by the wonder in his voice as the truth in his words. She didn't speak but looked around again and cocked her head to listen. He was right. Nature and creation spoke to her. God spoke to her. She was already coming to love Cowboy Creek.

Dominic stepped onto the narrow porch. He opened the cabin door and waited for her to go in ahead of him.

Bridget lifted her skirts as she stepped onto the porch and went inside. The cabin was tight and small and sparsely furnished. A small table and bench stood near a large cookstove. The opposite wall was dominated by a stone fireplace. The only adornment was a rifle over the mantle, hewn from a yellow pine log. Through one open doorway she saw a bed and a few pegs on the wall where Dominic hung his clothes. There was no empty peg. No wardrobe or bureau, or even space for one. She could see why he hadn't wanted to bring her trunks of books. There was barely enough space on the floor for the trunks and bags of clothes she had brought. How in the world would two people walk around in the small space without bumping into one another?

What would she do with her furnishings coming from Cincinnati? She hadn't lied when she told him she left most of her life behind, but there were some things she simply couldn't part with. Mother and Father's portraits. The sewing machine. The chifforobe she had hidden in as a child that she couldn't leave behind no matter how hard she tried. The curtains and bedclothes that would remind her of home through the years. They were coming, along with other treasures and mementos. If she and Dominic married, they would have a lot more to make room for than two trunks of books.

She pushed aside the worry and focused on the craftsmanship inside the cabin. A man who could build this place could easily add on as needed. She ran her hand over the smooth river rock of the fireplace.

"It's lovely. Did you build this yourself?"

He smiled with pleasure and pride. "Took two months of toting rocks up here from the river whenever I had a spare hour or two."

"Well, it's beautiful. I can't imagine all the work that went into it."

"Do you think—you'll be at home here? That you'll want to build a life here? With me?"

Her breath caught in her throat. Was this her marriage proposal? The moment she would remember the rest of her life? It wasn't as romantic as the proposals in novels. He didn't get down on one knee. Real life probably always paled in comparison to stories people made up. She hadn't expected love and passion the first day, but she hadn't expected Dominic either. A kind, hard-working man who seemed to see past her plain appearance and into her heart.

She looked from him to the stove. She was a good cook, having shadowed Frances most of her life. But she had never been completely responsible for preparing food for a family from scratch. She had never done all the shopping, growing, tending, and preserving of foodstuffs. She'd never given a moment's thought to the fully stocked coalbin or the hot stove and how they came to be that way. Those tasks were delegated to others. Out here, it would all be on her. She would have no Frances or Maggie or Pete to call on when she ripped a hem or dropped her hat in a puddle or ran out of firewood or ice.

Panic struck her heart. What if she wasn't up to it? What if she let Dominic down and he regretted asking for her hand? What if she couldn't get used to a cramped, remote cabin with no writing desk, wardrobe, bureaus, or indoor water? How would she live without the city and its shops and museums and amenities?

Despite her worries of disappointing Dominic and all the things she'd miss, a bubble of excitement rose in her breast. This cabin would be hers. Hers and Dominic's and someday their children. Not built with Father's money or run by Mother's capable hands. She envisioned a huge book and the hand of God turning the page. She could even see her parents smiling down at her. She would no longer be just their daughter but her own person. Dominic's wife.

She tentatively lifted her hand, and he took it. She would worry about space and storage and loneliness and keeping a fire going through the night later. For now, Dominic was waiting. So kind and handsome and thoughtful. For the first time in her life, she saw in a man's eyes that he wasn't disappointed. She prayed she wouldn't let him down.

"Yes, Dominic, I do want to build a life here with you."

He smiled and her heart swelled, crowding out her doubts.

Chapter Six

Bridget swept her hair onto the top of her head and turned from side to side to study her reflection. It had been four days since Dominic proposed, and she still couldn't quite get used to the idea of becoming a man's wife. By the time she reached her mid-teens, she had stopped imagining herself in a pretty dress, standing at the front of a church next to a man ready to vow he would love and cherish her until death parted them. That was exactly what was about to happen. She still wasn't sure when the nuptials would take place. They hadn't talked about that. Dominic's cabin was too small, for one. Bridget knew how marriage worked. Once they married, it would be expected that they share a marriage bed. Not only were the logistics against them, she couldn't imagine lying with him in that narrow bed in his tiny bedroom. The thought excited and terrified her at the same time. She liked Dominic, but she needed time before they took that step.

Oh, how she wished Mother were here. Marla was wonderful. She was kind and patient, but she couldn't take the place of Mother, who knew Bridget better than she knew herself. She would know just what to say to ease Bridget's fears and doubts. She would tell her she had done the right thing by coming here to build a life of her own instead of closing herself up in that big house in Cincinnati, living in the past until they were reunited in Heaven.

She didn't love Dominic; not in the way Mother loved Father. That would come later. She hoped. For now, the breathless delight at hearing his horse coming down the street would have to do. The only thing that threatened her excitement and anticipation of the adventure she'd embarked on was the shipment coming from Cincinnati.

In a journal, she had cataloged every item, and the list was long. In her big house overlooking the Ohio River, the items she hadn't sold or given to Charles hadn't taken up much space. Less than enough to furnish one large room. But here. Here, it was a different story. When she thought of Dominic's tiny cabin or the crowded trading post, so tightly packed that she had to turn sideways to fit between some of the shelves, she shuddered. What would she do with it all? Worse, what would Dominic think when it arrived? She had seen his reaction at the two trunks of books. He had been too polite to question her sanity for going to such an expense for *books*, but she knew he shared at least some of the driver's incredulity.

The shipment of household goods wasn't due for another month. If then, since there were always delays in shipping. That gave her plenty of time to figure out how to explain everything to him, and hopefully come up with a solution. She needed him to understand why she couldn't leave behind the special items that reminded her of her parents. Was she wrong? Her parents' memory was in her heart, not in material possessions. Still, she couldn't part with every physical reminder of them. Would Dominic understand? Or would her need to feel and touch items from her past hurt his feelings? She couldn't very well accept his proposal in one breath while in the next, tell him she needed a bigger house to fit all the furniture that meant so much to her.

Every day as she settled into the brides' house and helped Marla in the large garden behind the trading post, she fretted and prayed over how to handle the situation.

The week passed quickly. Bridget had never lived alone without a housekeeper or maid for company. It was different. Nice but different. Every evening Dominic rode into the settlement and sat for an hour or so on the trading post porch with her. Marla usually insisted he eat supper with them, but sometimes work on his farm kept him from arriving in time. The more they talked, the more convinced Bridget became that she had made the right decision. Marla was convinced of it as well and assured her Dominic would make her a good husband. Bridget wanted to believe it, but she wanted to make sure the Lord approved of the match and she wasn't marrying him because her pride wouldn't let her admit to Charles and Ellen she'd made a big mistake.

Yesterday, as a large kettle of roasted meat and potatoes bubbled on the stove for today's dinner after the church service, Bridget and Marla had gone into the meetinghouse to clean and prepare for today. They baked several loaves of zucchini bread, with an extra one for Dominic to take home after the communal dinner.

Bridget smoothed her hands over the soft fabric of her peach-colored skirt. It was her favorite dress. She believed the warm peach added depth to her sallow skin and brown eyes. She almost felt pretty when she wore it. She hoped Dominic liked it. There wasn't much she could do about her plain exterior, but a pretty dress covered a multitude of sins.

She took the loaves of zucchini bread from the basket and arranged them on the long table next to the piano while she waited for members of the community to arrive. She glanced anxiously at the door. She hadn't yet met another citizen of Cowboy Creek. Preach assured her everyone was busy and seldom left their farms this time of year. Not only was she eager to see Dominic, she wanted to meet the other brides. Dark clouds hung low in the sky. She hoped it wouldn't deter everyone from coming out today. She hoped she would at least meet Carrie Whitamore and the children who were her closest neighbors at the gristmill.

Dominic was the first to arrive. His eyes traveled down the peach dress and back again, pleasure evident on his face. Bridget blushed furiously. Was this how pretty girls felt when a man looked at them? Maybe it was just the dress. Whatever the reason, she could get used to seeing that look on his face.

The rest of the community began to filter in, laughing and joking about the wind tugging at their jackets and hats. The last man to arrive shut the door soundly and brushed raindrops from his shoulders. "We're about to get a gully-washer," he announced.

A few moments into Preach's sermon a crash of thunder shook the roof above their heads. A moment later the clouds burst forth and rain began to come down in earnest. Preach uttered a quick closing prayer. Even before the final *Amen*, everyone was gathering their wraps and jackets. Most had the foresight to bring slickers so they wouldn't get thoroughly by the onslaught before they got home. With a few hurried nods of greeting in Bridget's direction, the small group gathered the food containers they had brought with them and rushed for the door. Even Dominic hurried off without the loaf of zucchini bread Bridget set aside for him.

The skies remained open for four days. Every night Bridget fell asleep to the pounding of rain over her head and awoke to the pinging of drips in the buckets she had set on the floor under leaks. As she listened to the rain, she thought of her books in Good Hope and prayed the livery's roof above them would protect them from the rainstorm until Dominic was able to get there to rescue them.

No leaks could be repaired as long as the rain fell, but the men of Cowboy Creek still found work to do. Dominic and another bachelor—Sawyer Jamison, who raised hogs on a farm not far from town—showed up Tuesday to help Preach replace some rotted boards in the bedroom of the brides' house. To stay out of their way, Bridget went to the trading post and helped Marla prepare food for the men.

After lunch on Thursday when she threw the dishwater out Marla's back door, she nearly burst into song at the sight of the sun peering through watery clouds. She recognized the familiar sound of Dominic's horse coming down the road. She hung the dishpan on the nail under the porch roof and hurried around the side of the trading post to meet him.

"It stopped raining," she exclaimed as he brought the horse to a stop.

Dominic slid out of the saddle and looped the horse's reins around the hitching rail. "I see that."

Bridget's cheeks warmed at his teasing gaze. She liked him more and more every time she saw him. They hadn't talked more about getting married since last week when she accepted his proposal. Like her, he seemed content to take his time getting to know her before they made the move.

She looked at the brightening sky. "I can be ready in a few minutes if you came to take me to Good Hope."

His eyebrows arched under a heavy fringe of black hair. He looked down at his feet and made a show of lifting a boot out of the cloying mud. "I'm afraid it'll be at least a week before we can go anywhere. And that's only if we don't get more rain."

For the first time, Bridget looked past his face to the mud splattered up his boots and pants. Even his shirt and vest were splattered, as was the horse and saddle. There was so way a wagon could make it to Good Hope with the condition of the roads, and then back loaded down with books.

"I'm too far behind on my chores to spend a day going that far anyway," Dominic went on. "I just came into town to help Preach patch the hole in the barn roof while the ground dries out another day. And I came to see you." He touched her hand.

Bridget's heart fluttered, pushing away her disappointment. She wanted to go to town. She wanted to see for herself that no moisture had gotten into the trunks to bow the book covers and ruin the pages. One of the hardest things about living in Cowboy Creek, she realized, was the distance between it and everywhere else. Even if it didn't rain another drop, she likely wouldn't get to Good Hope until mid-June. For now, she could enjoy another day with Dominic.

Bridget's second Sunday in Cowboy Creek dawned bright and clear with an azure blue sky that seemed to stretch on forever. There was no zucchini left for zucchini bread. Marla had cocoa powder, so she made a huge chocolate cake. Bridget was so eager to meet the other brides she barely heard a word of Preach's sermon. She had just returned her Bible to her crocheted bag when a woman with tawny brown hair fashioned into a long braid marched up to her. She wore a simple green dress that accentuated her snapping green eyes. The woman extended a work-roughened hand and enveloped Bridget's, pulling her to her feet. At twenty-six, Bridget had thought she was too old to become a bride. This woman looked several years older and completely unapologetic about it.

"I'm Eliza Waring," the woman declared. "I'm sorry I didn't get to meet you last week. As I'm sure you've learned, the weather can turn on a dime around here. It makes all our decisions for us. My husband Adam and I live close to town, but it's a long ride with the rain pouring buckets and the creeks rising as fast as they did last week."

Before Bridget could agree or disagree, Eliza pulled her away from the row of chairs the congregation used in place of pews and turned her toward the tables where the food waited. Bridget cast her eyes about for Dominic. He was at the back of the room, seemingly trapped between two men. He shot her a quick look and a smile.

"We can talk and get to know each other while we set the food out," Eliza said. "Tell me the news from the city. There were murmurs of a dock workers' strike when I left. Did it happen? That useless city council should stand up for the workers who keep the economy moving instead of the shipowners. I guess we know who has the deeper pockets, don't we?"

Bridget couldn't believe it. Another woman in Cowboy Creek as interested in civic matters as she was. She opened her mouth to tell Eliza it wasn't that simple. Yes, the dock workers deserved fair pay and working conditions, but if the shipowners didn't turn a profit, they would move their operations downriver. What would become of the city's economy then?

"You didn't happen to bring a newspaper with you, did you?" Eliza asked before Bridget could put the words together.

"No, I—"

Eliza blew out a puff of air. "No matter. Everything in it would be outdated by now anyway. But I sure would like to hear some news about the world beyond Good Hope. I think I'll write to Nan Canfield and give her a list of things to send with the next brides."

A pretty young woman with rich brown hair that looked nearly black, huge brown eyes, and creamy ivory skin stepped between them. "Oh, Eliza, stop bothering everyone about newspapers. Dock workers' strikes don't mean anything out here. Thank goodness," she added exaggeratedly. She took Bridget's hands and squeezed.

"I'm Rennie Campbell. You must be Bridget. We're pleased to finally meet you. I was so disappointed when the rain prevented us from welcoming you properly last week."

Bridget estimated Rennie's age at no more than twenty. Her eyes were wide and expressive and her smile effervescent. Bridget smiled at the good-natured ribbing between Rennie and Eliza. It was like the women were family already. The next few minutes were a flurry of activity as the women set out plates and took covers off the different dishes they had brought to share. While working, Carrie Whitamore introduced herself along with the three children flittering around the room.

"I've heard the children calling back and forth to each other from the brides' house," Bridget told her.

"I hope they didn't disturb you."

"Oh no, on the contrary, I wanted to climb the hill to meet them, but it's been so muddy, the street was nearly impassable."

"That happens a lot around here," Carrie said with a chuckle. "The children are equally anxious to meet you. Since we lived in the brides' house a few weeks, the younger children still believe it belongs to them."

It was Bridget's turn to laugh. "They can come visit anytime. I'd love the company."

"Oh, they will. But with the river overflowing its banks last week, I thought it best to keep them close to home."

The men joined the women at the table, talking and teasing and everyone having a good time. Several times after the meal began, Bridget caught Carrie's oldest daughter, Candace, watching her. Each time, she gave the girl an encouraging smile. She remembered what it was like to be young and shy around new people. Out here, one would have to get over that quickly if they planned to make friends.

Bridget sat between Dominic and Lonnie, the community's blacksmith. Lonnie looked like the oldest among the bachelors. He had a long, wide nose and pointed chin. His large hands and forearms were roped with muscles from swinging a hammer all day long. Despite his disproportionate features, he had a kind smile and quick wit that drew Bridget in. He was shy at first but opened up with some encouragement from Dominic and shared stories that made Bridget laugh out loud.

After dinner she wove through the crowd to Candace where the young girl was sweeping crumbs from under the table. The two younger children dragged the chairs across the floor to where the men stacked them along the wall. The noise and half a dozen lively conversations forced Bridget to raise her voice to get Candace's attention. "Hello, Candace, I'm Bridget Reidy. I'm sorry we didn't get to talk during dinner."

One corner of the girl's mouth quirked into a shy smile as she continued to sweep. Bridget immediately recognized a kindred spirit in the girl. One who felt overlooked by the world, but a possessing a keen mind and unending curiosity.

"It's all right. Everyone wants to meet you. We don't see many new faces."

Bridget grabbed another broom from against the wall and stepped into line with her. "I sure get lonesome for the sounds of the city, especially at night. My church congregation back home had over three hundred members. My mother and I belonged to several clubs and civic groups that kept us busy all over the city. This is very different."

"I bet your mother misses you."

Bridget sighed. "She passed away in December. My father died a few months before her."

Candace stopped sweeping. "You don't have any family?"

Bridget touched her tongue to the corner of her mouth. "Not really. That's why I came here. I thought it was time I start a new life. Something of my own. I miss my home in Cincinnati, but I like it here too. Everyone I've met is so kind. Especially Marla. She tells such interesting stories."

Candace chuckled. "I think so too. She's teaching me to knit. I'm not very good yet, but…"

"Knitting takes a while to master. I'm sure you'll get the hang of it in no time. I brought some yarn with me. I can give you a few skeins to practice with if your mother doesn't mind."

Candace gasped. "Really? Oh, no, Mama won't mind. Thank you, Miss Reidy. We have a lot of chores at home, but in the evenings, there isn't much for me to do after dinner besides minding my brother and sister." She leaned on the broom and turned her face to watch the younger children. "I miss my friends."

She looked at Bridget from under a heavy fringe of blond bangs. "I hated school. Sometimes, my friends and I got into trouble. Well, I guess we got in trouble a lot. But now I miss it. I even miss my teachers, though they got to where they didn't like me much. Mama tries to keep us up on our studies, but mostly the only thing she has time for is helping Annie with her letters and J.T. with his multiplication tables. I already know all that."

"Candace, if you like to read, I brought some books with me. History and art, but some stories too. I can lend you a few books if you think you would enjoy reading them."

Candace nearly dropped the broom. "Oh, thank you, Miss Reidy. That would be wonderful. I haven't had anything to read since we left Cincinnati except for the Bible." Her face flushed. "Not that I don't like reading the Bible."

Bridget smiled. "It's all right. I understand. The Bible is full of romance and adventure, but there's nothing wrong with reading stories told through the eyes of young girls with big dreams."

Candace's eyes grew large as if Bridget had been reading her mind.

"The biggest part of my collection is still in Good Hope, but I have a few books with me. Come over whenever you have time. I'm sure you'll find something of interest."

Candace blushed red. "Oh, Miss Reidy, I can't wait to tell Ma. She and I can even read together. She likes stories too."

The rest of the afternoon Bridget visited with and got to know more of her new neighbors. She didn't get a chance to speak privately to Dominic until he walked her back to the brides' house. The afternoon was nearly spent. They only had a few minutes to chat outside since it would be inappropriate for him to go into the brides' house without a chaperone. As Bridget watched him walk back across the street to his horse, she marveled at how much at home she felt in Cowboy Creek. Like she mattered to someone for the first time since Mother died.

A smile on her lips, she went inside to find a book that might appeal to Candace Whitamore.

Chapter Seven

Bridget didn't see Dominic for the next few days. She knew he was busy with work on his farm now that the rain had moved on, but she felt a little left out. After they married, he would have just as much work to do, and he wouldn't have time for sitting and keeping her company like he had the first week. She would be busy as well with the work of a frontier wife.

Once the babies came, oh, she'd have so much to do. She was accustomed to staying busy from daylight until dark, just not the kind of work required here. She tried to ignore her loneliness by writing in her journals, Bible study, and helping Marla. One warm, sunny afternoon Candace arrived to get a book. Bridget already had three set aside she hoped the girl would like. They had an enjoyable afternoon, talking about books and school and all the things they missed from the city.

Candace invited her to lunch the next day at their house next to the gristmill.

At breakfast the next day Marla assured her she needn't worry about checking with Carrie to make sure the invitation wasn't a burden. Out here the social dictates of the city seldom kept residents from doing whatever they wanted when time allowed. Only the weather did that. If Candace had invited her, she would be accepted by everyone.

Bridget slid the kettle over the hot plate to warm dishwater for the breakfast dishes. She saw movement out of the corner of her eye at the same time Marla did. "Well, look who's here so early in the morning," Marla said. "I don't expect you'll be going to the Whitamores' for lunch after all."

Bridget couldn't suppress the smile on her face. "You'll excuse me, won't you, Marla? I'll be right back to finish these dishes."

Marla was already shooing her out the door. "Don't you think a thing about it. These dishes are nothing I haven't handled for fifty years. You go see what your young man has planned."

Bridget couldn't get over what the sight of Dominic did to her. She stopped in the threshold and adjusted her light shawl around her shoulders. What she really needed was a moment to catch her breath and get hold of herself.

Dominic raised his fist to knock just as she pulled the door open. He looked as unsettled as she felt, but she was sure with his good looks, he'd had plenty of attention from women over the years.

He tipped his hat. "Good morning, Miss Reidy."

Bridget pressed her lips together to hold in a very childish giggle. "Mr. DeSantis."

He removed his hat and held it with both hands. "I don't reckon you've got time to ride over to Good Hope to collect your trunks this morning?"

Bridget gasped aloud. She grabbed hold of his arm, then released it immediately, embarrassed. "Oh, Dominic, do you mean it?"

"Sure do. The ground's good and dry. The wagon's waiting around front with two pulling horses. I have a few errands in town, and I thought you might want to get a few things too. For the wedding."

She blushed furiously. Neither of them had mentioned the wedding since his proposal last week. Sometimes she feared he'd forgotten that he asked. "I have thought of a few things I'd like to get."

"All right then. I'm ready if you are unless you have something else planned today."

Bridget loved the teasing gleam in his obsidian eyes. "I need to get my reticule. And another wrap in case it rains." She took a step toward the street but stopped mid-stride. "I should tell Marla we're going and ask if she needs anything while we're in town."

The smile on Dominic's lips warmed her to her toes. "I'll pop my head in and speak to Marla. You go ahead and get your things together. It's a long ride there and back."

Bridget smiled appreciatively and hurried around the barn, fighting back excitement that made her want to squeal like a schoolgirl. She was getting her books! And spending the day with Dominic!

A few minutes later she was seated on the narrow wagon seat next to Dominic. The folded blanket under her provided little cushioning, but she barely noticed the discomfort.

Low spots in the road were still clogged with patches of mud, and limbs from trees littered the sides of the road. Twice, Dominic had to get out and move branches. Bridget held her breath every time the horses paused to throw their weight into a pull. She prayed they would get there safely, and back home again with the added weight of the trunks.

"I've been thinking about our wedding," Dominic said when they reached a high part in the road and the horses didn't have to struggle to move forward.

"You have?"

"Why sure. That's about all I've been thinking of. Haven't you?"

She started to answer until she recognized the teasing gleam in his eyes.

"Do you think you'd be ready by the end of the month. June usually gives us nice weather with only the occasional afternoon storm. We can have a ceremony at the church on the last Friday. We'll invite everyone in the community. Friday should work well for everyone. Then we could spend a few days alone together that weekend."

He glanced at her mouth. Bridget looked away, knowing what he was thinking. The same thing had crossed her mind more than once. Oh, how she wished she could talk to her mother. Her only experience with marriage came from watching her parents. They seemed to have it all figured out. Did they know something other people didn't? Or had they started out like her—confused, overwhelmed, and a little terrified?

"Do you need to buy a dress or anything for the ceremony? I thought I might get a new shirt."

He was so thoughtful. "I don't need anything. I already have more dresses than I know what to do with."

"If you're sure."

"Very sure. I brought too many things with me." She tipped her head apologetically. Now would be a good time to tell him about the shipment she expected. It would arrive in a few weeks, probably about the same time they married. She didn't want to spoil their day together, though, by starting him worrying about what to do with everything. She'd tell him on the way home.

When they reached Good Hope, Dominic led her through some of the shops. There weren't many so it didn't take long to see the entire town. Bridget helped him pick out a peacock blue shirt that went beautifully with his dark eyes and hair. He laughed and said it was the first shirt he ever bought because of the color of his eyes. Bridget resisted the urge to buy fabric and notions for a new dress. She didn't need one, and she had no place to store it if she did. The brides' house was already crowded, and about to become a lot more so once the rest of her furnishings arrived.

She bought a couple skeins of yarn for Candace and sets of jacks for the younger children. She had the clerk bag up candy for all of them. All children liked candy, even twelve-year-old girls who thought they were grown up. She tucked everything into her bag before Dominic could see and insist on paying for it.

They ate their noon meal at the only restaurant in town. Though Good Hope was small and didn't offer many options for shopping or socializing, the experience helped salve Bridget's homesickness.

After the waitress cleared away their plates and went to get them a slice of pie, she looked across the table at Dominic—her future husband. She still nearly needed to pinch herself to believe she was getting married in a couple of weeks.

"I thought it would be nice to throw a dinner for our guests after our wedding. I know everyone brings food to share on Sundays, but I'd like to do something special. What do you think? While we're here, I want to buy some extra sugar, lard, flour, and vanilla to make some cakes and frosting. A couple of hams would go a long way in feeding everyone."

He nodded thoughtfully. "I'll have Sawyer Jamison set aside a few nice-sized hams and pay him the next time I see him."

"Oh, no, this was my idea. I want to pay for everything."

His gaze darkened. "I can't let you pay for food for our neighbors. I'm the man. It's my responsibility."

"Not traditionally. This will be our wedding ceremony. Back home, it's customary for the bride's family to pay for the wedding. I have the money my parents left me. If they were here, they would insist on paying for whatever I wanted. I want to take care of it."

He stiffened in his chair. The waitress appeared with two slices of rhubarb pie. Dominic waited until she set them down and moved away before looking back at Bridget. His mouth was set in a hard line. "I have money, too, and you'll be my wife. I will pay for anything you need. If your father were here, he and I would discuss the matter. But he isn't, so the wedding and everything associated with it are my responsibility."

What he wasn't saying was that *she* was his responsibility. Bridget knew that's how marriage worked. The wife was the responsibility of the husband. Even the Bible said the man was the head of the woman, and the husband was to love his wife as Christ loved the Church. But if she couldn't spend her money on what she wanted, what was the point of having it? Mother and Father had wanted her to be taken care of. It was why they left her the money. Now that she was marrying, did that mean she turned over all rights and decisions concerning her inheritance to her husband? That put her in the same position she'd been with Charles.

Is that what Mother and Father intended?

Oh, she wished they were here. They would know how to handle the situation without offending Dominic.

Mother and Father weren't here. She had no one to discuss it with but her future husband. If he had money—and maybe he did—she would consider it hers. Whatever wealth and possessions she had would belong to him as well once they married. Maybe that was the answer to her question. Either way, she planned to honor and respect him as the Bible dictated. The same as Mother respected Father.

Now to make him understand the prickly situation.

"My parents never thought I would marry." She glanced at the untouched pie. "Neither did I. They wanted to ensure I never had to worry about money. My brother Charles made poor financial decisions. He kept getting into fixes, and then coming to Mother and Father to bail him out.

"I shouldn't speak ill of my brother. But since we're about to be wed, I want you to understand why Mother and Father were concerned he would squander any money they left him. A few years ago, he made a particularly poor financial decision. My parents decided it was the last straw. They feared Charles would never grow up and act responsibly as long as he had them to bail him out. They made the very hard decision to cut him off financially."

She looked earnestly at Dominic. "It was the hardest thing they ever did. They discussed the matter with me. They wanted me to know what was happening since it affected me too. Charles and Ellen were very angry. They stopped visiting. It broke Mother and Father's hearts. They believed they had done the right thing to force Charles to stand on his own two feet. Over time, Charles and Ellen came around, but it was never the same between them. Or with me. I always suspected they believed I turned Mother and Father against them. Which I didn't! More than likely, they resented that the bulk of the inheritance had been left to me.

"Father and Mother didn't completely forget Charles. They gave him and his wife a small award and put money into an account under their attorney's control for their three children for when they come of age. Mother and Father weren't rich by any means, but the estate was enough to provide for me as long as I lived. It's why Charles and Ellen wanted me to move in with them after Mother's passing. It wasn't me they wanted; it was control of my finances."

Bridget shook her head. "I couldn't let that happen. If Charles had control of my money, it would be gone within five years. I wanted to do what Mother and Father wanted. It's why I came here. Charles and Ellen would never have respected me. I never would've had my own life living with them."

She steeled herself. Talking about the money and inheritance was hard enough. Now she needed to tell him about the furniture coming. "That's part of the reason the books mean so much to me. They brought such joy and pleasure to my parents. They didn't mean anything to Charles and his family. Charles was more interested in impressing people around town. He had no patience for sitting in the parlor discussing philosophy or art or the Bible. He found it tiresome. When I asked if he wanted any of the books I couldn't bring with me, he said I could burn them for all he cared."

Tears filled her eyes. "It would've broken Mother's heart if she heard him say that. It wasn't the books so much as what they represented. It was as though Charles didn't care anything about Mother and Father, and losing them was no more of a heartache than losing a shelf full of books."

Dominic reached for her hand.

"I'm sorry you had to leave a single one of them behind."

Tears stung her eyes. "I know they're only books, and nothing can take away my memories of Mother and Father, but they'll always mean so much to me. When I hold them in my hands, it's like I'm touching Mother and Father again."

"We'll find a place to store them until I can build you a proper bookcase. I'll do my best to make sure you don't lose a one of them."

She started to tell him she already had a fine oak bookcase, and it was on its way. What she needed was a place for the bookcase. There was no way it would fit in Dominic's small cabin with its low ceiling.

"So, you don't mind if I buy the food for our wedding dinner? It'll be like a gift from Father and Mother. A gift they would give us if they were here."

She held her breath as he considered it. "I don't mind," he said finally. "I believe you're right and it's what they would want."

"Oh, thank you, Dominic. I...I wish my parents could've met you."

As soon as the words were out of her mouth, she realized if Father and Mother were alive, she wouldn't have left Cincinnati to become a stranger's wife. She loved Mother and Father deeply and missed them, but she anticipated her new life nearly as much.

He signaled for the waitress who brought the check. He paid the woman and pushed out his chair.

The stationmaster was busy when they reached the livery, so they went straight to where the books were stored without bothering him. Bridget held her breath as Dominic slid the first trunk out of the cubby. The trunk showed no sign of water damage, but she knew dampness could seep inside and ruin the books. She unlocked the latch with the key around her neck and eased back the lid. She opened the first book on the stack. She smiled up at Dominic in relief. No damage. She dug into the truck a few rows down and grabbed another volume of renderings of paintings and sculptures from around the world.

She opened the book and turned it around so Dominic could see the colorful pages. "Isn't it beautiful! This was one of Mother's favorites."

She clasped the heavy volume to her chest as tears stung her eyes. "If all the other books were lost, this is the one that meant the most to me besides the family Bible, which I already have with me in Cowboy Creek."

She placed the book carefully into the trunk and closed the lid. She stood and brushed her hands together. "We'll need to find someone to help you load the trunks.

"Miss Reidy. Dom," the stationmaster said from behind them.

They turned to face the stooped man. "Dale," Dominic returned.

The stationmaster nodded at him before turning his attention to Bridget. "A shipment arrived for you yesterday from Cincinnati."

She felt the blood drain from her face. "A shipment? Already?"

"Yes, and I sure am glad you came when you did. Your stuff took up an entire storeroom. I don't have room to store it here."

Dominic's eyes slid from the man to Bridget. "What shipment?"

Dale didn't look away from Bridget. "It's not everything from what I gather. You can go through what came and check it against the invoice to see what hasn't arrived yet."

Dominic stiffened beside her. "There's more coming? What is it? More books?"

"Well, no. Not exactly," Bridget said.

Dale headed into the depths of the building. They fell into step behind him.

Bridget hoped to have this conversation on the way home today. She sure didn't want Dominic to find out like this.

"There's Father's desk. Not the one from his office. The smaller one he kept at home. It was built by a premier furniture maker in Cincinnati, specifically from Father's design. I used to tuck myself in the cavern at Father's feet and play while he worked. There are a few other pieces of furniture that hold great sentimental value. I'm sorry I didn't tell you, Dominic. It's only a few pieces. I sold nearly everything else. Charles was only interested in the more valuable pieces and artwork."

The stationmaster rounded a corner and took a ring of keys from his vest pocket to unlock a closed door. He pushed it open and stepped back. Bridget winced. Dominic's eyes bulged. The room was packed. There was barely room to move around.

"Which pieces are yours?"

Bridget gulped. "All of it."

His eyes narrowed.

"Everything looks so much bigger than it did back home," she said.

"And there's more on the way," Dale reminded them.

Bridget wanted to tell him he wasn't helping. She thought of Dominic's small two-room cabin and knew the contents of the storeroom would never fit. Not even if he built two more cabins.

Chapter Eight

Dominic whirled around to face Bridget. "What do you suggest we do with all this?" Bridget flinched. Dominic immediately regretted his outburst. He hadn't meant to scare her. Or to lose his temper in front of Dale. He didn't want to lose his temper at all, but this was too much. What in the world was he going to do with a storeroom full of fancy furniture and paintings? Some of it didn't look like it'd survive the rough trip home.

He lowered his voice. "I'm sorry, Bridget, but there's no way we can tote all this to Cowboy Creek."

She looked close to tears. He hated to disappoint her, but what had she been thinking, paying freighters good money to haul all this junk here? Two trunks of books had been bad enough but this was insane.

"It's a fine collection of furniture," Dale said. "I can find buyers by the time you leave town today." He ran his hand down the side of a buffet cabinet. "For a small commission, of course, but it'll bring a pretty penny."

"No!" Bridget shrieked. She looked like she wanted to slap his grimy hand off the polished wood. "My grandfather built this cabinet himself and gave it to Mother and Father as a wedding gift."

She cast desperate eyes at Dominic. "I couldn't leave it. I tried. God help me, I did. But I couldn't leave any of it. Charles would've sold it like a bunch of castoffs. Sold Mother and Father's life. I know it's too much. I know it's impractical, but—but I didn't know what else to do."

The stationmaster held up his hands in surrender. He arched his eyebrows at Dominic as if to say, *'You know how women are.'*, turned, and walked away. Dominic ran his hand over his face. No, he didn't know how women were. Not really. Ma never disagreed with Pa—not in front of the children, anyway—and the situation of what to do with expensive furnishings never came up.

He couldn't break her heart. He couldn't ask her to sell what meant so much to her. She had left her home and life behind. Though it filled the storeroom, it wasn't too much of that life. But they had to be realistic. The furniture wouldn't fit in his cabin or the barn or sheds, and they sure couldn't leave it out in the rain.

"I don't know what we can do with everything. There's no room in the wagon, even if every piece fit in my cabin once we got it there."

"I know. I'm so sorry. I didn't think it would come this soon. They said it would take weeks and weeks. I thought by then I'd figure out what to do."

"Well, we can't leave it here either. They need this room for storage."

"I'll talk to the stationmaster. I'll pay whatever storage fees he requires until we're able to move it."

Dominic shook his head. "No. You're going to be my wife. Your debts are my responsibility. I'll work it out."

"No! This is my fault. It's my problem. I'm the one who should fix it. And I have the money."

He wasn't sure how he felt about that. He supposed she was right, but it grated against everything within him to think of his bride paying a debt on her own. As she talked at the restaurant about her family's inheritance, he had wanted to ask just how much money she was talking about. It must've been a substantial sum if it was enough to turn her brother against the family. He figured it was more than a plow and a goat and a little cabin, which was all his family ever owned. The only problem his family ever had with money was not having enough of it.

"Storing your things won't solve the problem of what to do with it once we take it home. And you have more coming?" He set his hand on an ornately trimmed china cabinet. "Where in the world will we put this? It looks like something you'd see in a museum, not in a cabin in Cowboy Creek."

She closed her eyes as if in pain. "I know. Believe it or not, it isn't much at all when you consider it filled a ten-room house."

Dominic was getting a little tired of hearing about her sumptuous life back in Cincinnati. "Well, I don't know what I'm supposed to do with it now. It sure won't fit in the wagon. It'll take a four-oxen team and fifteen trips to haul half of it."

She twisted her fingers around the straps of her reticule. "Maybe some of the other men can help."

"Or we can sell some of the bigger pieces. You heard Dale. He'll get you a good price."

Her jaw clenched. "I don't care about the money. I already sold or gave away every stick of furniture I could bear to part with. This is all I have left of Mother and Father."

Each word brought her closer to tears.

Dominic gritted his teeth. What kind of delusional, spoiled princess would part with good money to haul this junk halfway across the country? Had she actually thought she was moving into another extravagant ten-room house like the one she left? He already knew he wasn't smart enough for her. Now he found he was too poor and small for her too. How would she ever be satisfied with a simple man like him in a plain, little cabin in the middle of nowhere?

Maybe this whole thing was a mistake. She loved books and art and philosophy, and he could barely write his name. Cowboy Creek didn't have the cultured things she was used to. She would grow to hate it and eventually hate him. She'd resent him for forcing her into this life. They needed to face facts before it was too late.

As soon as the thought crossed his mind, he knew it was already too late. He couldn't send her back. He cared for her. He might even love her, if that were possible to fall in love with a woman after only a few weeks of knowing her. He looked at the genuine pain in her bottomless brown eyes and knew he'd do whatever it took to make her happy, even if he had to haul that monstrous cabinet to Cowboy Creek on his back.

He stroked his chin as he looked around the storeroom. "The only place to store everything—if we can get it to Cowboy Creek—is the barn and the trading post with Preach and Marla, and it isn't fair to ask them to make room."

Bridget stuck her tongue out of the corner of her mouth in thought. After a moment her eyes lit up. "What about one of the empty buildings in town? I saw one right next to the meetinghouse. No one is doing anything with it."

"No one but the possums and raccoons and snakes." She grimaced.

"I suppose we could make it work," he said quickly. "I'll have to patch a few holes in the roof and board over the broken windows first so nothing gets wet until we figure out how to fit your most prized possessions in the cabin."

He shook his head at the enormity of the situation. "I'll ask Rase and some of the other men if they'll help me get everything there whenever they have a spare day. Everyone's so busy this time of year. I reckon we'll figure something out."

Her eyes lit up. "Oh, Dominic, do you mean it?" She threw herself into his arms.

The breath rushed out of him. Not from the impact of her body but from the feel of her slender body against his. He wrapped his arms around her and held her close, marveling at the way she fit in his arms.

Too soon, she pulled away. Her eyes were bright and warm. The color in her cheeks softened the sharp angles, making her look soft and feminine. And desirable. Her lips parted slightly. Dominic wondered what it would feel like to kiss her. What would she think if he did? They were due to marry. It wasn't improper. But he didn't have the nerve. Not yet.

She pulled back, seemingly unaware of how much he wanted to kiss that mouth. Or maybe because she was aware. "Thank you, Dominic. It means so much that you're willing to do this for me."

"I'll check with the Dale to see what he'll charge me to store everything a few more days. Or weeks, if that's what it takes."

She squared her slim shoulders. "You mean what he'll charge *me*. This is my debt. *My* problem."

He squared his shoulders right back. "No, Bridget, it's my problem. *Our* problem. Now that we're getting married, I expect us to face every problem together. It worked for my parents as I'm sure it worked for yours."

"You're right, of course. Father was the head of the household, but they made every decision together. Mother wasn't shy about speaking her mind. And making her own decisions about money."

His jaw twitched. Money again. He'd never given the subject much thought before when he didn't have any, but apparently it would factor in a lot with Bridget. "I guess my folks never had enough money to make decisions about it other than how to keep us little 'uns fed."

She took a small step toward him. "I'm sorry, Dominic. That's not what I meant. I just mean these things here. You had no say in me bringing so much with me, and I'm sorry for that. Now that it's here, it's only right that I figure out what to do with it until we can make permanent arrangements. Together."

He nodded. "I'll go find the man and see what we can work out."

She smiled sweetly. His foolish insides melted like butter. "Do you think I could take a few things with me today that will fit in the wagon? Maybe these chairs and that small table. They should fit in the cabin without any trouble."

Dominic thought of the hard bench seats and rough table in the cabin. Hers would make a nice replacement. Taking his silence as assent, Bridget went to a heavy highboy and pulled open a drawer. "The bedclothes are in here. Quilts and pillowcases Mother and I made together. I have a few tapestries in here somewhere. And rugs and curtains. They won't take up any space in the cabin once I hang them or put them on the floors."

She pulled out a heavy set of curtains and draped them over her arm for him to see.

"Curtains and rugs sound nice, and tapestries too— whatever those are. They'll brighten up the place and help you feel at home."

"Oh, they will, and they won't take up any space in the wagon."

She paused a moment before stepping into his arms. This time he was ready. He breathed in the scent of her. He did care for her. He wanted her in his life, but what if he disappointed her? He could never offer her a life like the one she couldn't let go of.

"I want you to be happy, Bridget. My cabin will be your home, and I want you to make your mark on it. I don't want you to think you have to give up your life with your parents. But this isn't Cincinnati. Everything is different here. We have to be realistic."

He wiggled the lock on a small trunk. "I suppose I could wrangle this into the back of the wagon if it's something you can't live without."

She nodded eagerly. "It's pots and pans. I'll put them to use straightaway."

He looked at her. His expression sobered. He imagined a life with this woman on the edge of the mountains, and for a moment saw their future together.

"You probably have some dresses and shoes and other things you'd like to take with us today, too."

She laughed out loud and clasped her hands in excitement. "I won't take much, I promise."

Chapter Nine

Bridget looked around the tiny cabin. At home the kitchen had been lined with tall windows that offered breezes in the summer and views of the hills in the distance all year long. Here, she could practically lie flat on the floor and touch the table with her toes and the fireplace on the opposite wall with her fingertips. And there was no view outside the window. All she saw through the small two-foot-square pane was muddy fields drenched with rain.

But this would be her home in a few weeks. She needed to banish her complaining spirit and accept this new life. A life she wanted very much.

Yesterday at the livery, she was sure Dominic meant to kiss her. She could almost feel his breath on her skin. His hand on her cheek. His lips on hers. She'd never been kissed. No man had even looked at her like he was thinking of kissing her. Dominic's body had tensed, and

Bridget hoped he would pull her against his hard body and capture her mouth with his. Both times they embraced she had initiated the contact. It had been thrilling and left her wanting more. Left her wondering about the mysteries shared between men and women that she had never dwelled on before because those things didn't happen to women like her. Plain women, too smart for their own good. Women who didn't know how to talk about anything but books and art.

Dominic would have to kiss her on their wedding day and surely many times after that. If he didn't kiss her often enough, was it acceptable for her to kiss *him*? Her pulse raced. What was she doing thinking such scandalous thoughts? Women didn't go around kissing *men*. Not decent women raised by God-fearing parents.

Did they? Oh, she wished she knew. She should've asked Mother when she had the chance. If she had, Mother would've been too shocked to answer. She might've washed Bridget's mouth out with soap. Or she may have admitted she kissed Father all the time when no one was around.

Bridget laughed out loud as she stepped down from the stool Dominic had fashioned to make it easier for her to hang curtains. When they got back from Good Hope, he cut some dowel rods to length to hang curtains and fashioned wooden pegs he hammered into place above the windows. Bridget had brought hooks and ties with her but hadn't thought of rods. In her naivety, it hadn't occurred to her that every window ever hung didn't come equipped with curtain rods.

All morning while Dominic went about his chores and she hung her things around his cabin, she tried to think of a tactful way to ask him to let her use her money to build another room onto the cabin. A room facing east. How she enjoyed watching the sun rise in the morning with all its promises of a new day. She could set up Father's desk and line one wall with bookshelves. She could put a beautiful rug on the floor and sit in Mother's chair as she read stories to their children.

Children, she thought dreamily.

She looked around the tiny cabin with its rough walls and two small windows. Could she raise children in this cramped space when there was barely enough room for her and Dominic inside at the same time? Children wouldn't come all at once, of course. She supposed all families went through similar growing pains. They built on as the need arose. Soon she would have a large cabin with a long kitchen and long table to fit as many children as the Lord gave.

She lifted the lid from the pot on the stove and stirred the stew inside. A sigh escaped her lips. She had seen yesterday when she had to convince Dominic to let her pay the stationmaster to store her furniture that he didn't like using her money for anything—even settling her own debts. She couldn't suggest she pay to have improvements done to the cabin. At least not right away.

Patience. That's what she needed to ask for in her prayers.

She'd never had trouble with patience before. Maybe because she'd always gotten what she wanted when she wanted it. There were no shops or businesses to immediately fill her needs, and she would have her husband's pride to consider in the matter. Naturally Dominic would want to provide for her instead of her providing for herself from her parents' wealth.

She replaced the lid on the pot and went back to cleaning. It didn't take long since there was so little to do. The bed in the tiny bedroom filled up nearly the entire space. If she moved it against the wall, there might be enough space for her wardrobe. Dominic would have to move the nightstand next to the bed. On top of it was a folded handkerchief, a pocket watch, and a folding knife. She sat on the edge of the bed and picked up the handkerchief. Inside was something hard. She unfolded it and found a tiny tintype of a severe looking dark-haired couple. Dominic's parents. She spotted the resemblance right away. She ran her thumb over their faces and wished she could tell them she was marrying their son. She was sure they'd be happy.

She opened the narrow drawer to put the things away. She gasped in delight at the sight of her letters. She pulled them out of the envelopes, feeling like an interloper even though she was the one who had written them. A smile played across her lips as she scanned the familiar words.

From the wear of the pages, she could tell they'd been folded and refolded dozens of times. He must've read them over and over. She folded them carefully and slid them back into the envelopes. She carefully put them back the way she'd found them before going back to the stove to finish the stew.

"I now pronounce you man and wife. You may kiss the bride."

Bridget had been looking forward to this moment and dreading it at the same time. She didn't think of the crowded meetinghouse behind her. Of the chairs pushed together on one half of the room to make space for the tables laden with the wedding feast on the other side. She didn't think of Preach smiling at them. She focused only on Dominic, standing at the same height as she since she wore her best boots with a bit more heel than usual. He looked nearly as nervous as she felt. Tentatively, he put his arms around her and drew her close. The kiss was soft and brief, barely a whisper against her lips but enough to set her heart to pounding in her chest.

The entire wedding had been a blur. She could scarcely imagine it was happening to her. She almost wished Charles and Ellen were here. Despite the differences between them, they were her only family, and she wished they could share this moment in her life. They would find a way to spoil her happiness, though. To make her doubt she had done the right thing. She wouldn't think on them today. She wouldn't think on anything outside her control.

After the kiss, the women and three children surrounded her, hugging and kissing her and welcoming her to the community. She'd been here for four weeks, but now it was official. The men slapped Dominic on the back and wished the couple well before turning their attention to the food.

"Congratulations, Miss Reidy. I guess I'll have to call you Mrs. DeSantis now."

Bridget looked down at Candace, bright eyed and smiling. "Mrs. DeSantis," Bridget echoed. She leaned in close to the girl and whispered. "I don't know how long it will take me to get used to it."

Candace grinned as if they were co-conspirators.

"I hope you'll come visit me soon at the cabin. I know it's a fair walk, but I can let you borrow more books."

"Mama says you won't have time for that anymore."

"Nonsense. I'll have plenty of time for visiting with you, Candace. As long as your mother doesn't mind you venturing out from town."

"She won't mind. Thank you, Mrs. DeSantis."

Bridget kissed the girl's cheek before she rushed away to help with the food. Bridget thanked the rest of the women and exchanged a few words with each before taking her place next to Dominic at the head of the table. The moment was bittersweet. The only thing to mar her happiness was the absence of Mother and Father. They wouldn't want her to spend the day missing them. They would want her to focus on her husband and the blessings God had given her.

Bridget brought the ax down as hard as she could. It banged benignly against the chunk of wood. A sliver of bark landed at her feet.

She growled in frustration. Over the last week, she learned even the simplest task took her three times as long as the average person. Dominic cut and split all the wood for the cookstove. All she had to do was keep the kindling box filled. Gathering the scraps of wood left from his splitting was usually enough. But in the mornings when she needed to get the fire going to fix breakfast, she needed a few substantial chunks. At this rate, she would never have breakfast ready by the time Dominic came in from the barn. At least it wasn't cold out. She hoped by wintertime when the cabin needed a roaring fire all day long, she'd be better at swinging the ax.

No amount of hacking away at the pieces of wood would produce the results she needed, so she leaned the ax against a log and filled her bucket with chips of bark and splinters. Hopefully they would create enough heat to fry the eggs she'd gathered this morning.

Despite her frustration and lack of skills at the simplest chores, she couldn't keep a smile off her face. While wood splitting hadn't gotten any easier than her first attempt, she loved being Dominic's wife.

She carried her half-filled bucket back to the cabin. It wasn't only the wood splitting that put her behind schedule. There was so much to do from the moment Dominic rolled over to her, kissed her soundly, and slid out of bed, until she heard the thud of his boots on the porch at the end of the day. It didn't help that she continually got distracted from the endless chores.

Before the wedding, he had fashioned a bookcase out of scraps of lumber and she filled it with her favorite books from the trunk, which now sat in the corner of the room. Though she tried to ignore their siren song, every time she had a spare moment, she slid a book off the shelf.

"Just a paragraph or two while the water heats," she'd tell herself. The next thing she knew, she'd smell something burning or notice the patch of sunshine had moved across the floor, and she had forgotten what she'd been in the middle of before the book found itself in her hands.

Several times she tried to interest Dominic in reading with her after breakfast or before bed, but he either said he was in a hurry or too tired. Apparently, he wasn't much of a reader. The only book he owned was a worn, cracked Bible. She hadn't found any pencils or writing paper around the cabin either. She hoped once they settled into a routine, they'd find more time for her to share her favorite pastime with him.

She dumped the pail of wood shavings into the kindling box and slid the skillet onto a hot stove plate. She had just poured the corncake batter into the skillet when she heard Dominic's footfalls outside. The sound released a firestorm of butterflies in her stomach.

"Morning, wife," he called as he threw open the door.

"Morning, husband," she said back. Her heart warmed at the daily ritual. She had grown up seeing how a strong, mutually committed marriage was meant to work. With Dominic, it was even more amazing and rewarding than what she witnessed between her parents. She hoped like her parents' union, it would only get stronger and better with time.

He came to the stove, set his hands on her hips, and leaned around to kiss her cheek. Bridget leaned into him for a brief instant as she stirred the potatoes before he moved to the washbasin to clean up.

"I hope to find some time tomorrow to ride into Cowboy Creek and check out that little building next to the meetinghouse. I should be able to scrounge up enough lumber to patch any holes in the roof and walls. It'll just be a matter of time before the other men and I can make a trip to pick up your furniture."

She left the stove and threw her arms around him. "Oh, Dominic, really? I'm so happy. Hopefully everything else will have arrived by then."

He hugged her back, but she didn't miss the tightening around his mouth. "Yes, the rest of it. It's not too much, I hope."

"I don't think so. Most everything was already there, except for Father's desk and Mother's quilting loom and maybe a few more trunks I've forgotten about."

He glanced away. "We'll work it out. I've been pondering on where to set another cabin."

"Another cabin? You mean for us? I never meant for you to—"

He cut her off. "This one's always been too small, even for me. I built it right where the last one sat, but there's a spot on the grade above the barn I always thought would be a nice place for a house. Maybe a two-story with front and back porches. Now that you're here, there's no point in putting it off. I thought I'd break ground once the planting's done."

She wanted to tell him she had enough money to buy whatever materials he needed. She could hire a crew of carpenters from Good Hope and the surrounding area to complete the project by winter. She quickly decided to keep those ideas to herself. She wouldn't offend him when he was being so thoughtful.

Instead, she tightened her arms around his neck. "You're too good to me."

He laughed as he pulled her closer and nuzzled his nose into her neck. "With everything you brought, I won't have to worry about furnishing a house, no matter how big we build it."

She laughed and snuggled against him. His mouth found hers. Only the smell of burning potatoes broke them apart.

Chapter Ten

The tiny, rough cabin looked more like a home every day, but after Dominic put the idea of a proper house in Bridget's head, she couldn't think of much else. She knew without asking that he would not want her to contribute any of her inheritance to building the house faster with ready-made materials. Men were so sensitive about such matters. She hoped after he got used to the idea of the money, he wouldn't feel so insecure about letting her spend it to make their lives better, faster. She didn't want her inheritance to be a stumbling block between them. Nor did she believe Mother and Father left it to her to sit around in a bank doing nothing.

With talk of money and a new house set aside for now, the next few days slid by while Bridget acclimated to her role as wife. The hardest part were the empty hours when Dominic was out of the house. There was plenty of work to occupy her time. She just wasn't used to doing it in complete isolation. By the time she finished weeding the beans, carrots, and potatoes in the kitchen garden outside, the sun had slid past the point in the sky where she knew it was time to start supper. She washed her hands at the outdoor pump and hurried inside, chastising herself aloud for letting the day get away from her. Again.

No matter how hard she tried to focus, she was always running behind. Yesterday she had taken a walk up the hill to where Dominic planned to build their new house. She walked the perimeter of the imagined house before she finally sat down under a tree and fell asleep. The day before that, while creating a pattern for slipcovers for the kitchen chairs, she had burned their dinner.

She wouldn't let it happen today. Her husband worked hard. He deserved a wife who worked just as hard. She knew when she came here her life would be a world different than the relative comfort she left behind. She was eager to keep a neat cabin and provide a hot, delicious supper for both of them at the end of each day.

She went to the sink and poured hot water over the dishes from the noon meal. She should've washed them right away after Dominic had gone back outside, but she needed to weed the garden she should've done yesterday. She cut a chunk of bacon and dropped it into the kettle of beans to simmer while she washed the dishes.

A soft knock sounded at the door. She shook the water off her hands and dried them on the towel over her apron sash as she crossed the room.

Candace stood at the door, holding a quart jar against her chest. The girl smiled shyly up at her.

Bridget's heart burst with joy at the sight of another human face. "Candace! How lovely to see you."

"Mama and I made pumpkin butter yesterday from the pumpkin Papa canned last fall before we moved here. I've never done pumpkin butter before. It turned out pretty good. I wanted to bring you some."

Bridget smiled, warmed by the girl's thoughtfulness. "Thank you so much. Please come in."

The girl stepped over the threshold and looked around the room. Her eyes stopped at the bookshelf, bulging with the books from the two trunks.

Bridget followed her gaze. "I ran out of space before I ran out of books. But I found a few..." She went to the shelf and pulled off a volume. "I thought you might enjoy this one. It's called *Black Beauty*. Have you read it? It's a beautiful story. You can take it home if you like."

Candace's eyes widened. "Are you sure?" She smoothed her fingers over the etched cover. "I would hate to get it dirty."

Bridget laughed. "Nonsense. Books are made for reading, not sitting on a shelf. Please take it. And let me know what you think when you're finished.

"Oh, I will."

"Come sit at the table and we can chat. You're my first guest. I have biscuits left from lunch we can eat with some of this delicious looking pumpkin butter. Dominic will be thrilled to see it when he comes in for supper."

"Thank you, Miss—Mrs. DeSantis."

Bridget was happy for the company. Candace was just as eager to talk to her. In what seemed like no time at all, Bridget smelled the beans on the stove. She jumped up and peered down into the pot. She quickly added more water, hoping she hadn't scorched them. The water in the sink with the noon dishes had gone cold. She looked at the watch on her bodice. She grimaced. Nearly an hour had gone by. Dominic would be in for supper soon.

"I'm sorry, Candace, but I really must get to my chores. Your mother is probably wondering about you as well."

Candace stood. "Yes, I told her I'd only be gone a little while. Thank you for the book, Mrs. DeSantis."

"Anytime, dear. Don't forget to tell me what you think of it."

She nearly pushed the girl out the door. She added more wood to the stove for a fresh batch of biscuits. The cabin was already so stifling she hated to add more heat, but she and Candace had eaten most of the biscuits left over from lunch, so she had no choice. She opened the cabin door and went back to work. An open door was an invitation to flies, but she'd simply melt if she didn't get cross ventilation through the cabin. Back home, they had screens on the kitchen doors and windows. In the new house, she would make sure they installed screen doors, too, even if she had to send all the way to Cincinnati for them.

Just as she pulled the new biscuits from the oven, she heard Dominic's boots at the door. She dried the perspiration from her face on her apron and hung it over the back of a chair. The kitchen was tidy, the lunch dishes washed and put away, and fresh biscuits waited on top the stove. Except for a few scorched beans, he need never know she'd nearly let another afternoon get away from her.

He fanned his face with his hat. "You baked again?"

"Candace Whitamore brought us a jar of pumpkin butter. I thought that warranted fresh biscuits."

He combed his fingers through his hair, wet from cleaning up at the pump, as he pulled out a chair and dropped into it. "It's been a long day. Seems like everything that could go wrong did."

Bridget went to the table and covered his hand with hers. "I wish I could do more to help with the outside work."

He looked up hopefully. "It'd be great if you can help me tonight. After supper I want to plant more beans and tomatoes."

"More beans?" She thought of the blisters on her hands from hoeing around the plants already coming up.

"Now that the cold rains have passed, we have a small window to plant some late lima beans and a few others. Believe me, you'll be happy for the variety this winter. They're thirsty plants. If the summer's dry, they'll need watered every day. If you can take care of that work, it'll free up my time for bigger jobs."

"Like starting our house?"

He laughed and pulled her into his lap. "Like *thinking* about our house. We'll have to get through the summer season first. It's always busiest. Not only growing but canning and preserving. I was never able to do much of it myself, but with you here, I hope to have more to eat than beans and jerky all winter again."

She wrapped her arms around his neck. "You will. We'll build an empire. Together."

"Thank you, Bridget. I know this life is different for you, but the more we do together, the faster we'll be in the bigger house and the more time we'll have for other things." He arched his eyebrows playfully.

Bridget laughed, delighted by the light in his tired eyes. The work was hard, but she knew the rewards would be greater.

The next night Dominic worked two hours later than usual, and it was full dark by the time he came inside. After supper, Bridget ushered him to his chair and read a book by lamplight. When he looked ready to nod off, she closed the book and turned down the lamp. She looked forward to bedtime as much as Dominic did. Maybe more so, though she scarcely admitted it to herself. She wasn't sure it was proper for a woman to enjoy intimate times with her husband as much as she did. Maybe she appreciated them so much because she never thought she would be loved by a man. Or maybe the acts between husbands and wives were designed to be equally pleasurable to a woman and no one had let her in on the secret.

She spent her Friday morning adding more rows to the garden with a shovel. Like Dominic, she didn't want to spend a long winter eating nothing but beans and ham. The clock was ticking if she hoped to get squash and peppers into the ground. The garden was already huge. She hoped it wasn't more than she could take care of, especially if the summer turned dry. But it wasn't fair for Dominic to do all the hard work.

After the noon meal, she hurriedly washed the dishes and grabbed her gloves. She opened the door and stepped outside. Across the field she saw three children coming down the hill. She waved her gloves over her head in greeting. "Hello," she called out when they reached the barnyard.

"Hello, Mrs. DeSantis," they called back.

The younger children reached her first but didn't speak until Candace stopped in front of her. "You know my brother and sister, J.T. and Annie."

"Yes, of course. Hello, Annie. J.T. It's so nice to see you both."

"Thank you, Mrs. DeSantis," J.T. said. "Candace has been reading that book you sent over to us."

"Oh, how lovely. Are you enjoying it?"

"Yes, ma'am," Annie piped up. "We love it. Candace says you have more books. Lots of them. Do you think we could look at them?"

"Why, of course. Come inside."

Candace looked at Bridget's soiled dress and the turned earth behind her. "We didn't mean to interrupt you from your work. We just wanted to ask. We can come back another time."

Bridget glanced at the garden. Guilt pricked her. She wanted to finish her work before she started supper, but surely a few minutes with the children wouldn't put her that far behind. She was so lonely for company, and she was thrilled at the opportunity to share her love of literature with an eager young audience.

J.T. and Annie whooped and ran toward the house. Bridget laughed at the joy in their voices. She turned back to Candace. "You aren't keeping me from anything. It won't take long."

She was wrong. Nearly an hour passed before the children left. Bridget couldn't blame them. When she set them at the table and opened one of Mother's art books, they were immediately enraptured by the pictures. She laughed and talked and explained every picture that caught their eye, remembering the way Mother had done the same with her.

Candace gazed intently at a science book. She seemed to understand more of the concepts than Bridget thought possible for a girl her age. "I miss school more than I thought I would," she confessed, her cheeks coloring. "Not just because of my friends. I miss learning."

"Maybe you could come in the afternoons, and I could help you with some of the principals in this book. We could study your reading and arithmetic, and we could both help the younger children. If your ma doesn't mind."

"She won't care," J.T. said. "She's been trying to help Annie and me, but she's so busy, she doesn't have much time for it."

Bridget didn't really have time for it either. She was supposed to be working in the garden right now. If she managed her time better and got started earlier in the mornings, surely she could carve an hour or two out of her afternoons.

She didn't mind working in the garden and making a nice, comfortable home for Dominic, but the days sure were long and lonely, even with all the work to occupy her time. She missed hearing other people in the house. She missed her afternoon tea with Mother. She missed the stimulating political and societal conversations with Father. An hour or two with the children every afternoon would be an exciting break in her routine.

She closed the book she'd been reading to Annie and moved the child off her lap. "I think that's all for today. Your mother will wonder what's keeping you."

"Already?" J.T. protested.

"Can't we stay a little longer?" Annie asked.

"Mrs. DeSantis is right. We've taken enough of her time. Let's put these books away and get going."

"That's all right, Candace, I'll get them," Bridget said. "You children run along."

J.T. turned imploring eyes on her. "Can we come back tomorrow?"

"Can we take some books home with us?" Annie wanted to know.

Bridget's eyes widened.

"No," Candace said quickly. "These aren't storybooks. They'll be safer right here."

They said their goodbyes and headed out the door.

Bridget turned to the cold stove. The last two nights Dominic had worked late. Maybe he would tonight as well and never know she was late starting supper.

Outside, she heard J.T. call a greeting to Dominic. Her heart sank. She hurried to the stove and stoked the fire. She had let it go out after the noon meal to cool off the cabin. As the fire blazed to life, she lifted the lid over the roast venison from lunch. There was enough for a sandwich for Dominic. She would make do with some broth and bread for herself. She grabbed two potatoes and a knife and hacked off the eyes.

The door opened behind her. She painted a welcoming smile on her face. "Good evening, husband," she said when he didn't speak first.

He glanced at the table still crowded with open books. "I see you had company today."

"Candace has been reading *Black Beauty* to the younger children and they wanted to see what other books

I had. We had a nice afternoon looking through Mother's art books. You're home early today."

He advanced into the room and dropped into a kitchen chair. "I was going to show you some berry bush thickets."

He didn't look angry, just tired. Bridget felt terrible.

"We can still do that." She gathered the books on the table into a pile. "Those children are so bright and inquisitive. They miss going to school. That gave me an idea. I thought they could come over a few afternoons a week and I could teach them some things. Not that I'm a teacher, but I have all these books. It doesn't seem right to keep them to myself when we have children in the community eager to learn. What do you think?"

"What do I think?" He looked around the messy room. "What I think is, you don't seem to have time for your own work without taking on more. What about the cooking? And the garden? And everything else that needs done around here?"

She jammed the books into place on the shelf. "It won't be for the whole afternoon. Just an hour or two. It won't interfere…"

She glanced toward the stove. It had already interfered. If she prepared one big meal in the morning, they could eat on it all day. But that wouldn't help with the wash and gardening and splitting wood and everything else she needed to do.

Dominic made a visible effort to rein in his irritation. "I appreciate your worries about the children, but if you have that much free time in the afternoons, I could use you outside. I came across some felled trees down by the creek today. They need hauled up the bank and split before they clog up the creek or block the cattle from getting to the water. There are always a hundred jobs that would go a lot easier if I had an extra pair of hands."

"Then why didn't you ask me?"

"I didn't think I had to." He exhaled between clenched teeth. "I'm sorry, Bridget. I'm trying to give you time to get used to life out here. But work has to be done. Especially now. A wife's life is just as hard as the husband's, maybe harder. We're both going to have to work more than we ever have before—together—if we want to have something to pass on to the next generation."

Bridget looked longingly at the door. "You're right. I want the same things as you. It's just that I hate to disappoint the Whitamore children. They're bored and lonely for their friends. I wanted to give them a little education from everything I have."

"I appreciate that, Bridget, but other things need taken care of first. You said you were going to dig a few more rows for the garden today."

She stiffened her shoulders. "I did most of it."

She held her hands out to him. "My hands are so stiff and blistered I can barely bend my fingers. It was nice sharing the books with the children and telling them the stories Mother used to tell me. They're actually interested in my books."

Dominic's dark eyes flashed. "I'm sorry I don't feel like sitting around reading every night. When I come in at the end of the day, I want to relax without a history lesson on the Ming Dynasty. I thought having a wife meant I'd come home to a clean cabin and food on the table."

"And I thought I'd be more than a maid and a fieldhand."

"That's not what I said. Even when we only had beans to eat, my pa always came home to a hot supper."

"My father did too, but he realized there was more to life than food and work. A person's mind needs stimulation. A good education was important to my family. That's all I'm trying to do for those children."

"They are not your responsibility. I am. This cabin. You won't be able to help anyone this winter if we don't raise enough food for us or hay for the animals."

She threw down the potholder. "I can't believe you're being so selfish."

"I can't believe you're being so unrealistic." He stood. "Call me when supper's ready. I'm going to turn over a few shovels in the garden."

"Don't do that. I'll fix you a sandwich and have the potatoes ready in a few minutes. Then I'll go out to the garden and finish my work."

He shook his head. "I won't ask you to do anything you don't want to do. I don't want you to feel like a fieldhand." He stomped outside.

Part of Bridget wanted to go after him. She sensed he needed time to cool off. He was right; she had come here to be a wife, not a schoolmarm. She just wished he could understand she wasn't only doing this for the children. She needed more from life than cooking and gardening and hauling trees out of the fields.

Chapter Eleven

Bridget hurried through her morning chores, determined not to lose the day. If she wanted Dominic to understand her, she needed to make a concerted effort to understand him. As she hoed neat rows in the newly turned earth and planted radishes and onions that would grow quickly and catch up to the rest of the vegetables, she pondered on how she could help the Whitamore children without taking time away from her chores.

The most logical way involved the money that sat safely in the bank in Cincinnati and what she'd brought with her. If she could convince Dominic to invest her inheritance into this property, he could start building their new house without worrying about a long winter or all the calamities nature might bring. It would free up their time and ease the worries on his mind. But how could she make him see what was right in front of him without offending his fragile male pride?

By the time Dominic came in for the noon meal, he seemed over his anger. They laughed and talked while they ate, neither mentioning yesterday's fight. When Dominic got up from the table, he took her in his arms for a long kiss. Her body immediately responded.

When he suggested they lay down for a nap, even she knew what that meant. How perfectly scandalous! Did other people know this occurred in the middle of the day? She supposed things truly were different here. Or maybe it happened in her own neighborhood, and she had been completely ignorant.

Later, as Bridget pinned up her hair, Dominic asked if she had time to help him pile brush from some of the trees he had felled for burning later. Bridget didn't know how much help she'd be, but she'd do anything to get out of the stuffy cabin and into the fresh air.

The next day he gave her another riding lesson astride Ginger. After lunch on his way out the door, he pulled her into his arms for a toe-curling kiss.

"Will you have time to wash and iron my shirt for tomorrow?" he asked as they drew apart.

Bridget was startled. "Wash your shirt? Do you mean the new one? I planned to make Monday my laundry day, just like back home."

He smirked and tweaked her chin for a quick kiss. "It's the only nice shirt I have."

"The only nice shirt? I had no idea."

"That's why I bought it."

She watched him walk out the door, whistling. She couldn't believe her husband only had one decent shirt for Sundays. Something would have to be done about that.

She had just dumped the first kettle of hot water into the tub for laundry when she heard the Whitamore children coming across the meadow. She refilled the kettle, dried her hands on her apron, and went to the door. All three of them broke into a run at the sight of her.

"Mrs. DeSantis," Annie called out before throwing her arms around Bridget's legs.

Her heart melted at the love in the little girl's voice. She leaned over and swung the child in a circle. "Annie. Children. It's so good to see you today. I'm sorry, though, I don't have time for schoolwork."

Their faces fell in unison.

"I found another book for you to take home that you can study on your own," she said in concession. "It's science, and I think you'll find it very interesting. Maybe your mother or father can help you with it."

"They're too busy," J.T. told her.

As I should be, thought Bridget.

"What do you have to do today, Mrs. DeSantis?" Candace asked. "Maybe we could help you with your chores and still have a little time for schoolwork. That way we can do both in the same amount of time."

They looked hopefully up at her.

"All right. But this will be the last day for a while. I've started helping Mr. DeSantis in the fields in the afternoons."

She finished filling the tub and put Dominic's shirt and a few other things in to soak. When she got back in the cabin, the children had several books strewn across the tabletop.

Annie was running her dirty fingers down the page of a heavy volume. "I don't like this book, Mrs. DeSantis. It doesn't have any pictures."

Bridget grabbed the book from her and wiped away the smudges with the heel of her hand. "Don't be so careless," she scolded. "You'll ruin it."

Annie's bottom lip quivered.

Bridget swallowed her impatience. It wasn't the child's fault. She hadn't instructed her on how to handle the books. "This book is too advanced for you, Annie. You need to wait and let me pick out books for you to read. All of you," she said to the other children.

"Yes, ma'am," they replied.

"We're sorry," Candace said. "We were just excited. We've never seen this many books in somebody's house."

"I understand. These books are very valuable to me. They belonged to my parents, and most of them would take a lifetime to replace."

She reshelved most of the books they had picked and made a mental note of a few that were better suited for curious fingers. "Don't forget our bargain," she said. "Housework first. You can sweep the floors while I wash Mr. DeSantis's shirt."

"Yes, ma'am."

Bridget went outside to scrub the blue shirt and a few of her chemises, since she'd gone to the trouble of heating water. It wasn't long before she heard squabbling inside the cabin. She hurriedly wrung the water out of the clothes and threw them over the clothesline. Inside the cabin Annie and J.T. had positioned the chairs into an obstacle course and were crawling through the legs while Candace worked to sweep around them.

Bridget had only been gone five minutes. How had her plan broken down so quickly? "You two go outside and gather the scraps of wood around the woodpile to fill the kindling box. Candace and I will finish in here."

The children got off their hands and knees and ran for the door, thrilled at the opportunity to get out of the cabin and away from any real work. Bridget noticed their dirty hands and reminded herself to have them wash up before they touched her books again.

At least Candace was a hard worker. Washing the windows and rubbing linseed oil into the chairs and bookshelves went much faster with her help.

In no time at all, Bridget called the little ones back inside and washed their hands and faces before setting them at the table with a pile of books. She kept an eye on the clock over the mantel as she went through the books with the children.

J.T. was very advanced at reading for his age and Annie quickly grasped the basic reading skills Bridget gave her. They were all very bright. She could see how much they would benefit from regular schooling. She hoped by the time she and Dominic had children of school age, there would be somewhere for them to get a proper education.

Dinner bubbled on the stove as they worked, and Bridget was confident their visit wouldn't interfere with her chores. On rainy days or days that Dominic didn't need her outside, maybe she could let the children come over so they would get a little bit of schooling.

At the end of the session, she gave the children bread and pumpkin butter while she added potatoes and turnips to the bubbling stew and slid a loaf of fresh bread into the oven. It was so nice having a full table. She daydreamed about her own children someday seated around this very table.

"Thank you, Mrs. DeSantis," they said.

"Thank you, children, for helping with my chores. "I'll see you tomorrow at church."

Bridget tidied up the cabin and looked around satisfied. Everything was in its place and dinner would be ready when Dominic came in from work. When she saw him coming across the field, she filled the wash pan with warm water and hurried outside so it would be waiting for him. She was getting better at this wife stuff every day.

She crossed her arms over her stomach and watched him approach. When he caught sight of her, he lengthened his strides.

Bridget's insides warmed, still amazed at the man God had given her when she had expected a life of spinsterhood.

"Evening, wife," he called to her.

"Good evening, husband. It looks like you had a good day."

He reached the porch and looked up at her. "It's much better now." He grabbed a porch post and swung himself up. With one hand on the post, he wrapped his free arm around and pulled her in tight. Their lips met and he kissed her hungrily.

Bridget pulled back, embarrassed. She hoped the children hadn't turned back for something. What would they think witnessing such a display in broad daylight?

Dominic released her and went to the washtub at the corner of the porch. "You must've had a good day too. I could smell that stew all the way at the barn."

"I made double so we can take a dish of it with us to church tomorrow."

He set his sweat-stained Stetson on the porch and rolled up his shirtsleeves. "I'm looking forward to showing off your cooking skills to the other men."

"Now, Dominic, God doesn't favor a braggart," she teased.

"It's not bragging, just stating the obvious. I've got the prettiest, smartest cook in all of Cowboy Creek."

She laughed. "As long as you believe it, that's all that matters."

"I do believe it." He looked about to lunge at her again when something caught his attention.

His brows slid together. Bridget followed his gaze to a crumpled pile of fabric under the clothesline.

"What…"

Bridget gasped. His shirt. She lifted her skirts and ran to the pile of clothes. She jerked Dominic's shirt up out of the dirt along with her best chemise and shook them out to survey the damage.

Dominic looked around. "What happened? I wonder if an old dog saw them flapping in the wind and—"

"It wasn't a dog. The Whitamore children came over to look at the books. I told them they had to help me with my chores first. Annie and J.T. filled the kindling box while…"

Their eyes went to the woodpile. Dominic crossed his arms over his chest. "Doesn't look like they did much of a job of it."

Most of the chunks of wood lay where they had been this morning. "I'm sorry, Dominic. I didn't do a very good job supervising. Candace and I were inside cleaning where I could keep an eye on the stew so it would be ready for you. Oh, dear, the bread."

With the wet shirt and chemise clutched in her hands, she ran into the cabin and jerked the pan of bread out of the oven. Smoke rolled off the blackened top. She dropped the pan on the table with a bang.

That's what she got for thinking too highly of her cooking skills.

"It's ruined." She looked at the two other loaves of bread rising on the sideboard. She could bake one of them, but if she did, she'd have to make more for the church dinner tomorrow, and she was low on yeast.

She looked at Dominic, expecting him to say it was all right. He could eat his stew without bread. Instead, his eyes were narrowed and dark.

"I thought you were going to tell the children you had enough of your own work to do without teaching them."

"I did. But Candace said they could help with the chores for an hour and then we'd do an hour of schoolwork."

"We see how much help they were with the chores." He glared at the shirt as huge drops of muddy water puddled on her clean floor.

Tears welled in her eyes. "I thought I had everything under control. The schoolwork didn't interfere with my work in the house. The cabin is clean, and supper was right on time."

"Except for the laundry for tomorrow and no bread for supper."

Bridget grabbed the clothes off the table. "I'll take care of this right away." She started for the door but realized there was no hot water left to wash his shirt again. After getting trampled in the dirt, it might need repairs. She hoped it wasn't ruined.

She dropped it back onto the table and grabbed the bucket to head to the well. How she wished they had an indoor pump. It would save her so many steps.

"I'll fix a batch of cornbread while you do that," Dominic said.

"No, Dominic, it's my job. I don't want you to help me."

His eyes flashed. "There's no point in being stubborn. You need the help and I'm capable of giving it."

"I'm sorry. I just didn't want to disappoint the children."

"So you disappoint me instead."

"I don't mean to. It just keeps happening. If you had more than one shirt, I could've waited until Monday to do the wash like I intended. When we go back to Good Hope for the rest of my things, I'm going to buy you five new shirts."

He bristled. "Oh no, you won't."

"Why not? I have the money."

His jaw tightened. "I didn't marry you for your money."

"No one thinks you did."

"They will when I show up at church dressed like a dandy in a wardrobe of ready-made clothes. No, Bridget, you won't buy me one thing with your money."

"It's *our* money. We're married. If you had money, I would consider it just as much mine as yours. Isn't that how marriage works? What's the difference since it's mine?"

"Because your parents left it to take care of you, not me."

"They left it to ensure I had a good life."

"That's what husbands are for."

She exhaled loudly in frustration. "Dominic, money is made to be spent. My parents worked hard their whole lives. They made good financial decisions. They would consider it an honor to know we were using their inheritance to carve out a good life for ourselves. For their grandchildren. What difference does it make where the money came from?"

The vein in his neck throbbed. He had gone beyond frustration to barely concealed anger. "*My* parents didn't raise me to take something for nothing. DeSantises work for everything we have. We don't take handouts."

"I'm not offering one. We're married. What's mine is yours, and what's yours is mine."

He made a sweeping gesture with his hands. "Well, here you go. It's all yours. But I'm not taking anything I didn't earn myself."

"Now who's being stubborn?"

"Not me. You're the one who brought half the city of Cincinnati with you. I don't know what possessed you to come here when you obviously knew from the beginning it wouldn't suit you."

"Of course it suits me. It's just different is all. I didn't know exactly what I was getting into when I came, but isn't that why any of us do anything? I wanted adventure. A new life. *You*! Back home, every morning I woke up I knew would be the same as the one before. I didn't want that for the rest of my life. I came here and met you. I wouldn't take that life back for anything."

"You could've fooled me. Every day you act like you'd rather be doing anything else. Like what we have here isn't enough to please you. That I'm not enough."

She started to tell him he was wrong. He wasn't a mistake. Coming here and leaving Charles and Ellen was the smartest thing she'd ever done. But was it? At least living with her brother and his family, she could spend every day reading and going to civic meetings instead of scrubbing her hands raw on a washboard.

While water heated to rewash the clothes, she gathered the other garments out of the dirt. "God, why do I keep messing up?" she prayed. "Why do I keep saying the wrong things and hurting either Dominic or the children? Teach me to be a good wife. This life is good enough for me. Dominic's good enough. He's just so hard-headed."

She didn't know what to say when she got back in the house, so she didn't say anything. For the first time since they said their vows, they turned on opposite sides in the bed that night and went straight to sleep.

Chapter Twelve

Dominic tossed the water from his shaving pan out the door into the yard the way he'd done every morning for the last four years. Even in winter, he kept his face cleanshaven. It was a small thing heating the water and going to the trouble, even though most days before Bridget came, he never saw another living person. His mother had instilled in him a desire for things to be neat and orderly, even if no one was around to appreciate it. That went for his whiskers too. He hung the pan on the nail on the side of the house and ran his hand across his smooth jaw.

Inside the cluttered cabin, where he could no longer turn in a full circle without risk of banging his knee on a new piece of furniture, he heard his new wife moving around, fixing breakfast, getting ready for the day. For the life of him, he couldn't understand that woman. Still, he loved having her around, fancy furnishings and all.

After rewashing his shirt, she had hung it in front of the stove to dry. It was still damp when he checked it on his way out to his morning chores, but the iron would warm it enough to it put on.

He sat down on the edge of the porch and looked toward the horizon, just pinking as the sun made its appearance.

Last night had been the longest twelve hours of his life. "I shouldn't have been so hard on her, Lord," he mumbled aloud. "She's working hard to get used to this. I know she's lonely. And she's smart. She can't get any of her learning through my thick head, so it makes sense for her to reach out to those children."

He glanced toward the cabin door. Wouldn't do any good for her to hear him out here talking. She'd think he'd completely lost his mind. He should tell her he did that sometimes. Talked out loud to the Lord. It came from spending so much of his time alone. The fellas in the Bible did it all the time. If it was good enough for them, well, he supposed it was the way the Lord preferred it.

She needed to know. She needed to know a lot of things. Like how this place, this life, was all he ever wanted. Besides a woman to share it with, of course. He was crazy about her. It was all he could do to keep his hands off her every minute of the day. There were times he had to force himself to stay in the field and see to his work instead of riding back to the cabin and taking her in his arms. He should tell her that, too, though he suspected she already knew and enjoyed their time together as much as he did. Just one more thing he hadn't suspected about women. They sure were a mystery. Any man who said they weren't would lie about other things too.

She was just so different than him. Unbeguiling to a fault, she couldn't see why he didn't want her to spend a dime of her parents' money. She thought he was stubborn and proud. His family pride had little to do with it, despite what he said last night. The truth was he didn't want anyone thinking that's why he loved her. He knew she wasn't what most men considered pretty and feminine. To him, she was the prettiest gal in the world. No one else knew it though. Once they found out she had money, they'd assume that's why he chose her. To get his hands on her money and the easy life it would provide.

He didn't have money or brains or anything to offer her but a strong back and his two hands. It wasn't enough for a woman like Bridget who grew up in a fancy house in the city with everything she desired at her fingertips. Pretty soon, the shine would wear off and she'd figure it out. Then where would he be?

"I don't know what to do, Lord," he said under his breath in case she was close to the window and might overhear. "Pretty soon she'll figure out she married a dummy who can't read or write. I'll let her down and she won't want to stay."

He scrubbed his hands over his cleanshaven face. "I don't know what I'll do then."

He got to his feet and paced to the barn unable to face his wife.

The sun shone brilliantly in the sky. A warm breeze ruffled the thin wisps of Bridget's fine brown hair that had come loose from the knot at the back of her head. She transferred a handful of soapy clothes into the tub of clear water to rinse. Monday had always been washday back home, but she'd never had to do much of the work. She didn't mind the mundane chore as much as she thought she would, at least not on a beautiful day like today. It gave her a sense of accomplishment, much like the tidy rows of sprouts in the kitchen garden.

She and Dominic hadn't talked much since Saturday. She didn't think he was still mad. Like her, he just seemed unsure of how to proceed. Whether he liked it or not, she still had her parents' money. And whether she liked it or not, he didn't want to spend any of it. They were at an impasse. Neither knew what to say, so they didn't say anything.

It wouldn't be long before they'd have to go to Good Hope to collect the rest of her things. Maybe she should relent and let the stationmaster sell some of the bigger pieces. That would make Dominic happy, but how would she choose what to sell? Everything she brought meant so much to her. Thinking of Father's desk sitting in someone else's parlor nearly reduced her to tears. But if that's what it took to make her husband happy, she might need to consider it. Of course, after she sold the items, Dominic would see the proceeds as hers and not want her to spend it. They'd be right back where they started.

She stepped back from the washtub and heaved to pull the heavy sheet out of the water, twisting out the water as she went. She threw the tail of it over her shoulder to keep it out of the dirt while she worked on the rest. This would not be a pleasant task in February with a raw wind tearing down from the mountains.

Over the grunting and splashing, she heard someone call her name.

Oh, no. Not the children. Not today. She had too much to do to have them underfoot. She didn't look forward to sending them away either.

"Here, let me help." A pair of feminine hands reached into the water and took the other end of the sheet. Bridget sighed in relief at the sight of Carrie Whitamore, the children's mother, at her side.

With Bridget holding one end and Carrie the other, the two women stepped away from the washtub. They twisted in opposite directions as they carried the sheet to the clothesline. Between them, they shook out the water and wrinkles and threw the sheet over.

Bridget rotated her shoulders. "You came at just the right time."

Carrie secured her end with a clothespin. "An extra set of hands comes in handy with a job like this. Let me help you finish."

Within minutes the last of the wash was flapping in the breeze, sure to dry in no time.

Bridget put her hand on the small of her back and stretched. "Thank you so much, Carrie. Now we have time for a cup of coffee if you have a few minutes."

"I'd love it."

Inside the cabin, Bridget went to the stove while Carrie sat at the table. "It's the least I can do after all you did for the children last week. They finished reading *Black Beauty* last night. They wanted to bring it back today and get something else, but I told them I'd do it. I figured you had enough work to do yourself without entertaining them."

No need for Bridget to tell her Dominic believed the same thing. "I love the children's company. It's nice having them here. But there is so much to do."

She suppressed a sigh as she took two cups from the shelf above the sink and set them on the table. She didn't have more work than every other woman on the frontier.

Carrie nodded in understanding.

Bridget reached for the cookie tin for the last of the molasses cookies she had baked Saturday. "No, please," Carrie said, stopping her. "The coffee's fine. I just stopped by to thank you for your patience with the children and to return your book."

"And to help with the wash." Bridget smiled and sat on the opposite side of the table while she waited for the coffee to heat.

After a moment of silence, Carrie cocked her head and studied her. "There is another reason I came." She toyed with her lip a moment before going on. "Is everything all right? Yesterday at church you looked a little glum. I know it can get—lonely out here, especially when you aren't used to it."

"No, well, yes, I suppose a little. There have been a lot of changes for Dominic and me."

The teakettle began to hiss. She got up and went to the stove, thankful for a chance to turn away from Carrie. She didn't want to complain about her husband to someone she barely knew. She didn't mean to complain at all. Dominic was a good man, a man she vowed to honor as long as she lived. That included not sniping about him behind his back.

She filled the cups with coffee and sat back in her chair. "Cream? Sugar?"

"Yes, please," Carrie said, helping herself. "At home with Whit I drink it black. This makes it feel like an occasion."

"It is an occasion. You're the first company I've had at my table. Besides the children, that is."

The women dressed their coffee the way they liked. "So..." Carrie said after she finished, "how are you getting used to married life? I know it's different for you than it was for me. As you know I was married before. I rather knew what I was getting into."

"Oh, I knew too. I think. My parents had a very strong union. I learned everything about respect and patience from them."

"Patience?"

Bridget stirred absently at the coffee. "I suppose one needs a lot of it when learning to share her life with a stranger."

Carrie pursed her lips before speaking. "You and Dominic seem well suited."

"We are," Bridget said quickly. She didn't want to give the woman the wrong idea. "He's..." She couldn't keep from smiling. "He's wonderful. He's the patient one. I'm...I keep doing everything wrong. I get distracted with my books and forget to wash his shirts. I burn supper nearly every night. I brought too much with me." She swept her arm around the crowded room. "There's more at the livery in Good Hope with more on the way, I'm afraid. I don't know what we'll do with it all."

"I worried the children were in your way and keeping you from your work. I'm so sorry. I'll be more mindful of them coming over all the time."

"Oh no, don't stop them from coming, at least not all the time. It's my fault. I love spending time with them. It's just...I have to learn to manage my time better."

"All young married people deal with this when they start out. I'm sure Dominic doesn't mind the burnt suppers one bit as long as you're on the other side of the table."

Bridget picked at a broken fingernail. She wasn't sure how much she should unburden herself, but it seemed like Carrie would understand. "It isn't just the burnt suppers or even how I run out of time. It's…we're so different. I love books and academics. Dominic doesn't seem interested in those things. I wonder how we'll find anything to talk about as the years go by. My parents had such stimulating conversations. It was wonderful. Our house was filled with lively debates. Dominic is so tired at the end of the day, he isn't interested in reading or discussing anything beyond the work he has for the next day."

Carrie patted her hand. "I'm sure your parents went through the same growing pains when they first got together."

Bridget took a sip of coffee. "Maybe, but they came from similar backgrounds."

"That doesn't always matter. Whit was a confirmed bachelor. He certainly didn't expect a woman with three children when he asked for a bride, but we're making it work."

"There's more, Carrie. There's also, um, money differences."

Carrie wagged her head sympathetically. "Whit and I have had a few of those difficulties ourselves. Providing for a wife and three children was a bit overwhelming for him to say the least. Money brings a lot of tension into a union."

"It isn't like that for Dominic and me. We have too much. Or rather, I have too much."

"Too much?" Carrie's look revealed she didn't know such an obstacle could exist.

"I inherited a significant estate from my parents," Bridget explained. "It was enough for me live comfortably on my own for the rest of my life. Now that I'm married, I don't know what to do with it. Dominic is offended if I suggest spending a penny."

She glanced toward the door. "I want to use it to make our lives easier. Dominic wants to build a new cabin on the hill. Do you know how much faster it would go if we used my money? We could put a pump inside. Screen doors. But Dominic is proud. He wants to provide for me himself. He doesn't want to spend anything he hasn't worked for."

"Men can be quite stubborn with things like that."

Bridget slapped the table, vindicated. "Thank you."

Carrie laughed.

Bridget smiled in return, relieved for someone she could talk to. "I don't know how to handle it. I don't want money or anything else to come between us. Sometimes I think things would be easier if I didn't have the money. I even thought of sending it to my brother and let it be his problem. He thought he should've inherited everything anyway."

"Don't do that," Carrie said quickly. "Your parents must've known what they were doing when they left the estate to you. And worse, you'll only resent Dominic if you forfeit your inheritance to suit his pride. You can't solve this issue through good intentions or rash decisions you'll regret later. You have to talk this over with Dominic. Understand where he's coming from and make sure he knows how you feel. Men are proud. That's a good thing. It means Dominic is strong and smart and will always provide for you the best he can."

Bridget smiled. "He is all those things. I don't want to hurt him with the money, but if we need something, I don't see any reason why we should do without when we can afford to have our needs met. It wouldn't make him less of a man in my eyes."

Carrie patted her hand. "You love your husband, and he loves you. That much is obvious. You want to make each other happy. You are not a terrible wife, and he's not a terrible husband. You'll work it out, but you have to talk to each other. You can't assume you know what he's thinking. You have to let him see that whether rich or poor, you'll be here for him. and you can count on each other."

"Oh, Carrie, you make it sound so easy."

Carrie laughed gently. "It isn't easy, but it is simple. As long as you put him first and he puts you first, neither of you will ever feel used or put upon or taken for granted."

She pushed aside her empty cup and stood. "I must be going. It was wonderful spending time with you."

"You too, Carrie. Please, come back."

Chapter Thirteen

Bridget watched Carrie mount her horse and ride away, then went to the clothesline to take down the wash. She spread everything on the bed to fold since it was the only flat surface in the cabin besides the narrow kitchen table. She'd iron later while Dominic rested.

She mixed up a batch of cornbread and slid it into the oven just as Dominic strode through the door, looking as determined as she was to work things out. "Smells good in here, wife," he said cautiously. He was obviously checking out her mood.

She smiled brightly. "I'm so glad, husband. I'm trying to keep ahead of the chores instead of them keeping ahead of me."

He wrapped his arms around her from behind and kissed her ear, tickling her into a fit of giggles. "I know it's been hard, being so far from everything you know. I talked to Rase and Sawyer today. They said they'll have time at the end of the week to ride with us to Good Hope to get the rest of your things."

Bridget turned in his arms and wrapped her arms around his neck. "Thank you, darling, but what will we do with it all?"

"I checked out the little building next to the meetinghouse. Rase said someone had used it for a tack shop and hardware store. Shouldn't take but a few hours to make it suitable. You might have to get in there and chase out a family of possums."

She wrinkled her nose. He laughed. "I'll help you. I want you to have your things close. Maybe we can break ground on a foundation for our house soon so you'll have plenty of space for whatever you want."

She gasped. "Do you mean it? Oh, Dominic, I love you."

He pulled her closer. "And I love you, Bridget."

"Maybe the tack shop has a counter and some shelves. Candace could help me clean it out, and I can create a lending library with some of my books. That way, the whole community could go in and borrow what they wanted to read. Mother and Father would be pleased to know more people than just us will benefit from their collection. It wouldn't take my time away from the house, especially since I'm going to be busy helping you build another house."

He kissed her soundly.

She put her hands on his shoulders and studied his face. "We're so different, but I think that will make our union stronger as long as we always talk through our differences. How did you know you wanted to marry me?"

"I knew the moment I saw you sitting in that wagon you were the one for me."

She playfully smacked his shoulder. "No. Before that. What about my letters? What in them made you think we were suited? That we could fall in love?"

"Every word you wrote." He glanced away.

She moved her head so he'd have to look directly at her. "Dominic? What's the matter?"

He let go of her and stepped away. He didn't speak for a long moment. When he did, he couldn't look at her. "I didn't read your letters."

Her forehead puckered. "But…I saw them folded in your drawer. I could tell from how worn they were you had read them over and over."

He exhaled. His jaw clenched. Bridget's stomach tightened. Had she done something wrong by going through his things? Were they about to have another fight?

He finally looked up, his obsidian eyes wounded. "I didn't read them, Bridget. Not once. Rase read the first one to me. I didn't read the others. I have no idea what you wrote."

Tears stung her eyes. "That doesn't…I don't understand. Didn't you—"

"I can't read, Bridget. Not a word. I barely know how to sign my name." He lowered his fist to the table and leaned on it.

She couldn't wrap her head around what he was saying. "What about the letter you wrote to me? It was short, but I read it a hundred times."

He turned back to her. He didn't meet her gaze right away. "I asked Marla to write it. I told her I was too busy and I didn't know what to say. I asked if she could write a few things about me, and I'd write a proper one later. I let her think I was too shy. Better her think I'm bashful than stupid."

"Don't say that! You're not stupid. I just don't understand how you can't... We talked. You knew so much about me. How did you know if you couldn't read what I wrote?"

"I can't read, but I know how to listen. Rase read the first one to me and I memorized what he read. It's how I've gotten through life without anyone knowing I can't read. I pay attention and listen to what people say and fake the rest."

Hurt pounded in her head. "Why didn't you tell me? All those times I tried to get you to read with me, you could've told me then. Instead you let me go on and on about books and art when you didn't care about any of it. You should've told me to shut up and stop embarrassing myself."

"You didn't embarrass yourself."

"Well, I'm embarrassed now. I knew you didn't want to read, but I thought you cared about what I was saying. Did you fake that too?"

"Of course not. I care about everything you say. I care about everything you are."

"Except for the most important part. All this time, you let me think you knew me. The whole time I talked about my friends, my church, my neighborhood, my beliefs, you didn't know what I was talking about because you hadn't read my letters."

He circled the table toward her. "That's how I got to know you. It's how anyone gets to know another person. By listening." He reached for her, but she backed up. He exhaled in frustration. "It's how you got to know me, isn't it? Even though I never wrote my own letter? I didn't want you to know you married a dummy who never took the time to learn to read."

"Is that all the more you think of me? That I'm so snobbish and petty, I would judge you for something like that? You should've told me the first day."

He reeled back. "The first day! Do you mean the day you showed up with two trunks of books it took a team of horses to get home? How could I admit I couldn't read my own name after you told me how important literature and learning was to you and your family? No one in Cowboy Creek knows I can't read but Rase. I sure couldn't admit it to you of all people."

"I'm your wife. You shouldn't have pretended with me."

"I never pretended. I just avoided it." Dominic ran his hand across his smooth jaw. "I didn't have much chance to go to school. When I did, I was so far behind the other kids, I pretended I didn't care about the work and got out of there as quick as I could. It's not something I'm proud of. I never saw a reason to point out I can't do something most children can do easily."

She hugged her arms around herself and looked away. She wasn't sure how to feel. Embarrassed for talking about literature so much, pity for him, or anger that he thought she wouldn't accept a man simply because he couldn't read.

"You weren't exactly forthcoming yourself," he pointed out. "You didn't mention a word about all the property you had shipped across the country to cram into this cabin."

"I didn't bring *all* my property," she defended weakly.

"And you didn't tell me a word of it. You let me walk into the livery to pick up two trunks of books only to find an entire storehouse of citified furniture."

"I told you why I couldn't leave it behind. It's all I have left of Mother and Father."

She saw the emotions play across his face. When he spoke, she heard defeat in his voice. "What did you expect to find here, Bridget? A big house like the one you left? A cultured cowboy who would discuss literature and art and politics the way your parents did? It wasn't fair. If that's what you wanted, you should've stayed in Cincinnati and married some educated fella in a suit coat."

"No!" she exclaimed. "That isn't what I expected. I expected…"

He tilted his head and waited for her to finish. She sighed, fighting tears. "I don't know what I expected. I guess all I thought about was getting out from under Charles's thumb."

She went to the table and slumped into a chair. "Oh, Dominic, I wanted my own life. That's what I came here to find. When my brother found out I inherited everything from our parents, he and his wife devised a plan to control me—and the money. I couldn't sit there and let them. I didn't just leave Charles and Ellen. Once people in our circle learned of my inheritance, suitors would've come calling. Men who never noticed I was alive before."

He reached across the table. "Bridget…"

She pulled her hands out of reach. "All I ever wanted was for someone to love me for me. Plain, homely, bookish Bridget Reidy."

"Not for your money."

"Exactly."

"When are you going to trust me, Bridget? When will you understand I don't care about that?"

"I guess about the same time you trust me enough to tell me you can't read."

He sat opposite her and took her hands. This time she didn't pull away. "How about we start over then?"

"I want to. I want you to believe me when I say coming here was the best decision I ever made. *You're* the best decision I ever made. But that doesn't change the fact of my parents' inheritance. I'm not going to throw it into the river to mollify your male pride."

He exhaled. "That would be ridiculous, wouldn't it?"

"Very. You said you'd been thinking of building a house even before I came. Now we have the means to build exactly what we want in a lot less time than it would take without money. I know your pride doesn't want you to take something you didn't work for. It's also prideful not to use what you already have because you're afraid of what people will think."

"It isn't just what *people* will think. I don't want you to think I chose you because of your money."

"Because I'm not pretty enough for you to have chosen on my own?"

"Of course not. I didn't mean that. You're beautiful."

"I'm also not stupid enough to let a man take advantage of me to get close to my money."

"You can say that again. You're the smartest, shrewdest woman I ever met."

"Shrewd enough to design and furnish a house just the way I want with an indoor pump and screens over the doors and windows? And to invest the rest so we can leave an inheritance for our children's children like the Bible says?"

He stroked his chin. "If we're going to have eleven young'uns, that'll make for a lot of grandchildren. I guess we best get started."

Bridget blushed. "On the children or the investing?"

He gave her a lustful smile. "Can't it be both?"

"Dominic, you're truly terrible. What am I going to do with you?"

"Come here and I'll show you." He took hold of her apron sash and pulled her toward him. She lifted off the seat to reach him across the table. She melted into his kiss. He put his hands on either side of her face.

A groan of pleasure escaped her lips as the kiss deepened. Her eyes began to burn. She blinked and pulled back. Smoke curled up from the stove.

She shrieked and jerked free. "My cornbread!" She jumped up and hurried to the stove. She pulled out the loaf and turned the pan upside down on the tabletop. A blackened brick landed on the table. "Not again."

Dominic broke off a corner and juggled it from hand to hand to cool it. "Just the way I like it." He popped the charred bread in his mouth and grimaced as he chewed.

"Oh, Dominic, I'm sorry. You deserve so much better than a wife like me."

He swallowed the lump as he circled the table. "I deserve you and I love you and I'm so glad I got you." He pulled her into his arms. His kiss was long and passionate.

Bridget tasted burnt cornbread on his lips. "Just don't come in here again and distract me while I'm cooking your supper or you'll never get a pan of decent cornbread again."

"I'll eat a mountain of burnt cornbread if it means you'll keep kissing me like this."

Bridget happily obliged.

The   End

Before You Go

If you enjoyed Carrie and Bridget's stories, please leave a review on Amazon or any other marketplace or blog that allows reviews. Even a short review proves to Amazon there is interest in the book, and they will display it to more readers and more people can learn about the *Nine Brides* Series.

The best way to support an author is still the old-fashioned method of recommending books to a friend. Share any of my links on social media outlets. Follow me on Amazon, BookBub and GoodReads. Give the books a thumbs up and leave a comment whenever you see them posted somewhere. No greater compliment can be paid to any author of stories you love.

I love hearing from readers. Email me at teresa@teresaslack.com anytime with your thoughts and input about my stories and series ideas you would love to read.

Read for Free

Sign up for my newsletter and receive a free download of *A Promise for Josie: A Willow Wood Brides Prequel*

After a broken promise and a broken heart, is love worth the risk?

Abandoned at the altar on her wedding day, Josie Segal doubts she'll ever find true love. When a tall stranger rides into Josie's life, her dreams of love and adventure are reawakened. Can she move beyond the pain and fear of broken promises to trust Owen Dutton, and her own heart?

About the Author

Teresa Slack loves reading, writing, and falling in love. Creating clean and wholesome western romances where cowboys still sweep independent women off their feet was an easy choice for her.

She writes from her home in the beautiful southern Ohio hills, which she shares with her husband and rescue dog and rescue cats. Any errors and typos she blames on the cats, randomly running across her keyboard.

www.ingramcontent.com/pod-product-compliance
Lightning Source LLC
Chambersburg PA
CBHW051243260626
47162CB00002B/576